Edited by Jennifer Collins, EJL Editing, and Represent Publishing

Formatted and Published by Represent Publishing

Cover Designs by 100bookcovers.com

LIVING SECRETS

LIVING SECRETS

A Thriller

S.F. BAUMGARTNER

PUBLISHING

AUTHOR'S NOTE

To all readers, especially residents and those familiar with the state of Florida, I wish to clarify that the town of Marian and the Mirror Estate are purely fictional creations for this series.

All characters and events depicted in this novel are born from my imagination. Any resemblance to actual people, living or dead, or to real-life events is entirely coincidental.

RECAP

BURIED SECRETS - WHERE IT ALL BEGINS, BOOK 1

Twenty-five-year-old Dylan Roche barely has time to mourn his mom before an attorney appears with an invitation to his long-lost maternal grandmother's opulent estate. Eager to learn about the family he believed dead and armed with a mysterious key his mom gave him before her death, he's ready to uncover what he believes are buried family secrets.

After a lifetime of scraping by with his mom, he's shocked she grew up wealthy. But, while the estate is lavish, something's off, and he can't shake the haunting feeling that he's being watched. As he delves deeper, he unearths his family's dark history tied to organized crime. His focus, however, remains unshaken, latched onto what the mysterious key unlocks.

At last, he locates the buried box the key opens. Then, along with those buried secrets, he discovers the ever-present, sinister aura he's been sensing is his mother's twin sister, believed to have died shortly after birth. Very much alive, this ghost is now a criminal mastermind out to kill him. Although he dodges her murder attempt, he's left questioning everything he thought he knew about family, trust, and his past.

PRAISE FOR BURIED SECRETS - WHERE IT ALL BEGINS: BOOK 1

I felt that the author wove a story that had twists and turns with unexpected moments sprinkled here and there.

— DELPHIA, GOODREADS

They say that dynamite comes in small packages. This one was definitely loaded with plenty of information that will blow your mind.

— TAMMY, GOODREADS

What a great story! This had enough thrill and mystery to draw me in even though it was a short novella.

— MEGAN, GOODREADS

PRAISE FOR LIVING SECRETS: BOOK 2

"In the field of biological weapons, there is almost no prospect of detecting a pathogen until it has been used in an attack."

– Barton Gellman

CHAPTER 1

USA/CHINA

THE GHOST

"Status?" the Ghost demanded.

"He needs more convincing."

"Use leverage. Anything. Make him cooperate. We've got friends in that part of China. The triads owe us. Call them in if you have to."

Silence for a beat.

"You're not really planning to use his notes, are you? We don't have the resources to build something like that. And the Chinese won't appreciate you hijacking their research."

"That's not your concern. Get it done." She ended the call.

Marge Beaumont, the Ghost, leaned back in her chair. She'd watched the video in secret, footage smuggled out of a hidden Chinese lab.

A grotesque display—test subjects convulsing, bleeding, dying.

The scientist behind the camera had promised a perfect storm —smallpox, cholera, Ebola rolled into one.

Without the antidote, death was inevitable. The timer ran forty-eight to ninety-six hours.

One hundred percent fatal.

She'd shuddered when she watched it. Now, the memory hardened her resolve. She needed that bargaining chip.

CHAPTER 2

MIRROR ESTATE

DYLAN

Dylan Roche sat at his cluttered desk, thumbing through a set of handwritten notes. Even in these photocopies, the faded ink hinted at secrets and mysteries buried deep within his family history. The past couple of months had shaken him to the core. Now, he sought answers, resolution, and perhaps even closure.

His fingertips traced the notes' outlines. These had once belonged to his grandfather, a decorated police officer in the organized crime unit. The FBI now held the originals as evidence, but he'd made copies before handing those over to FBI Special Agent Ron Peters. Dylan had to protect himself, to have something tangible to hold onto as he ventured down this treacherous path.

But now, at this crossroad of his investigation, he needed more help, a connection to his roots, to the fragments of his shattered family.

"Fr. Phil," Dylan muttered. The priest knew more than he

revealed. After all, Dylan's mother had entrusted the priest to deliver her email to him after her death.

He put the papers away and pushed to his feet to head to the chapel, a short walk from the estate.

His phone rang. Agent Peters's contact flashed onto the screen.

Dylan answered. It was a short conversation. Fr. Phil would have to wait.

CHAPTER 3

CEMETERY, HONG KONG

LILY

"It's not fair."

Lily Tso stared at the plaque with her uncle's name, the dates etched in bronze like a final sentence. He'd been all she had since Auntie Elsie died. Now, even he was gone.

"…you'd be so proud of her…" Sr. Marie Ramos—Auntie, to Lily—kept talking, but Lily had already tuned her out.

They'd eaten lunch at a picnic table near the base of the columbarium, and the scent of leftovers still clung to their bags. Lily barely touched her food.

Her mother had died right after she was born. She'd never known her father, although she suspected he wasn't Chinese. Her reflection hinted at a mixed heritage, rounder eyes, soft brown hair. At her American school, no one cared. Foreign kids were common. But back at her local primary school, she'd fielded questions.

For years, she'd thought Auntie was her aunt by blood, same mixed features. Later, she learned Auntie's father was Portuguese. That explained part of it. But not all.

"Lily!" Auntie's voice snapped her back.

"Yeah. Sorry. Just thinking. It's not fair. God already took my mom and other aunt. Now he's taken my uncle too."

Auntie, ever calm, placed a hand on her chest. "They're not gone, Lily. They're with the Lord and with you. Always."

It'd be nice to believe that. But believing didn't bring them back.

Her phone buzzed with a calendar reminder. "I need to go soon."

Auntie caressed the plaque. "Happy heavenly birthday, big brother."

Lily echoed the words, her throat tight.

"Tell me about your promotion," Auntie said as they exited the cemetery.

"It's not a big deal. A new title, small raise. Same work. Just me and one other person at the business center. We mostly help guests print stuff or act like secretaries for the tech challenged."

"You're building experience. The future holds more." Auntie gestured toward the tram. "I'll take this way. You?"

"MTR."

"Take care." Auntie placed a gentle hand on Lily's arm.

Lily patted her hand. "Bye, Auntie."

She walked alone toward the MTR station. Just before descending the steps, something made her pause.

A prickle ran down her spine.

She glanced over her shoulder.

The street behind her bustled with people, none paying her the slightest attention. But the feeling lingered, like someone was still watching.

She shook it off and kept walking. It was nothing, wasn't it?

CHAPTER 4

MARINO HOTEL, HONG KONG

DYLAN

Dylan adjusted his tie. The stiff collar felt foreign. Back home, business casual was enough. But here in Hong Kong? Every veteran in the upper ranks had made it clear. Suits were expected.

"Tell me again why the proper authorities aren't involved." His best friend, Tommy Rivers, questioned from the living room.

Dylan exhaled through his nose, gave the knot a final tug, and stepped out. "Because Agent Peters said it'd be a hassle. Bureaucracy, paperwork, delays."

Tommy rummaged in the mini-fridge like he was hunting for treasure. "Wouldn't it go faster if you just told them you own the place?"

"I don't own the place. My grandmother does. And I'm not about to cause a scandal and tarnish the family name after everything she's worked to rebuild."

Tommy shut the fridge. "So you're letting the guy off the hook?"

"No, I'm finding out who's dirty. Quietly."

Hotel-grade coffee scented the suite. Dylan checked his pockets, phone, wallet, key card, then nodded toward the door. "Let's go. We're meeting Larry for breakfast."

Tommy fell into step in the hallway. "Whatever happened to your game thing? The reality-show idea?"

"Dropped it." Dylan pressed the elevator button. "Agent Peters made a good case for why it was a stupid idea."

"I told you it was a stupid idea before the good agent did."

Dylan rolled his eyes. "Thanks for the support."

The past few months had been a blur. Soon after his mother's funeral, a grandmother he'd never known had located him. After a few eventful weeks, including almost getting shot by a deranged woman, he'd accepted his grandmother's offer to stay and work for the family business.

They reached the café, where a breakfast buffet was already in full swing.

"We're meeting Larry Tan," Dylan told the host.

The staff seemed to move telepathically. A man in a black suit approached. "Mr. Roche? Right this way."

Dylan still wasn't used to that, being called Mr. Roche.

The man led them to a blocked-off corner. A server poured coffee, and Tommy ogled the buffet before remembering their mission.

"Circling back." Tommy poured sweetener in his coffee. "I went over the accounting files. Nothing flagged. All clean."

"Yeah, but this is going to be local. Agent Peters said to look for symbols, ghost-themed stuff. They hide things in plain sight, in inconspicuous accounts. Old-school gang trick."

Tommy stirred his drink. "You do realize I'm twenty-five and barely look the part of an international forensic auditor?"

"You're here as my guy. That's enough. Throw around some IRS jargon. They'll be too scared to question it."

"Still. If I find anything, it won't hold up in court."

"We're not going to court. This is about exposure. If we prove someone's on the take, Peters takes it from there."

"Got it." Tommy sipped his coffee, then lowered the mug. "Oh, and for the record, call me Tom Rivers while we're here."

Before Dylan could respond, Tommy nudged his elbow. "That him by the door?"

Dylan glanced up. "I think so."

"He's staring at you and not in a good way." Tommy stood up. "I'm going to check him out."

"Tommy, wait." But he was already gone.

A few minutes later, Tommy lowered himself back into the seat with deliberate nonchalance. "He was on the phone. Speaking English, weirdly. I couldn't catch much, but he said something about not being sure he could do it. Then he mentioned a name, Lily So."

Dylan raised an eyebrow. "So?"

"He also mentioned *you*. Said you were here. Said he had to be careful not to raise suspicions."

Now Tommy had Dylan's full attention.

"Now I need to know who this Lily is." He reached for his phone. "And what she has to do with any of this."

LILY

A man paced outside the business center before Lily Tso even reached the doors. Suit. Agitated. Westerner. And ignoring the Open at 9:00 a.m. sign.

"Excuse me, ma'am. Are you opening?" American accent, mid-fifties, probably a conference guest.

She gave him her professional smile. "If you'll give me a minute to get settled, I'll be right with you."

"Sure."

He followed her in anyway.

Breathe. She loosened her shoulders. *Gonna be a long day.*

"I apologize for barging in this early, but my partner, who normally takes care of this stuff, bailed. I need this faxed over to this number here ASAP."

He kept rambling. She didn't catch most of it as she focused on putting away her bag, logging into the system, and getting her workspace in order.

Once her screen lit up, she folded her hands on the desk between them, posture erect, mind ready. "What is it you need faxed?"

He held out his phone. "Can I send you an audio file? You type it up?"

She frowned. Definitely not a listed service. The center had guest-use computers. Typing it for them? Not standard. Not preferred.

"I know it's not listed. Special request maybe?"

"I'll have to check with the manager. Room number?"

He handed over his key card. "Nick Thomas."

She swiped it. Marketing VP, according to her screen. Fancy.

"Would you like to wait while I get a quote?"

"No time. Charge it to the room, thanks. I've got a meeting. The conference room's on the second floor?"

She hesitated, then remembered. American.

"Yes, second floor for you. But if you're using the lift, uh, elevator, press one."

He grinned. "Thank you, Lily." He'd read her name tag. "You don't sound local. American?"

"No."

"Could've fooled me."

"I went to an American school."

"Ah. What's the best way to send the file, email or text?"

She gave him the email and watched the screen. Within seconds, the file appeared.

"Would you like me to email you a draft first?"

"Nah. Make it a final copy. I'll reach out if I need edits."

"Yes, sir."

He nodded and hurried off.

She called her manager, got a price, and entered the charge.

What a boring life. Same routines, different guests. If not for Mr. Thomas, someone else would've wanted something done. Still, no reason to complain.

Her setup was decent. Unlike the small banks of computers on American shows, the Hong Kong center had desks, chairs, and actual space. It looked like a real office.

Winnie Tang walked in, phone pressed to her ear. "Yeah, Ma, I will. Gotta go."

She dropped into the chair across from Lily. "My mother is meddling again. Anything interesting this morning?"

"Same old, same old." It'd be nice to have parents. Even annoying ones.

As Winnie powered up her computer, Lily turned back to hers. A new internal memo had arrived in her inbox.

VIP Guest Alert: Dylan Roche, Marino Hotel Group,
Orlando HQ.

No photo. No details. Just a name.

She'd never heard of him. Something about the vague alert gave her pause.

She flagged it, then returned to her inbox.

DYLAN

Halfway through dialing Agent Peters, Dylan hesitated, thumb hovering just above the screen.

What time was it back home?

Hmm, 9:16 p.m. Orlando time. Late, but not outrageously so. Peters had told him to call anytime. Still, Dylan wasn't used to contacting federal agents at night from a hotel room halfway around the world.

This wasn't what he'd signed up for.

He was here for a routine visit to walk the property, put some faces to names, and shake a few hands. Tommy was already in the accounting office, combing through financial statements. Dylan would spend the afternoon touring the upper floors, chatting with department heads, and getting a feel for the staff.

Now, he just wanted to touch base with Agent Peters.

He pressed call.

The line barely rang.

"Dylan," Peters answered. "I was just about to call you."

That threw him. "Oh, uh, good timing, then."

"Listen. An officer from the US consulate, James Conway, is going to reach out. He has important information. I'm texting you his photo now. When he arrives, check his credentials."

A buzz in Dylan's hand signaled a message. He tapped it open. A photo popped up. Conway could've been the most average man alive. Late thirties, clean-shaven, bland suit. More like an insurance underwriter than a government contact.

"What's going on?" Dylan rubbed the back of his neck. "Why is someone from the consulate coming to see me?"

"A senator requested your help. That's why."

He blinked. "My help? Why? That doesn't make any sense. I'm not—"

"You're the perfect cover. You're already overseas, legitimately. You're not law enforcement, not intelligence. That gives us options."

"I work in corporate hospitality."

"Exactly. We need someone at your hotel relocated to the US

on the DL. It has to look routine. Conway will brief you when he gets there."

"Relocated?" Dylan repeated. "You want me to make up a reason to send an employee back to the States?"

"Yes."

"Can't you just extract them?"

"If we do that, we risk exposure. This is a covert operation. Conway will explain the stakes. But we need this person moved on a moment's notice and without raising flags."

Dylan exhaled, pacing toward the window. Down below, Hong Kong's lights pulsed and glittered like a circuit board even in the daylight.

Who was this employee? What kind of situation required this level of secrecy? And why him?

"How's it going otherwise?" Peters asked.

"Tommy's working in the back office, checking the accounts. I wandered around the property. Everything looks fine on the surface. I'm getting an escorted tour this afternoon."

"Keep it that way. Just play your role."

Dylan didn't respond right away.

A knock startled him.

Not housekeeping. No cheerful voice from the hallway. Just two quiet, deliberate raps.

He crossed the room, phone still in hand, and looked through the peephole.

It was him. Conway.

And he wasn't alone.

Standing just behind him was a younger man, mid-twenties, maybe. In a suit, posture alert, eyes sweeping the hallway like he was casing it.

Dylan lowered the phone, pulse ticking faster.

A senator needed his help?

He wasn't sure he wanted to know why.

CHAPTER 5

MARINO HOTEL, HONG KONG

KYLE

Kyle Peters had been briefed, cleared, and warned. None of that prepared him for this.

As he stood beside Officer Conway outside the Marino Hotel's Presidential Suite, his thoughts kept circling back to the moment it all began. A closed-door meeting with Senator Simon Roth launched him into a covert mission halfway around the world.

Why him? Sure, his probation had just ended, a milestone he hadn't had time to acknowledge, but he was still new, still proving himself. So many agents with years of experience would've been better suited for this. Maybe that was the point. A fresh face. Off the radar. No reputation yet.

Following protocol, he'd contacted the consulate and received a final briefing from Officer Conway.

Conway elbowed him. "Let me do the talking."

"Yes, sir." Kyle straightened up.

The door opened, but only as far as the chain allowed.

"May I see your credentials, please?" came a calm, steady voice.

Kyle fumbled for his FBI cred pack. Conway already had his ID in hand. After the occupant gave a moment's inspection through the narrow gap, the chain slid free, and the door opened fully.

Even knowing who they were meeting, surprise still jolted Kyle. So this was Dylan Roche, the recently discovered heir to the Marino business empire. According to the file, Dylan had survived a brush with death and now worked for the family business. They were about the same age, but their lives couldn't have been more different.

Stepping inside, Kyle stifled a low whistle. No wonder they called this suite presidential. It wasn't just a hotel room. It was an apartment in disguise. A sleek living area with a couch and TV where a wide window framed the glittering skyline. A kitchenette with a minibar and a full dining table. No doubt, the bedroom and bathroom would also be five-star luxury.

"Mr. Roche?" Conway extended his hand.

"Dylan, please."

"This is Special Agent Kyle Peters."

"Peters?" Dylan cocked his head to one side. "By any chance, are you related to Agent Ron Peters?"

"That's my dad." Kyle nodded. With the resemblance, no use pretending otherwise.

Dylan broke into a grin. "I know your father. FBI your family business? Following in the old man's footsteps?"

Kyle dipped his chin. People always assumed that made things easier. It didn't. If anything, it raised the bar.

"Speaking of family business..." Conway rubbed his hands together and got down to business. "We're here to request your assistance."

Dylan gestured toward the couch. "Yeah, Agent Peters mentioned something. What do you have in mind?"

"I spoke with him as well." Conway crossed the room. "He assured me you'd be cooperative and understand this operation's classified nature."

"I understand." Dylan settled into the couch.

"The person we need to extract, Lily Tso, works here in the business center. Kyle will be escorting her back to the States."

Dylan held up a hand. "Where do I come in? I don't know if I have any authority here to give anyone a vacation."

"Here's the sticky part. We can't let anyone know she's going to the States on government business. It'll need to be an undercover operation. That's why the senator picked young Kyle here. He'll pose as her boyfriend."

"What?" Kyle blurted, sitting straighter. So much for easing into post-probation fieldwork.

Conway gave him a sidelong glance. "Or a friend."

Dylan obviously tried not to laugh, but amusement gleamed in the guy's eyes.

"That's why he asked if I could come up with an excuse for her to go to the States." Dylan leaned back, staring at the ceiling. "Hmm, some sort of training program?"

"I've done some research. The hotel used to send employees to their US headquarters for training. Not in a while, though, but it wouldn't be suspicious if the practice resumed."

"Will she come back?" Dylan asked.

"No."

"I hope she knows that and is prepared for it."

"I don't know about that. And it's not our concern. We need to make sure she gets stateside safely. To keep her behavior natural, you shouldn't tell her anything until it's necessary."

Dylan rubbed his chin. "Okay. Let's see... I assume the employees used to return after training. I could have the hotel offer her a job in the States, make it look like a promotion or extended internship. That might work."

He scooted forward, elbows braced on his knees, and locked

his sights on Kyle. "You're supposed to be her friend. Have you met her?"

"No." Kyle squirmed.

Dylan raised an eyebrow. "Then we'll have to find a way to introduce you to your friend." He smirked. "Before that, you'll need to be mine."

Kyle managed a smile, but his gut tightened.

This wasn't just an awkward cover story. It was a test of timing, trust, and his ability to protect someone who didn't know she was in danger.

LILY

For the second time that day, a man in a suit was waiting for Lily outside the business center. This one looked younger, maybe not much older than her own twenty-two years, and far more important. And this time, Larry was also there.

"They're waiting for you," Winnie whispered as she left to go on her break.

"Ah, Lily, here you are." Larry beckoned her forward. "This is Mr. Dylan Roche. And this is our business center supervisor, Lily Tso."

She knew the name. She mentally scrolled through everything she'd read that week. Yes, the memo! Dylan Roche was the owner's grandson. Or was it the hotel president's grandson? Either way, he was a VIP.

She placed her to-go cup on the desk and shook the hand extended toward her. "Nice to meet you, Mr. Roche."

"The pleasure's all mine. And please, call me Dylan." His smile brought warm crinkles around his brown eyes.

Larry shuffled his feet, more ill at ease than she'd ever seen him. "Dylan here would like a chat with you, to see what you do here, you know."

Why would a VIP want to talk to her? "Of course. Please have a seat." She gestured toward a chair on the guest's side of her desk. At least her work area was organized, everything in its proper place, outgoing items stacked in the outgoing tray, and her incoming tray emptied.

"I'll leave you two to it." Larry excused himself from the conversation.

"About what we discussed earlier?" Dylan inquired.

"Absolutely," Larry confirmed. "I'll make sure it's on the agenda for our meeting this afternoon."

"Thank you." Dylan acknowledged with a nod before Larry left. Then Dylan slid into the offered chair and gestured to their surrounds. "Nice. This is more than a business center. I see you offer secretarial services."

"Yeah, the basics. Mostly typing, printing, that sort of thing. We also provide translation services."

"Cool. Do you handle that too?"

"Not personally. We have a few people on contract." She braced her hands on her cool desktop. "Why? Do you need something translated?"

"No. You know, you sound American. Most people here have a British or local accent."

"I try." The desk warmed beneath her palms. "American TV shows help. Plus, I attended an American school with lots of expat kids."

"I have to tell you, I would have thought you were still in high school. Are you sure you're not one of those prodigies who graduate at age twelve?"

Her cheeks flushed. "I get that a lot, mostly from foreigners. I'm older than I look. I'm twenty-two."

"Twenty-two? Have you recently graduated from college?"

"No, I obtained an associate degree in hospitality management."

"Good for you. Do you enjoy your job?"

"Yes, sir." She smiled out of habit. *It's boring.*

Their conversation continued with Dylan displaying genuine curiosity about her work, the hotel, and how the management treated the staff. He seemed refreshingly friendly and down-to-earth, unlike many wealthy playboys in Hong Kong. His attractive appearance didn't hurt either.

But why was he so interested in what she did? He wasn't trying to eliminate the business center, was he?

Someone was approaching the center, and she was the only one there. What to do?

Before she figured out a polite way to tell Dylan she had work to do, he beckoned the fellow forward. "Lily, allow me to introduce you to a friend of mine, Kyle Peters."

The name meant nothing to her. But something in Dylan's tone made her sit up straighter.

KYLE

Lily wasn't what Kyle had pictured from the file—prettier, sharper, and more composed than any photo could show. A natural beauty, she wore no heavy makeup and only the faintest flowery scent, maybe her shampoo.

This assignment wasn't bad after all.

Dylan asked her, "What kind of movies do you enjoy?"

She didn't reply right away, probably wondering why Dylan wanted to know. "I love thrillers and action films. How about you?"

"Same here!" Dylan uncrossed his legs. "Do you have any favorite actors?"

"No. You wouldn't know the Hong Kong actors anyway."

Kyle tugged at his collar. He'd better not tip her off yet, not while this was going smoothly and she was opening up.

She moved her monitor aside to see them both sitting across from her. He'd had to pull up a chair since Dylan already claimed the guest chair. Glass panels framed two sides of the business center, leaving them sitting in a fishbowl.

"It doesn't appear you're very busy here," Dylan said.

She shrugged. "It depends. Guests don't all come down to place an order. A lot of them call or go online. We've had a few translation requests. Mostly, guests want something printed." She gestured toward the computer stations. "As you can see, we offer those stations with desktops for the guests who want to take care of their own business. But, now and then, they need technical help."

"And you're the technical help?"

"I can be." She offered a polite nod. "Most of the time, it's user error."

A young man strode toward them with purpose.

As soon as Tommy Rivers pushed open the door, Dylan stood up. "My lunch appointment is here. Before I go, let me introduce you."

Dylan introduced Tommy to Lily, but not to Kyle. Must be part of their ruse that he and Tommy were already acquainted.

"Hey, Kyle. Good to see you." Tommy played it casual, as planned.

"Same here." They shook hands.

"We're going to lunch," Dylan said. "Kyle, stay and hang out."

"Maybe for a moment." He took the opportunity to learn more about Lily, who seemed friendly enough. She'd fielded a couple of calls, but no guests had come in for services. She seemed to consider this a nice change of pace.

He was suggesting lunch when the other two men returned.

This time, Dylan didn't sit down. "Sorry to bother you again. You said you went to an American school, but I hope you can read Chinese."

She dipped her head. "Yes, sir."

"Can you see this?" Tommy showed her an image on his phone. "Is this a Chinese character?"

Kyle leaned in, curious himself. He hadn't seen the image yet.

She took the phone and enlarged the image. "Yes. *Gwei*. It means ghost."

A chill coursed through Kyle, though he couldn't say why.

CHAPTER 6

MARINO HOTEL, HONG KONG

DYLAN

The word *ghost* hit harder than Dylan expected. He exchanged a look with Tommy—confirmation.

"Why?" Lily asked. "Where did you see it? You came back for this?"

"Never mind." Dylan waved her off. "We're only curious. We'll be going now."

They took off before she could question them further. Once out of earshot, Dylan said, "Tell me what you found out."

Palms raised, Tommy made a nothing-much face. "This checks with the symbol. Everything else seems to be in order. The other reimbursement accounts all need approval. For some reason, Larry's is exempt. He's treating it like his personal ATM. A lot of his checks with that symbol on the memo line. I bet you the company he's making payments to is a front for something."

"We should inform Agent Peters. He'll know how to handle this or how to initiate an investigation." Dylan diverted from the café. "Let's go back to the suite. We can order room service and avoid having our conversation overheard."

"Okay." Tommy veered left toward the elevators. "Speaking of Agent Peters, is Kyle—"

"Yeah, Kyle is his son. I can see the resemblance."

"Didn't Fr. Phil think you resembled your dad too?"

"He did. Even Grandma Carol mentioned it."

"Wait, you're calling her 'grandma' now?"

"Still getting used to it."

Back at the suite, they placed a lunch order. Dylan sank deep into the couch, arms spread across its back. "You know Larry's phone conversation you overheard?"

"Sure, and I told you what I heard. He seemed reluctant about something and mentioned Lily."

"I'm calling Agent Peters to update him."

This was their second time reaching out to the agent, hoping that it wasn't too late. The agent did say to call anytime. Once again, Agent Peters answered promptly.

"Agent Peters." Dylan sat up straighter and slid to the cushion beside Tommy. "I'm putting you on speaker. Tommy is here with me."

They told him about the checks with the Chinese character on the memo lines and the overheard conversation.

"Okay, good work. I'll let the appropriate agencies know. You let them do the investigation. These people are dangerous. You hear me? Don't try to play detective."

After his brush with death, Dylan wasn't planning on going solo again in any adventure. And if he knew his best friend, Tommy wouldn't do anything stupid.

"No worries there."

"Oh, by the way, we met Kyle," Tommy said.

After a grunt, but no response, Dylan asked, "What do you make of Larry mentioning Lily's name to the unknown person on the phone?"

"That's worrying. I'll alert the appropriate people. Did you manage to secure her leave of absence?"

"I'm about to find out after a meeting this afternoon."
"Text me updates. Call if it's urgent."

CHAPTER 7

TOWN HALL, FLORIDA, USA

SIMON

"Thank you." Senator Simon Roth maintained his smile, exchanging handshakes and fist bumps and posing for photos as he maneuvered his way out of the town hall. His shoulders loosened once he reached the waiting car with an aide as his driver. He'd grown accustomed to the routine, even though he never enjoyed it.

But was he truly suited to a life in politics? Staying in the State Department might've been wiser. His mentor, retired Senator Roger Rifkin, had encouraged the move. Roger had groomed Simon as his handpicked successor.

By all accounts, Simon was thriving. His career was strong, and he owned a house while maintaining an apartment in DC. Coming from a humble background as a poor orphan, he'd aspired to climb the social ladder and enjoy the luxuries life had to offer.

Yet, now that he had achieved most of those aspirations, a touch of emptiness and dissatisfaction crept in. Was he experiencing a midlife crisis? Reluctant as he was to admit it, he was in the middle age at forty-nine.

Now and then, powerful attorneys tried to entice him to join their lobbying or law firms. He'd turned them all down. That hadn't deterred his campaign manager, Harrison Burke, who'd collected those attorneys' names and contact information and likely later approached them for support and contributions.

Simon rubbed his temples. His melancholic state began when Roger highlighted his absence of a family or, at minimum, a spouse. According to them, having a family image would always be more favorable.

Roger remarked that Simon was married to his job. Quite true. Since his time in Hong Kong, he'd never pursued a serious romantic relationship. Instead, he sometimes retrieved a faded photo from his wallet and ached to turn back time.

As he exited the car, he hoped something, anything, would change soon.

Outside his office, a staffer, Lucia, intercepted him. "Sir, urgent message from Langley. Says 'Nightingale is humming.'"

He'd prepared for this. And hoped it wouldn't come. He mumbled his thanks and hurried to his office. "Office swept?"

"Yes, sir," answered an aide.

Since he'd started serving on the Senate Select Committee on Intelligence, his office had undergone a regular sweeping of eavesdropping devices. Now, he closed the door and settled behind his desk. He went through the security protocol to connect.

Todd, his contact on the operation, appeared on the screen and said, "I see you got the message."

"What did you hear?"

"Decoded something from Phoenix." He checked a piece of paper. "Intel acquired, operative in danger, will deploy backup asset, Lily Tso."

Simon searched his memory for the particulars from the

operation briefings. Their undercover operative, Phoenix, might be in danger. The one photo etched in his mind was that of Lily Tso. "Do we have any information about the specific danger the scientists are facing?"

"Nothing at the moment. We'll continue to monitor the situation. Phoenix will provide further guidance on what to do with the scientists. They could be arrested, killed, or simply vanish as did many others in China."

"Maybe the scientists got cold feet. If that's the case, could Phoenix's cover be blown?"

"No evidence suggests that. We're flagging everything remotely related to this operation. If we uncover any indication it happened, we'll take appropriate action." Todd paused. "What still puzzles me is why Phoenix chose Lily Tso. According to her dossier, she works at a low-level position in a hotel. She's never even been to China."

His mind drifted back to a place and time where he'd professed his love to a woman. It must be a coincidence, but Olivia and Lily Tso possessed an uncanny resemblance. Too uncanny to ignore, especially with the shared last name. As far as he knew, Olivia had died.

At least, that's what Roger told him. The only person he knew who had details about Olivia's demise was Marie Ramos, her best friend. He'd better meet with Roger and inquire further. Could it have been a false rumor? Was Olivia still alive? Or perhaps Lily was Olivia's niece?

"Sir?" the voice interrupted his thoughts.

"Oh, sorry." He rubbed his temples and refocused. "What were you saying?"

"I was asking why you think Phoenix selected Tso for this role."

He had his suspicions, but offered none. "I don't know."

"I guess we'll need to come up with a new plan, then."

He nodded. After some deliberation, they reached a plan of action.

If circumstances had been different, he'd have been confined to receiving briefings and reports. However, he was now entangled in a crisis that had reached the White House, either due to being at the right place at the right time or perhaps the wrong place at the wrong time, depending on one's perspective. The president selected him to take charge of the situation.

Marge Beaumont, known as the Ghost, was a criminal mastermind fueled by a deep-rooted hatred of her biological family. After years of evasion, she'd been caught. Raised by a deranged woman who'd stolen her as an infant, she'd surpassed her mentor in cruelty and control. However, her personal vendetta against her biological nephew became her downfall.

Simon heard enough stories about the Ghost to know she didn't bluff. When she threatened something, she had the means to back it up. Her team of skilled lawyers claimed a fail-safe plan, her bargaining chip to evade severe penalties, including death. Everybody was on edge, even though she was being held without bail, awaiting further legal proceedings.

Simon checked the time. Still early Tuesday evening here—Wednesday morning already in Hong Kong.

As he drove toward the nondescript warehouse, his phone buzzed.

"Don't forget about your fundraising event tomorrow!" Harrison exclaimed as soon as Simon answered.

"I won't. Although I might have to leave early. I'm dealing with an emergency, and I have another meeting to attend."

He wasn't looking forward to that meeting. Supervisory Special Agent Ron Peters, leader of the elite Task Force 629, had been pressuring him for updates.

Technically, the elite task force had been disbanded following the Ghost's capture. However, Ron's team, along with some support staff and occasional assistance from other agencies, was still working to tie up loose ends. The higher-ups were unaware that dismantling the crime boss's organization would take months if not years. The national consequences of her threats were far from ordinary.

"How do you plan to insert your undercover agent?" Simon asked after delivering his report.

Seated at a conference table in a secure room, the agent clasped his hands on the desk before responding. "We don't need Eva yet. Dylan is as good a contact as any. Since he's embraced his heritage, he's determined to clean up his family's business." Ron's thumbs tapped against each other. "The matriarch has been dealing with health issues. Once Eva is ready, Dylan will offer her the assistant position. She'll go in as an aide to Boss Lady Marino."

Simon shifted in his chair. Eva, not Higgins. Ron's longtime family friendship with the girl showed in his use of her first name. Simon tapped his pen against the table. "If Dylan is willing, why not make him the primary contact?"

"For one, he's a civilian." Ron spread his thumbs, palms open, knuckles against the tabletop. "He has no prior military or scouting experience. No training with firearms or serious criminals. The Ghost is ruthless and connected with dangerous individuals. We need someone with the right training. That's why I sent Eva to receive specialized training from our Langley colleagues."

Hmm. Simon exhaled. "I understand your point. How do you plan to utilize Dylan?"

"Dylan is aware individuals within his family business are still working for the Ghost. He's determined to clean house, and that should be his role."

"All right." Simon nodded. "Does the matriarch still have access to valuable intelligence?"

"Definitely. She's been around a long time. With the attorney gone, they don't trust Dylan, a newcomer, especially someone that young."

"Okay, you didn't choose Eva Higgins for this operation solely based on your connections, did you?"

Ron gave him a knowing look. "You should know me better than that."

"I do." Simon did. However, Eva practically grew up with Kyle, Ron's son, and Simon must consider that fact.

"Now, it's your turn."

Simon briefed Ron on the latest developments. The Ghost had claimed to possess the power to unleash a deadly biological weapon if her demands were not met. The intelligence received, via Phoenix, confirmed the existence of the plan to deploy the weapon. Their operatives recovered the virus, but the Chinese scientists involved lost their lives in the process.

Most alarmingly, Ghost's trusted lieutenants already possessed a test batch of the virus. "Intelligence hasn't confirmed whether that batch is fully active or capable of mass transmission."

Simon fell silent. No need to say they had to assume the worst. "Phoenix has, however, secured an antidote and tasked Lily Tso with delivering it."

Ron's thumbs had stilled again. "Any luck in tracking down those lieutenants?"

"Not yet. All ports of entry are under surveillance. However, they always find ways. This operation will require a two-pronged approach—capture those individuals and retrieve the antidote. One way or another, we must prevent a catastrophe."

"The way I see it"—Ron's thumbs pressed to each other, their tips turning white—"time is running short. If Tso doesn't arrive in time, those lieutenants may release the virus, and the consequences would be catastrophic before we could contain it."

"Agreed. That's why she should be on the way soon."

"Do you trust this operative, Phoenix?"

Simon redirected his focus to the agent's face. "I've never met Phoenix." Which made it difficult to trust the person fully. However, he did have faith in the intelligence agents who'd vouched for Phoenix. "But I trust the intelligence people I work with. It's a complicated situation. Don't ask too many questions."

"Interesting. The other agencies will handle the operational details, then."

"Exactly. Now, let's discuss Lily Tso. The Company is taking care of arrangements for bringing her here. However, I do need your assistance." Long ago, Simon learned the insiders referred to the CIA as the Company.

Ron cocked his head. "Yes?"

"Could you ask Dylan to provide assistance if the liaison requires it?"

"Of course."

"That would be great. I've already assigned a young agent to accompany Lily covertly."

Ron frowned. "Why? I thought the Company already had officers in place."

"They do. However, we're aiming to avoid drawing unnecessary attention. Having a young agent pose as her boyfriend will help maintain a low profile."

"A young agent. Which agency? Us?"

"Yes. I would've told you earlier, but my mind was somewhere else. For that, I'm sorry."

Ron narrowed his eyes. "Who did you send?"

"I conducted thorough research for the right person. I needed someone young, someone who visited Hong Kong a couple of times before, which makes it easier to establish a believable backstory in case anyone investigates. Plus, this person must have experience interacting with the local population." It sounded bad, but he hadn't made the decision lightly.

Ron's frown deepened. "Who? Please tell me you didn't send Kyle."

CHAPTER 8

TASK FORCE OFFICE, FLORIDA, USA

RON

Ron Peters waited until the senator left before reaching for his phone. Then he stopped, his chest tightening.

As much as he hated to admit it, Simon was right. Kyle was an FBI Special Agent. He had training. And the job was simply to babysit the girl. How dangerous could it be?

However, as a father, he couldn't help worrying. He'd been tracking the Ghost and her crime syndicate for years. He knew how ruthless she could be. He could only hope Kyle wouldn't encounter her minions.

He paced the room, trying to quiet the unease twisting in his gut.

He'd better check on Eva. The program he sent her to wasn't typical, but his retired spy friends were skilled. They offered to help when he explained her role.

He picked up his phone and dialed a contact. "Hey, how's Eva doing?"

"Everything's going great," the voice on the other end

assured him. "She's eager to learn and proving to be a quick study."

He exhaled. He hadn't been sure using a fresh agent was the right choice. With the Ghost's network, most seasoned agents were on their radar. But he'd known Eva through his son and ran her background. She appeared to be a good choice.

He'd passed her profile to Fr. Phil, the pastor of the church next to Mirror Estate, and asked for a favor to make sure she got selected. He and Phil had served in an operation or two together back when Phil had still been with the SEALs.

Phil persuaded him Dylan was a stand-up guy, something Ron concurred with after getting to know him. Good thing he'd persuaded Dylan the reality show was a stupid idea. Of all things! A small smile tugged at his lips.

Nathan Tanner, his senior agent, poked his head in after a knock. "Boss, if there's nothing else, I'll be heading out."

"All right. Good night."

As Ron entered his home late that evening, his thoughts turned to Simon. They'd known each other professionally for decades. Back when Simon had been with the State Department, they'd even worked together a few times.

And right now, the senator was hiding something or not telling him the whole story, particularly when it came to the Tso girl. Could it be something beyond his security clearance?

His phone beeped with a reminder to check on Dylan. And he remembered the senator's request.

He was about to call when his phone rang.

CHAPTER 9

MARINO HOTEL, HONG KONG

LILY

Lily smiled more than she'd expected during lunch with Kyle. They hadn't gone anywhere fancy, just the hotel café, and it wasn't a date. She tucked a slippery strand of long hair behind her ear. "I'm surprised to hear you've visited Hong Kong before. Do you have any favorite spots?"

The café was quiet at this hour, its small tables arranged beneath warm recessed lighting. The faint aroma of freshly brewed coffee and baked pastries lingered in the air. Soft instrumental music drifted in from the lobby, blending with the low hum of conversation from distant reception desks.

"A few I loved, I'm sad to say, no longer exist. I still remember the first time I landed at the old airport." Kyle stirred the ice in his coffee with the straw, the cubes clinking as he leaned forward, eyes distant with memory. "I sat by the window, staring out—buildings were practically right next to us. My dad said it was one of the hardest places for pilots to land."

"I heard that too." She lowered her spoon into the steaming bowl of wonton noodle soup, swirling the thin noodles before setting the spoon back down. "Now we have a nice, spacious airport." She caught Kyle watching her lunch with mild curiosity and gave a small smile. "This is Hong Kong. We serve a blend of Western and Cantonese food. By the way, which school did you go to? Or were you only here during summer?"

"Just summers. Why?"

The fragrant broth rose in a cloud of warmth, scented with shrimp, pork, ginger, and a whisper of sesame oil. She picked up her chopsticks and lifted a wonton, its delicate wrapper slick with broth, revealing the plump pink shrimp nestled inside. As she bit into it, the savory filling burst with juicy sweetness, mingling with the soup's comforting, salty warmth.

"Curious. I went to an American school. Thought maybe we crossed paths without knowing it."

"I think I'm older than you. We wouldn't have been in the same crowd anyway."

"I'm twenty-two. You can't be that much older." She studied him, sandy brown hair, warm brown eyes. No crow's-feet, no thinning. Broad shoulders. He must live at the gym.

In front of him sat a piping hot bowl of congee topped with slivers of ginger and bright green scallions, alongside a small bamboo steamer of sticky rice wrapped in lotus leaf. The savory aroma of tender pork, mushrooms, and glutinous rice drifted across the table as he unwrapped the parcel.

"Four years doesn't sound like much now, but back then, it was practically a generation." A beat. "You ever go on any adventures?"

"Not yet. But I'd like to try something thrilling." She glanced discreetly at the time.

"I see you checking the clock." He signaled for the check. "Lunch hour's over?"

"I work for a living. You're on vacation."

"Hardly."

"You're here on business? What do you do?"

He didn't answer right away. "I'm in law enforcement."

"You're a cop?"

"Not exactly." He paid the check too fast. "Should we go? I'll walk you back."

Her brow furrowed. Not exactly? What did that mean?

Her phone buzzed. She picked it up. "Thanks. I need to take this."

He nodded and gestured toward the restroom.

"*Wei*, Auntie," she said into the phone.

"Listen, Lily—" That wasn't Auntie's voice.

"Who are you?"

"—you need to be careful. You're being watched. Go to Marie. She'll explain. Tell her Phoenix said it's time for the truth to come out… and for you to meet your father."

Click.

The phone shook in her hand as she gawked at it. The contact on-screen said Auntie. But that wasn't her voice.

KYLE

After their conversation, Kyle adjusted his first impression. Lily clearly wasn't a teenager.

She carried herself with confidence, had insights about Hong Kong only a local would, and asked astute questions. The lunch hadn't been a date, but it wasn't awkward either. He'd even enjoyed himself.

When he came back from the restroom, she stood outside the café, holding her phone, brows furrowed, mouth parted, eyes wide.

"Everything all right?" he asked.

She jumped, blinking as if pulled back to the present. "Er, er…"

Kyle located a quiet corner and guided her back inside to an empty table. Once they sat, he kept his voice low. "What happened?"

"It doesn't make sense." She waved her phone. "Someone called using my godmother's number. She said I was being watched and to be careful. I don't understand."

Kyle's instincts kicked in hard. Spoofed number? Surveillance threat? Who knew her contact list? "Did you try calling your godmother back?"

She shot him a look. "Why didn't I think of that?"

The sarcasm was automatic, but the tension didn't fade. She tapped her screen, held the phone to her ear, and spoke rapid Cantonese, throwing a few English words in. He caught "Auntie" and then "Phoenix."

His focus sharpened. That code name wasn't supposed to be in public use.

While she was still on the line, he texted Officer Conway.

> Possible breach. She got a warning call.
> Phoenix is mentioned.

Then one to Dylan.

> Heads up. We need to move now.

She hung up. "She's fine. But guess what, she told me to be careful too. And she wants me to come see her."

"I don't blame her." Kyle kept his tone even. "Are you going?"

"After work."

He nodded.

His mission was clear: Get Lily to the States safely.

From now on, he'd be her shadow.

Without her knowing it.

CHAPTER 10

THE RIFKIN RESIDENCE, FLORIDA, USA

SIMON

Simon always made time to visit Roger Rifkin. Since Roger retired and moved back to Florida full time, it felt like the least he could do. The old man lived alone now, no more staff bustling through the halls, just one housekeeper and many rooms full of memories. His wife died years ago, and he never remarried.

More than once, he'd said his biggest regret was not having children. Maybe that's why he'd taken to Simon the way he had, like family, like a son.

Simon approached the million-dollar home in one of Orlando's most exclusive neighborhoods, gated and guarded. The first time, he'd driven past the guardhouse in awe. To a former orphan who considered a sit-down meal a luxury, this kind of opulence still made an impression.

Now, it was time to ask about Olivia. Despite his standing invitation to dinner, he always texted ahead out of courtesy. He turned into the driveway and pulled up alongside Harrison's car and another vehicle he didn't recognize. A guest, maybe? Occasionally, others showed up. Usually, it was just the three of them, Roger, Harrison, and Simon.

Harrison had been Roger's campaign manager, then his chief of staff. After Roger retired, he coaxed Harrison into running Simon's campaign.

Simon parked and approached the door. Before he could knock, it swung open. Congressman Adrian Pearson stepped out, flanked by his aide and a man who looked like a bodyguard.

"Hello, Adrian. Didn't know you were coming." Simon offered his hand.

"I'm leaving. Another event to run to. Remember Evan?" He gestured to his aide.

"Of course." Simon nodded.

"Enjoy your evening," Adrian said as they moved. Evan gave a nod. No one introduced the third man—too much in a rush.

"Same to you," Simon replied.

Inside, Rosa, the housekeeper, led him to the dining room. Spa-like music played in the background. Saffron and garlic scented the air. Muted lighting cast the trim work on cream walls into shadow and glowed along the twelve-seat mahogany table. Roger and Harrison were already seated at one end.

"I saw Adrian leaving." Simon joined them.

"I invited him to stay, but he had another commitment. Rosa made paella. Wine?"

"I'll have what you're having."

As Rosa served, Roger asked, "How's the case with the Ghost going? Is she gonna skate?"

Simon shrugged. "Hard to say. We're working hard to prevent that."

"I hear she has something up her sleeve."

Nursing his drink, Harrison watched the exchange.

Simon said nothing until Rosa left the room. "How did you hear that?"

Roger waved, wineglass in hand. "Come now. You don't think I'm that out of the loop?"

Fair point. Roger had been a power player for decades. Influence lingered long after retirement.

"Then you know I can't talk about it."

"Oh, I know. Just curious." Roger twisted his glass. Straw-yellow chardonnay sloshed side to side. "My guess? She's got dirt on some powerful people. If that kind of scandal leaked online…"

Simon crossed his legs and settled back in the plush seat. That angle hadn't occurred to him. "Scandals happen all the time. Doesn't mean they threaten national security."

Harrison reached for the wine bottle, the Vie di Romans label crisp. He poured Simon a cup and passed it across the table. "I remember one of her underlings—supposed to stand trial. But the evidence vanished, and so did the prosecutor." He saluted with his refilled glass. "Right after the midterms, I think. No one noticed. Everyone was too busy celebrating."

The conversation continued through dinner until Harrison excused himself, citing work.

Roger moved to the living room with his wine. Simon, sensing the night wasn't over, asked for coffee.

As he sat sipping the warm brew, his thoughts turned inward again, questioning whether he was cut out for politics. Telling voters what they wanted to hear just to win votes? That wasn't who he was. There were issues he couldn't ignore, promises he wouldn't break.

Roger waved in front of Simon's face. "Where'd you go?"

"Sorry, spaced out." A beat. "Do you remember Olivia?"

Roger set his glass down. "The fling you had in Hong Kong?"

It wasn't a fling. No matter how many times Simon had tried to explain that, the man had never taken it. He exhaled. "It wasn't a fling, and you know it."

Roger raised a brow. "Okay. What about her?"

"How did she die?"

Roger was quiet. "That's ancient history. Why dig it up now?"

Simon couldn't explain without revealing classified intel. "Just curious."

Before he could press further, his phone vibrated. He swiped the screen, then stood. "Sorry. Duty calls."

TASK FORCE OFFICE

The task force building was nearly empty when Simon arrived. He went straight to the secure comms room.

"Report," he said as soon as the screen lit up.

Todd, the CIA contact, looked exhausted. "We've lost contact with Phoenix. No one on-site knows anything. No messages, no chatter."

"Last confirmed contact?"

"Four days ago. The message about Lily Tso. Now we're hearing whispers. Phoenix went on some important trip."

Was Phoenix dropping breadcrumbs for them or false leads to throw off the Ghost? More importantly... "Status of Lily?"

"We've got eyes on her. So far, so good. Nothing on the scientists."

"Was Phoenix compromised?"

Todd shook his head. "Nothing to suggest that."

This was unusual. Where was Phoenix's handler? As far as Simon knew, the handler was the only one who maintained contact with an undercover operative and acted as a conduit of information. However, with Phoenix, it seemed all standard operating procedures went up in flames.

Simon frowned. "Who's Phoenix's handler?"

"Burns. Jay Burns."

Whoa. Simon blinked. "*The* Jay Burns?"

Everyone in the community knew the name. His reputation—and that of his longtime partner, Patty Helms—was the stuff of legends.

"Is Helms still active?"

"She is, but currently out of the country."

Simon nodded. "Send me Burns's contact."

"Yes, sir."

As the screen went dark, Simon leaned back. If anyone knew who Phoenix really was or what happened to Olivia, it would be Burns.

They needed to talk.

CHAPTER 11

ASSUMPTION CONVENT, HONG KONG

LILY

After work, Lily headed straight for the convent, still haunted by the caller's voice. Rather than taking her usual stroll from the MTR station, she flagged down a taxi.

She had started her schooling here, at the Catholic school connected to the convent. By Hong Kong standards, the campus was large, complete with a chapel, classroom buildings, and the convent itself. After primary school, her uncle transferred her to an American school, much to her godmother's dismay. It had become common in recent years for Hong Kong parents, especially those who'd secured foreign passports, to send their children to international schools.

"Visiting Sr. Marie?" the woman who opened the convent door asked.

"Yes." Lily stepped inside.

She came often enough that the residents recognized her. Despite dwindling vocations in many religious orders, Auntie's community remained flourishing. Lily had often seen young women attending so-called come-and-see retreats here. Some stayed, though many didn't make it to final vows.

The convent also had space for lay consecrated women. The woman who had answered the door was likely one of them, dressed plainly, no habit. The nuns, both professed and discerning, wore habits. Lily had once learned there were subtle differences between them, but she couldn't recall what they were.

She approached the convent's guest parlor.

Auntie appeared a moment later and motioned toward her small office with its spare essentials—a desk, a cabinet, a pair of chairs, and a window overlooking the chapel courtyard. On the wall hung a crucifix and portraits of the Holy Father and the bishop.

After settling into one chair, Auntie leaned forward. "Tell me again exactly what the caller said about your father."

Lily sat across from her. "She said to tell you Phoenix said it was time for the truth to come out and for me to meet my father."

Auntie's expression didn't change, but she nodded once. "She said Phoenix."

"Yes. Does that mean something?"

Auntie sighed. "It does."

23 YEARS AGO

HONG KONG

CHAPTER 12

OCEAN CENTER CAFÉ

SR. MARIE/MARIE RAMOS

Marie Ramos dropped her purse on the empty chair and settled in at the coffee shop across from her best friend, sharing teatime. The warm aroma of freshly baked scones mingled with the sweet, buttery scent of fruit crumbles and delicate pastries displayed behind the glass counter. The fragrant steam of strong black tea with a hint of bergamot drifted from porcelain teapots on nearby tables.

Around her, the café buzzed with quiet chatter in English and Cantonese, the gentle clink of fine china, and the soft scrape of knives spreading clotted cream and strawberry jam. Beyond the polished wood and brass interior, large windows framed the steady flow of pedestrians and the distant honk of buses threading through crowded city streets.

"Ramos? That's not Chinese," said the American guy, her best friend's date.

It was the first time Marie had met Simon Roth.

Before she could respond to him, Olivia jumped in. "Her father isn't Chinese. You do know there are all kinds of people in Hong Kong, right? She wasn't even born here. She's from Macau."

Simon perked up. "Seriously? Let me guess—your dad's Portuguese?"

"Yes." Marie managed a polite smile. "I've heard a lot about you. I'm surprised Olivia hasn't told you about me."

He leaned out of the way, waiting for the waitress to finish refilling their tea. "Oh, she has, just not your background. I know you're a, uh… What do you call it? A nun-in-training?"

"As of last week, I'm a novitiate."

"That means she's passed the first stage of discernment." Olivia patted Marie's arm. "She's one step closer to the vows and all that."

"Enough about me. What about you?" Marie folded her fingers around a teacup. The delicate citrusy scent of Earl Grey tea, rich with bergamot, carried on the steam. "I heard you work at the American consulate."

"Yeah. Can't say what I do, but I've got the nice title of foreign service officer."

A phone rang.

"Sorry." He pulled a small flip phone from the suit jacket he'd slung over the chair.

"Isn't that cool?" Olivia whispered. "He has one of those new flip phones."

Marie had seen the chunky models some of Olivia's friends carried, but this one was different—sleek, almost futuristic, probably one of those expensive international phones she'd read about.

"Excuse me." Simon stepped away to take the call.

Once he was out of earshot, Olivia scooted her chair closer to Marie. "So? What do you think?"

Marie shrugged. "He's handsome. But I don't know him."

"He has a good job. He's American. You know my parents are always pushing me to study in the States like Andrew."

Olivia's brother had gone to the US for university, married a Hong Kong girl with US citizenship, and become a US citizen within months. A lot of families were doing that now, especially since the handover.

"You're saying marrying Simon could be your ticket out. Would your parents approve?"

"Come on, you know my parents don't want me dating *gweilo*." Olivia flicked her fingers, waggling three. "We've been dating three months on the sly."

"You never told me you were dating. I thought you were just friends."

"We were. At first."

Marie let the sweet steam bathe her face again. Then the liquid warmed her tongue in a burst of flavor. "Three months is something. But it doesn't mean love. Or does it?"

"I don't know. We click. He gets me. Doesn't care that most of my friends aren't Chinese. And—he knows about my hacking."

"You told him?" Marie clattered the cup back to its saucer and winced at the noise. "You never tell anyone."

"Yeah, it just kind of came out. I was, like, sixteen! And it's not like I hacked into government sites or anything. I just wanted to change a couple of grades."

"I know. You were lucky the school didn't report you."

"You know what he said? That his country could use people with my computer skills. And he knows I'm legit now, working in computer security."

But that didn't mean he loved her. He started walking back. Even though they'd been speaking in Cantonese, a language he probably didn't understand, she wouldn't risk continuing the conversation in front of him.

She leaned in and whispered, "To be continued."

A FEW WEEKS LATER
ASSUMPTION CONVENT

"Amen," the nuns responded in unison.

Evening prayers ended, and most of the women slipped out of the chapel. Some lingered, kneeling in private devotion. Marie rose and headed back to her shared room. Life in the convent had settled into a rhythm of prayers, studies, and chores. She still wasn't sure if she'd take final vows, but for now, she was committed.

Her roommate had kitchen duty tonight. Marie couldn't cook to save her life, though kitchen duty often meant cleaning. Most of the women here could cook. Everyone brought their own talents.

She stopped midstep. The doorbell? At this hour?

The convent's doors were open during the day but locked at six when the sisters gathered for dinner and evening prayer. Visitors weren't expected now.

A passing older sister poked her head into the hallway. "Marie, you have a visitor."

Her?

She made her way to the guest parlor. In the doorway, she froze.

Olivia.

She stood with her back turned, but the shape of her shoulders, the set of her stance, was unmistakable.

"Hi—" Marie started.

Olivia pivoted, and Marie's stomach dropped. Her friend's pale face and glassy eyes said something was very wrong.

"What's the matter?" Marie crossed the room in a few steps.

"What am I gonna d–do?" Olivia's voice cracked.

Marie reached for her arm. "Come with me."

She led her through the hallway. No one stopped them. There wasn't a rule against bringing visitors into dorm rooms, but even if there was, this wasn't the time to worry about it.

Once they were inside, she shut the door.

Olivia paced in quick, jerky steps, her hands cutting through the air as if forging a path. "I don't know what to do. They're gonna kill me. What do I do? What do I do?"

"Stop." Marie grabbed her friend's shoulders and eased her into a chair. "Take a breath. Talk to me."

Olivia sniffled, eyes brimming. "I took the test."

"What test?"

"I got it at the pharmacy. I took it twice. Then again at the clinic."

Marie blinked, trying to follow. "What are you—"

And then her heart stopped. Her hand reached for the cross at her neck.

"No," she whispered.

Olivia's silence was answer enough.

Marie stepped closer and lowered her voice. "You're... pregnant?"

A tiny nod.

Marie closed her eyes. *God, give me wisdom.*

Then she looked her friend in the eyes. "Does Simon know?"

Olivia shook her head. "I left a message at his office. He hasn't called back."

"What about his mobile? The one he always uses for work?"

"I don't have the number. It's only for government stuff."

He'd taken a call during their first meeting, pulling the phone from his suit jacket. She'd thought it was so modern, so out of reach.

"Can you go see him? You said he lives in one of those apartments in the Mid-Levels, right?"

"I guess. Should I?"

"Of course. He has a right to know. You can't go through this alone. He needs to step up for you and the baby."

She paused to let her friend say something. Nothing.

"And you need to tell your parents."

Olivia recoiled. "No way. They'll kill me."

Marie's heart ached. "They'll find out, Olivia. Better from you than someone else. But for now, let's focus on Simon."

LATER THAT EVENING
HUNG WAH BUILDING

OLIVIA

How long had she been standing outside Simon's high-rise? Olivia Tso shivered, out of time and out of ways to reach him.

Before leaving Marie, she'd called Simon again at both his office and his flat, but had been unable to reach him. She took a deep breath, braced herself, and stepped into the marble-floored lobby.

At one of the two intercom phones by the lifts, she punched in his flat number. Ten seconds, then twenty seconds, then thirty. No response. She sighed and put the headset back. What to do now?

"Hello, miss?"

She turned toward where a gweilo, an older one, maybe her father's age, distinguished and dressed accordingly, walked in from the street. She smiled tentatively, unsure if he was talking to her.

"Pardon me. Are you here for Simon? I've seen you with him."

"Oh yes. I think he's out."

"Here, let me take you to the lounge where we can talk. By

the way, my name is Roger Rifkin. Simon works for me. Not directly."

Rifkin… Simon had mentioned him. A senator. As with most Hong Kong people, she paid no attention to politics. Still, she hesitated.

He punched in the security code and opened the door to the lifts. "I keep an apartment here, excuse me, a flat, even though I'm no longer stationed in Hong Kong. Business brought me here this time. Simon is staying here as my guest. Rent is ridiculously high in this area, especially for a young officer. Why don't we sit in the lounge?"

This was new. Simon never mentioned staying at Rifkin's place. "I had wondered how he could afford such a luxurious flat." But she'd also thought he made good money.

Since he wasn't taking her to the flat, she relented and followed him. They wouldn't be alone. Residents were coming and going. The luxury building dedicated the entire second floor to residents' entertainment and health. A gym took up a good portion, while sofas, big-screen TVs, and a kitchenette formed the lounge in another portion. Several residents were working out.

He gestured to the sofa. "Would you like something to drink? I'm sure I can find something in the little fridge there."

She sat. "No thanks."

"I believe your name is Olivia. Is that correct?" As she nodded, he smoothed his slacks. "I'm surprised he didn't tell you. He's been reassigned to Singapore."

No! "Singapore? When?"

"Immediately. He would've told you if he hadn't had to leave abruptly."

"What do you mean? 'Leave abruptly'?" This couldn't be happening.

"He left yesterday."

No way would he have left without telling her or leaving a message. "Do you know how to get ahold of him?"

He gave a small headshake and exhaled. "I'm sorry. He hasn't called with his new contact info yet. Young love. You can't blame him. It's a great opportunity. He applied for that position last year, but got turned down."

She wasn't listening anymore. Her hand moved to her belly. All she could think of was how to get word to him about their baby.

The next day, she went about her business automatically. It wasn't easy, but she found Simon's work email. She emailed a cryptic message. They might assign him a new email address, but maybe, if that was the case, this was early enough they'd forward the message.

She still hadn't told anyone other than Marie. Last night, when she'd returned to her home, she'd relayed to Marie what Rifkin had said. While her friend said she would pray for guidance, Olivia would take a more practical approach. She wasn't giving up yet.

Usually, she left her workplace at five. Today, having nothing to do at home and no word from Simon, she stayed late. The work computer was far superior to hers at home, and the internet connection was much faster. She wanted to research the US Embassy in Singapore. Maybe she could find his contact information.

When she left for the day, she took her usual route to the bus stop. A hand came out of nowhere and covered her nose and mouth with a cloth. Was that a familiar figure, maybe the senator? She squinted, trying to focus. But the cloth cut off her air, and everything went black.

Olivia woke to the scent of antiseptics. Was she in a hospital? Other than a ceiling fan, some kind of machine by the bed, and a door, she didn't see anything else. What was this place?

A woman in a nurse outfit approached and checked her vitals.

Olivia was too weak to resist.

"Where am I? What happened?" she managed to croak out.

The nurse left without a response.

Then another gweilo strode in. This one was maybe a tad younger than Rifkin. Not another senator!

"Olivia? How are you feeling?" the man asked. Another American, his accent told her.

She had no energy to be nice. "Who are you?"

"I'm Jay Burns. Suffice it to say, I work for the USA and the good guys. Someone tried to abduct you. I got there in time to stop it."

That didn't make sense. Maybe she'd hit her head. Who would abduct her? "I… don't know. I think, er, you're wrong."

"Is Simon Roth the father?"

The name jolted her closer to full consciousness. "How, er, what?"

His demeanor was gentle, not at all threatening. "We've been keeping an eye on him and a few others. And the nurse told me about the baby."

Too shocked to speak, Olivia gawked. Behind him, a woman leaned against the door.

"I'll talk. You listen, okay? Let's assume Simon is the father. Let's further assume you failed to locate him to tell him the good news. We can confirm he did get reassigned. However, we believe he tried to have someone relay a message to you, but that person didn't do so."

She could believe he hadn't left without informing her, but who would stop a message between lovers? None of this made sense.

"By the way, your discreet visit to the clinic yesterday didn't go unnoticed." Jay Burns shifted his weight, resting a hand on the

IV pole as he looked down at her. "I'm sure that's how you became a target. We're not the only ones watching Simon. We have reason to believe he's serious about you. And you can assume the bad guys know that too. A baby would derail their plan for him." He held up a hand when she opened her mouth. "And before you ask —no, we can't pass on a message. Not now. Maybe someday."

"But he needs to know."

He nodded. "In time. What we can do now is give you an offer. If you're like most Hong Kong folks, I imagine you're hoping for a way out of here."

Olivia blinked. Her mind was foggy, but not gone.

Jay Burns stood calm, unwavering. "We know of your skills. Your current job lets you hack legally, testing client security systems. We can use that. You'll be doing meaningful work. And we'll make sure you're safe."

She stared at him, trying to find her balance in this strange shifting conversation. A moment ago, she thought she'd been kidnapped. Now she'd had a job offer?

"So let me get this straight"—her voice came out steadier than she expected—"you, the Americans, want me to work for you. To do what?" A pause. "And what do I get in return?

CHAPTER 13

CARITAS HOSPITAL

MARIE

Marie had been waiting for *the call* ever since Olivia's mysterious announcement that she needed to disappear. Olivia had refused to explain, saying only that she needed to go hide before anyone noticed her pregnancy. But she'd promised to let Marie know when she was in labor.

Soon after her best friend went into "hiding," Marie discovered Olivia's parents had immigrated to America. Never had Marie heard of them applying for immigration, and now they were gone. But she'd had no time to dwell on these strange happenings with her studies and preparation for her vows.

After hanging up, she informed her Mother Superior, who had already been briefed. And then she hurried to the hospital where she followed directions to the maternity ward. Andrew, Olivia's brother, and his wife, Elsie, were also there. Weren't they in America?

"Hello, Marie." Andrew waved. "Surprise!"

"Oh my! When did you get in? Have you been to see her?"

"We got in two days ago." Elsie sat down. "Andrew has a

business thing here. I don't know the area or anyone. He hasn't had a chance to touch base with any friends or relatives yet. We were going to contact Olivia and you when the hospital called."

"We just arrived," Andrew added. "The nurse told us she's in room 2."

Marie followed them to the room, but a nurse blocked their way in. Beyond her, Olivia lay in bed hooked up to some monitors. She didn't appear to be in pain, although she did look exhausted. She hadn't noticed them.

"Sorry, only fathers are allowed in here." The nurse put her hands up, then turned to Andrew. "Are you the father?"

"I'm her brother."

"Well, then, sorry. Please wait outside in the lounge."

Back in the lounge, Marie prayed for a safe delivery, focusing on her prayers, not the others waiting impatiently, though the teenager bobbing his head to music in his headphones kept drawing her focus.

She scooted closer to Andrew. "I'm confused. How did you find out about her? I mean, the pregnancy. Last I heard, your parents didn't know."

The couple glanced at each other. Elsie sighed. "From the Tsos. They asked if we would consider raising the baby. We were shocked, and Andrew asked a lot of questions. He wanted the father to be responsible."

Andrew patted his wife's hand. "It was all very strange. We never got to talk to Olivia. Nobody knows who the father is. Anyway, we debated it many times and decided it was only the right thing to do. I mean, if she wanted to raise her baby, we'd support her. In the States, being a single mother doesn't carry much stigma anymore. But here, I don't know."

But when and how had the Tsos learned of her pregnancy? Olivia had been so scared back when she'd found out. She'd never mentioned telling them. Maybe she had after all.

"Wait." She sat up taller. "Are you planning on taking the baby to America?"

They shared a look again. "No, we're moving back here." He laced his fingers through his wife's. "The company transferred me. And Elsie has accepted an offer, as of a week ago, to teach at the American school."

The tightness in Marie's chest loosened. "I suppose it all worked out... almost too perfectly." Perhaps it was divine intervention.

Andrew stood up to stretch his legs. "We've received ultrasound pictures. They appeared in our mailbox. No stamp or anything. I wonder what Olivia's gotten herself into."

Marie remained quiet.

A nurse approached the crowd. "Olivia Tso's family?"

Elsie and Marie stood beside Andrew. "I'm her brother."

"Congratulations! You have a niece."

Elsie grabbed his hand and squealed, "A girl!"

"How is Olivia?" he asked.

"She's doing well, resting."

Joy charged the waiting-room atmosphere as they reveled in the news. Andrew turned to the nurse, his eyes sparkling. "Can we see her? Both of them?"

"In a moment. She asked for Sr. Marie to go in first."

"Oh." His shoulders slumped.

"You two are welcome to see the baby," the nurse offered. "She's a little jaundiced. We took her to the nursery to put her under the bili lights. It's nothing unusual."

Inside the room, Olivia looked like she'd gone ten rounds in the ring.

Marie rushed forward. "Congratulations! How are you feeling? You wanted to see me? Andrew and Elsie are here. Don't you want to see them? Where have you been all this time? I thought you left the city."

"I do want to see them, but I need to talk to you first. And I did leave the city, moved to another island." Olivia checked to make sure they were alone. "One, I want you to be her godmother."

Marie's mouth opened wide. She clamped her hands over it. "I'd be honored."

"Two, promise me not to reveal the truth until it's time. Nobody can know about Simon."

She frowned. "Why?"

"Promise me. The truth would jeopardize his safety and possibly the baby's."

That sounded ominous. "Does he know?"

"No. Trust me. It's for the best. One day, when it's safe, the truth will come out."

How could she keep such a promise? Deny a man knowledge of his child? Marie opened and closed her mouth. Neither a yes nor a no would come out. "Where will you be? I mean, I heard your parents asked Andrew and Elsie to raise the baby. Did you not want to do that? Don't you want to be in her life?"

"Of course, but sometimes sacrifices have to be made."

Marie's chest tightened, a swirl of confusion and helplessness rising inside her. She wanted to honor Olivia's wish, but keeping such a secret would gnaw at her conscience. She clasped her hands, her fingers twisting together as she searched Olivia's face for answers that weren't coming.

"Olivia, you're not making sense. Besides, when the baby's older, she'll wonder. Especially when she's not fully Chinese. She'll have questions. What do you want Andrew and Elsie to say to her? And what am I supposed to tell her?"

Olivia closed her eyes, seemingly to gather her strength and resolve, and then reopened them. "Promise me, please. When the time comes—and it may be a long time from now—you'll get a message to tell her everything. But you must make sure the message comes from Phoenix. Remember that."

What could Marie do other than nod?

Andrew and Elsie joined them, but only for a few moments. They cooed over how cute the baby was and tossed around names.

Then the alarms were going off. Doctors, nurses, and technicians flooded the room, their movements swift and purposeful. The team crowded around the monitors, interpreting readings and exchanging clipped, urgent instructions. A nurse herded them out and closed the door.

Andrew tried to ask what was happening, but nobody would answer.

Marie stood frozen outside the door, unable to help, unable to forget.

PRESENT DAY

CHAPTER 14

ASSUMPTION CONVENT, HONG KONG

LILY

I'm dreaming. I have to be. Nothing this insane could be real.

Lily gripped her chair's hard wooden arms, needing something to balance her. Her gaze drifted to the cross on the wall while Auntie continued her narrative.

"The next thing we heard, she'd had some complications, and there was nothing that could have been done. Andrew was devastated. He demanded to see her body. After some back and forth, they let us into the room. She looked like she was sleeping —still hooked up to all the wires and tubes. But the flat line on the monitor told us otherwise."

She sighed. "Lily, I know this has already been an information overload, but you need to brace for what you're about to hear."

Lily sat completely still. "This… this… no. No." Then her head shook, as if she could erase the words.

"I'm afraid it is true." Auntie drank some water from her water bottle on the desk. "Here's the reason you're here and the message you received. I believed your mother was dead for years. Although, now that I think about it, I did sense her presence, but I chalked it up to my imagination."

A cold, trembling hope flickered through Lily's chest. But anger rose alongside it, hot and bitter, curling in her stomach. How could they have lied to her all these years? How could Auntie sit there so calmly while her entire life crumbled apart? "What are you saying? My mother is not dead?"

Auntie shook her head. "She's alive. The whole time. I only found out when you turned eighteen."

"What?" The office blurred around her, her breath catching somewhere between fury, disbelief, and fragile hope. "What about the funeral? There had to be a body!"

"There was no funeral, only a memorial Mass. As you know, she was cremated, or so we thought. I don't know if there was a body in the coffin at the service. We never saw."

Heat exploded inside Lily. "You've known for years—over four years—and you never said anything!"

"You don't understand. It was the only way to keep you safe. I understand your mother works for the American government now. I don't know what she does. I doubt she'd tell me if I asked. And I only saw her that one time. She had someone send me a message to meet the assistant bishop at the cathedral office. Of course, you can imagine my shock at seeing her alive. After I'd recovered sufficiently, she told me everything—well, likely not *everything*, but enough for me to know to keep the secret until it was time."

Lily's thoughts spun, crashing into each other faster than she could catch them. "Let me get this straight. Do you think *Po po* and *Gung gung* knew she was alive? Did *Kau fu* know?"

"I don't know what your grandparents knew, and we can't ask them now. They never said anything before their deaths, as far as I know. But whether they knew or not, they loved you. After they got their passports, they came back. You had a wonderful relationship with them. As for your uncle, I don't think so."

This was all too overwhelming. She pressed her hands to both temples, a whirlwind thrumming beneath them. Anger at the deception, joy at her mother's survival, relief at discovering her father's identity, and confusion surrounding the secrets. What was she supposed to think about everything right now?

"Your mother loves you, Lily. Whatever she's doing, she's been keeping tabs on you. She was there at your piano recital, your kung fu award ceremony, and your graduation."

"She was?" Her head jerked up. "I don't remember seeing her." She had pictures of her mother. She would have recognized her.

"She'd have worn disguises and changed her appearance. I never noticed her, either."

"This all sounds like spy stuff. This Simon… is my father?"

"Yes, Simon Roth. Keep this to yourself for now. You can go online and research him. I understand he's a senator."

Lily's fingers were already tapping at her phone. A moment later, she was scrolling through his website, drawn to the photo. She turned her phone toward her godmother. "Is this him? Do you see any resemblance?"

"Yes, that's him." She looked from the photo to Lily and back to the photo. "I see a bit of him, but you look so much like your mother. Just with a sprinkle of gweilo in the mix. You and I, we share that blend. It's rare, but beautiful." She stood up. "Evening prayer is in thirty minutes. Before that, I must give you something."

CHAPTER 15

THE BURNS RESIDENCE, FLORIDA, USA

JAY

Was it finally time to get out of the game? Jay Burns sat with his back to the desk in his home office, sipping a glass of scotch while gazing through the window. If he was wondering that—and wondered it a lot lately—the answer might be yes.

According to Patty, Phoenix was getting antsy. The young woman they had taken on long ago had proved to be the best recruit they'd ever encountered. Why had she now skipped her check-in? He hadn't heard any chatter about her being made, captured, or worse.

Then there was the girl. *Why* would Phoenix concoct such a plan to use the girl?

Yes, the Ghost had somehow found out about the girl. They had to extract the girl anyway. So why not use her to carry the intel? Every other operative would've been on the Ghost's organization's radar. They needed someone fresh.

An unfamiliar ringtone sounded. He turned back around, set

his glass down, and pulled out his bottom drawer to extract the secured phone.

After all the security protocols, he said, "Burns."

"I want out." Phoenix's voice came through smoothly. "Patty tried to talk me out of it, but gave up, so save your effort."

He huffed. Even though he didn't think Phoenix was in danger, hearing her voice took that extra edge off. "I'm glad you're okay. Why did you miss your check-in?"

"Unforeseen circumstances. I want out."

"I heard you. Your cover is taking a vacation, no?"

"They fired my cover for harassment. Jade had been an exemplary employee for decades. So instead of calling the authorities, they just quietly terminated her."

"Shouldn't you have checked with us first before pulling your stunt?"

"If I did, you'd have said no. I learned from the best. Better to ask for forgiveness than permission. I'm out."

"Why now?"

"They're watching her. She's in too much danger." Of course, Phoenix was worried about Lily. "I caught two tails on her. One good and one bad. They'll use her as leverage to force Simon to cooperate."

"They don't know she has the intel, correct?"

"Correct."

"Then we stay the course. We can't alert them that she's more than a pawn they can use as leverage."

"I will shadow her. This'll be my last mission."

"Not a good idea."

"I'll do it covertly. They won't know, but I need to do this. I owe her that much."

Jay leaned back in his chair, the weight of it all settling in. He should've seen this coming.

About an hour later, his security camera showed none other

than Simon Roth approaching the front door. His day was getting more interesting by the minute.

"Senator, what a pleasant surprise!" He opened the door wide. "Welcome to my humble abode."

"Please, call me Simon." He walked in. "I believe we met once in Hong Kong, Officer Burns."

"Indeed. And it's Jay. That was a lifetime ago." Jay led him to the living room and gestured for him to sit. "Scotch? Or you're a bourbon guy?"

The senator sat on the leather couch. "No thanks."

Jay poured himself a finger and sat across from Simon. "To what do I owe the pleasure?"

"I understand you're Phoenix's handler."

The younger man was on the Intelligence Committee. There was no use in lying. "Yes, sir."

"What do you know about him?"

"Her. What would you like to know?"

The senator's eyebrows lowered, and his eyes narrowed. His microexpression changed enough for Jay to know the truth would be coming out sooner rather than later.

"What is her connection to Lily Tso?"

"What makes you think there's a connection?"

He snorted. "I've seen Lily's photo. She resembles someone I knew."

"I hear us gweilo think they all look alike."

"That may be for average foreigners. Not for one who's spent a few years in the region. And Lily's features suggest she may have white blood."

Jay sipped his scotch. "Lots of those in Hong Kong do. The city is cosmopolitan. The Brits have deep roots there. Not to mention neighboring Macau with its Portuguese ties."

Simon rubbed the back of his neck, ducking his head. "I once knew a woman in Hong Kong whose name was Olivia Tso. She died when I was stationed in Singapore. I tried to get the details

—nothing. No death record, no burial location." He raised his chin, his gaze direct. "You were there. There weren't that many of us in Hong Kong at the time. Did you know her? Did you hear what happened?"

"It's classified. Need to know only."

"I have a need to know. Tso isn't a common name. Wait, you said… 'classified.'" Simon held up a hand. "I believe you recruited her. You staged her death. Olivia is Phoenix. And Lily…"

Jay didn't answer. He didn't have to.

Simon already knew.

CHAPTER 16

THE PETERS RESIDENCE, FLORIDA, USA

RON

Ron's phone buzzed on the nightstand—5:30 a.m.
What now?
He swiped to answer. "Peters."
The call was short.
As soon as he hung up, he made another one.

CHAPTER 17

ASSUMPTION CONVENT, HONG KONG

LILY

The office felt even smaller now, shadows deepening in the dim lamplight. Lily's gaze flicked to the wooden bookcase lining the wall, the scent of old paper and polished oak grounding her in the quiet room.

Auntie went to the bookcase against the sidewall, pulled out a thick Bible, and removed the small box hidden behind it. She set it on the desk.

"Your mother—or someone she sent—put it there and left a note." Auntie shook her head. "I still don't know how. My best guess is that, yesterday, we were hacked or something. All the computers went haywire. We called our service company. I was at a school meeting when the tech showed up. The sisters who were here didn't ask many questions—only that she fixed the computers and left."

"Did you open it?"

"No, the note said to wait for you." She pushed the box toward Lily. "You ought to open it."

Inside was something that looked like a mole. Lily recoiled.

Surely, it wasn't real—hadn't been cut from someone. "What do you think this is?"

Her godmother pointed to the other item. "Maybe that will tell you."

It appeared to be a key chain. Lily picked it up, turned it around, and poked at it. Something popped out. A flash drive. She held it up. "May I borrow your computer?"

With Auntie's permission, she plugged the drive into the desktop. After following the on-screen directions, she read the message.

> *Lily, I'm going to give you some instructions. It's vitally important that you read them carefully. The message will self-erase. It's a fake mole, and critical intel is embedded in it. Follow the directions in a separate file and put it on your body.*
>
> *You have three days to deliver the intel to Simon, your father. That is until Friday, 1700 hours, US eastern time. (That's 5:00 p.m.) After that, it'll be too late to prevent a national catastrophe. He has sent an undercover agent to escort you to the States.*
>
> *The agent must verify his identity by saying: "I hear it rains a lot in Seattle."*
>
> *Do not trust anyone except your father and his agent!*
>
> *Remember, three days. Godspeed.*

Her legs weak and wobbly, she had to sit down. Her arms crept across her emptied-out chest. She wanted to go home, crawl into bed, and pretend none of this was real.

"Are you okay?" Auntie gripped Lily's shoulder. "I need to go to evening prayer soon."

A few deep breaths filled the hollow in her chest. "Yes, I will be."

"If it's okay to tell me what she said and if you want to, I'm here."

She nodded. "Thank you. But I need time to process this."

"All right, then. I will keep you in my prayers."

"Wait—do you think I should do this? She said to deliver something important to my father." After her mother's message ran through her mind again, a perilous excitement shivered over her. Her imagination ignited. No doubt this could be the adventure of a lifetime.

"My child, it's not my place to tell you. You need to decide for yourself. Do you want to meet your father? Your mother wouldn't have involved you if the situation weren't dire."

"You think she wants me to be a spy, like her?"

"I don't think so. I do know she cares about you. No way will she not make sure you're safe." Auntie squeezed Lily's shoulder. "Lily, I'd be lying if I said I wouldn't worry, but I trust your mother."

Despite the thrill, the old warning—be careful what you wish for—echoed in Lily's mind. She'd thought her life boring. Could this be an answer to her prayers?

"She said three days. You think someone will come tomorrow and take me out of here?" Leaving Hong Kong. Facing an uncertain future. Yes, the idea appealed to her. "I'll check out the instructions for this mole."

"Come." Auntie enveloped her in a rare embrace. "God be with you!"

KYLE

She'd been inside too long.

Kyle shifted in his seat, one eye on the convent, the other on the tail across the street. The half-eaten bag of veggie chips in his lap had gone stale—like the air in the car.

He sat in the company car's front passenger seat, just down the street from the convent. In the driver's seat, Officer Conway pressed his phone to his ear. In the back, a tech tapped away on a laptop, cycling through surveillance feeds. The guy didn't know the full details—just that his job was to patch into nearby cameras and keep eyes on the exits.

Conway had spent most of the last hour on the phone.

"Yes, we see the other tail." Conway told someone on the other end. "No, we don't have eyes on her, but we're monitoring all the entries and exits. The other tail is sitting across the street. Watching."

Kyle had spotted the guy earlier, right after trailing Lily from the hotel. She'd taken a taxi—standard enough in Hong Kong. He kept his distance as the other tail started following her too. Whoever the guy was, he didn't look local.

"Yes, sir." Conway hung up. "Change of plans. We're going in."

Kyle's gaze flicked toward the street.

A shadow moved behind the second tail. Then the man staggered as if drunk. Swayed. Collapsed. Lay still.

Kyle blinked. What just happened?

A moment of hesitation. Was the guy unconscious? Hurt? Faking?

He gulped. "Should I check on him?"

"If he's still breathing, he's someone else's problem." Conway opened his door. "Let's move."

Kyle followed, heart kicking up. This just stopped being routine.

CHAPTER 18

MARINO HOTEL, HONG KONG

DYLAN

Was he really hearing this? Dylan leaned over the phone. "What? You want what now?" He'd put the phone on speaker. Tommy, the only other person in the suite, crossed to his side.

"There's a change of plans. Are you able to get her out tonight? Or early tomorrow morning?"

They exchanged a glance. Dylan paced. "I got word from the manager that they were going with the plan. Why the change now?"

"Because her life is at stake. And we only have a few days to thwart a deadly attack."

How was he to get her out of Hong Kong? Tommy gestured for his attention. "What?" Dylan lowered the phone. "Agent Peters knows you're here."

"Remember how the lawyer got you to Florida? A chartered flight."

Right. His pacing took him to the window and back. Even though that had been mere months ago, to him, it was a lifetime ago. And Tommy somehow remembered. "I've never chartered a flight. I wouldn't know how."

Tommy put his hands up. "Don't look at me. I couldn't afford to fly first class if you didn't pay."

"Dylan," Agent Peters cut in. "Can you authorize the expense?"

"I think so." Dylan pivoted, stopping square before Tommy. "I'll check with my accountant."

Tommy rolled his eyes. "Of course, you can."

"Okay." Agent Peters's clipped tone carried through fast, and something clicked in his background. "I'll have someone arrange it. I'll text you the details. If we can't get you guys out tonight, your time, it'll be first thing tomorrow morning. They'll keep her in a safe house overnight, if necessary." With that, Agent Peters hung up.

Dylan held the dormant phone as far from him as his arm could reach. "You know…" His droll words cut into the silence. "Moments like this almost make me wish I hadn't reunited with my grandmother. Being heir to a multimillion-dollar empire comes with responsibilities I never asked for."

Tommy spread his arms out to encompass the presidential suite and tsked. "Yeah, poor you. Having to charter a plane and stay in places like this."

CHAPTER 19

ABOARD PRIVATE JET

LILY

The mole clung to Lily's skin like a bad decision. Everything else was a blur.

One minute, she'd been following instructions, touching up the adhesive, packing her purse to go home. The next, Kyle and another man—Officer Conway, she learned later—had swept her out of the convent with no explanation. If it hadn't been for Kyle's confirmation that he was assigned by Senator Roth and her mother's message, she would've fought them every step.

She'd barely managed to pantomime a goodbye to her godmother who mouthed something vague about being safe. From the look Kyle gave her, he didn't know they had any connection. She filed that away.

They took her to an apartment close to the airport. That much she knew. Everything else blurred in adrenaline and confusion.

During the ride, they'd asked her for a list of essentials like clothes, personal items, anything she couldn't live without for a few days. Someone would collect them from her home. Apparently, they didn't plan to let her go back.

Sleep? That had been laughable. She'd spent the night upright on the edge of the bed, too wired to lie down. And when she'd drifted toward sleep, someone knocked.

Time to go.

She checked her phone. Already 4:16 a.m.

Kyle held her duffel bag at the door. "Need anything before I take this to the car?"

She retrieved a clean outfit, muttered thanks, and handed it back to him.

Outside, the sky was still dark. Instead of heading to the terminal, they drove straight to a private hangar. Her stomach flipped. What about customs? Tickets? Wasn't someone supposed to scan her shoes?

As the car pulled up to the steps of a waiting jet, a group— agents, probably—conferred outside. When they nodded, Officer Conway opened her door.

Kyle stood ready beside the steps, posture tense, scanning the shadows. He didn't smile.

The jet was smaller than anything she'd ever flown on. Sleek. Intimidating. The only other time she'd flown was a budget airline to Singapore, and that plane hadn't sparkled.

"Welcome aboard!" A cheerful woman, likely the flight attendant, beamed. "You may sit wherever you like."

The door closed behind them. Kyle stayed close, but Lily's eyes were already adjusting to the interior. With its polished leather, warm lighting, and actual elbow room, she might as well have stepped into a movie.

"Hey, stranger." Dylan stood at the cabin's far end, hands in his pockets like he belonged there. "Tommy's up front chatting with the pilot."

Of course he was.

Kyle extended a hand. "Thanks for the quick assist."

"Happy to help." Dylan's gaze flicked to her. "You look like you haven't slept. Feel free to nap. These chairs recline flat."

"I doubt I could sleep now." Not with how her nerves were still humming.

They buckled up as the pilot's voice came over the speaker, announcing takeoff. Lily took a window seat at the booth-like table. Kyle sat beside her. She couldn't see Dylan or Tommy anymore, which was fine. She needed a second to breathe.

She closed her eyes just to rest them. Maybe she dozed. Maybe not.

"She's sleeping," Kyle whispered.

"No, I'm not," she said, eyes still closed.

"You had me fooled."

She blinked and sat up. The seatbelt sign was off. Dylan was now sitting across from her with a coffee cup. Kyle still sat beside her, alert. Tommy had disappeared again.

"Want something?" Dylan asked. "Coffee? It's decent."

"Sure, thanks."

Nice that he didn't snap his fingers for the flight attendant.

A few minutes later, he returned with a steaming cup and a pile of packets. "Creamer and sweetener, just in case."

She accepted it, murmuring thanks. "You didn't have to get it yourself."

He shrugged. "Didn't want to wake anyone."

As he wandered off again, probably to find Tommy, she leaned toward Kyle and whispered, "I thought there was a flight attendant?"

"There is," he murmured. "Maybe Dylan requested her. Maybe it's for show."

"Right."

Dylan came back before she could ask more. She added sweetener and cream to her cup. "I thought you were staying in Hong Kong. Why are you flying with us?"

He shrugged. "Plans changed."

Vague, but she let it go. "I have to ask—you're not what I expected."

He raised an eyebrow. "That wasn't a question."

"You're right." She tested a sip. Hmm, more than decent—or maybe she was just overtired. "There was a memo going around. About you. The elusive grandson. I expected one of those spoiled playboys. Paparazzi, parties, scandals, naked women, and yachts."

A laugh exploded behind her. Tommy's head popped up, his grin wide. "That's because he keeps forgetting he's rich now!"

"Shut up." Dylan waved him off.

She might be overtired, but that wouldn't have made sense on a good day. She gestured with her cup, beckoning him to fill in the explanation. "How do you forget you're rich?"

Dylan hesitated, then launched into a version of his story, laden with credit card debt while helping his mom, scraping by, then being plucked from obscurity and dropped into this… empire. The way he told it was unpolished, honest. No bragging. Just facts.

How oddly comforting. Like her own story. The gaps. The lies. The ache of not knowing. "You've got a real Cinderella story. Weren't you angry? About the deception?"

"Of course. At first." He swirled his coffee dregs, then set it aside without finishing it. "I wasn't sure I'd stay. But… my grandmother loved my mom. She loves me. They had their reasons, even if I didn't like them. She asked for a second chance. I figured I could give her that much."

Lily folded her hands around her coffee cup. "You make it sound easy."

"It wasn't."

She paused, then tried another sip. Another question. "So… why are you with us? I thought Kyle was escorting me."

Kyle, who'd been quiet, leaned in. "He chartered the flight."

Her mouth parted. "Wait. I thought this was a government jet. You know, like in the shows."

"Yeah." Dylan cuffed Kyle's arm. "Don't you guys have jets?"

Kyle chuckled. "Above my pay grade. You're a tycoon. Flying private's expected. Makes our cover easier."

"Cover?" she repeated.

Kyle shot a look at Dylan, who seemed to remember something. "Oh, right. Under the radar. Totally casual."

She gestured with her cup between them. "What am I missing?"

Tommy slid into the seat beside Dylan, nodding toward Kyle. "He's posing as your boyfriend."

Her heart skipped. Kyle?

He rubbed the back of his neck. Was he *squirming*? "I'm sorry." He avoided her eyes. "Just following orders."

Dylan glared at Tommy, who shrugged. "She needs to know. They can't act like strangers."

Her coffee cup still warmed her palm, grounding herself. "Okay. No big deal."

Totally cool.

CHAPTER 20

MARINO HOTEL, HONG KONG

LARRY

"Where did they go?" Larry's voice cut through the hallway as he stood in the empty presidential suite, fists clenched at his sides.

The housekeeping supervisor shrugged, blinking eyes wide with confusion. "I don't know, sir. I just came on duty. The log says the guest checked out late last night."

"I can see that." Larry scanned the adjoining room, also stripped clean. "This one too?"

The man checked his sheet. "Yes. Checked out together, it looks like."

Larry marched over to the hotel phone and punched the button for the duty manager. "Why wasn't I informed that the VIPs checked out last night?"

Silence, then the voice came on, calm and bland. "We don't notify staff of guest checkouts, Mr. Tan."

"They were supposed to be here another three days."

"Plans change. There was no flag to alert you." A pause. "We follow protocol."

You're just covering for yourself. Larry didn't say it. He let out a tight breath. "All right. Understood."

He ended the call and dialed the business office.

No Lily. She hadn't shown up. Worse, she'd arranged for a sub.

He shut the suite door behind him, the soft click too final.

Then he pulled out his phone.

Time to make the call he'd hoped to avoid.

CHAPTER 21

PRIVATE AIRFIELD, FLORIDA, USA

KYLE

As soon as the wheels hit the tarmac, Kyle exhaled. The plane coasted down the runway, its brakes humming beneath them. No sudden instructions. No in-flight surprises. Just a smooth landing.

He hadn't realized how tense he'd been until now.

At the top of the cabin stairs, a uniformed customs officer approached. Kyle met him halfway, checking the man's ID against the dossier photo. Verified, cleared, and discreet. Just as it should be.

Still, Kyle double-checked. You didn't take chances, not with someone like Lily onboard.

He'd kept mostly quiet during the flight. Not out of disinterest, but calculation. Better to observe than to interrupt.

And Lily had been worth observing.

He'd learned more than she probably realized. She spoke fluent Cantonese, played piano since she was young, dabbled in kung fu, and seemed comfortable with IT. For someone who worked in the hotel's business center, she was sharp. Calm under pressure. Graceful. Friendly without being naïve.

And beautiful.

There was something elegant in the way she carried herself. But what most intrigued him were the questions Senator Roth hadn't answered. Who was she, and why was she important enough to trigger this level of security?

Lily had been warm with all of them. Dylan had kept her entertained with personal stories and self-deprecating charm. Tommy had tried flirting with the flight attendant, who was easily fifteen years his senior, but Lily laughed at his jokes all the same.

Kyle's role had been more peripheral. Present, quiet, watchful.

He wasn't the talkative one. That was Dylan. And Lily seemed to enjoy his company.

The realization hit like a sucker punch. Irrational. But there it was.

Outside, the air was thick with early morning humidity.

Welcome to Orlando.

"Are you guys coming to the hotel?" Dylan slipped on sunglasses like they were already on vacation.

"Let me check." Kyle stepped aside and dialed the encrypted number Senator Roth had given him.

A clipped voice answered. Kyle confirmed safe arrival.

"New destination," the voice instructed. "Safe house. Location's in the secure file."

Seconds later, his phone buzzed. A new message flashed on the screen with vehicle details and a GPS pin. The car was waiting in the airport lot, key fob tucked in the front wheel well.

Efficient. Quiet. How Kyle preferred things.

When he returned, he caught the tail end of a conversation.

"…Universal Studios. And if you're a Harry Potter fan, you *have* to see Harry Potter World," Dylan was saying.

"We'll show you around," Tommy added.

Lily's eyes lit up, and a bright smile spread across her face. "My first time here. That sounds amazing. I'd love to go."

Kyle's stomach turned over what he had to say next.

"Sorry." He touched her elbow. "Maybe later in the trip. We need to go somewhere else first."

Her face fell a fraction. She nodded. "Oh. Okay."

Dylan stepped forward. "You have your cell?"

She pulled it out. "Yes, but I'm not sure it works here. I don't have an international plan."

"Let me give you my number anyway." He rattled off the digits as she tapped them in.

"Kyle, you've got mine, right?" Dylan added.

Kyle nodded. "Yeah."

"Call if you guys need anything."

Kyle met his gaze, then gave a noncommittal nod.

Best to get her to the safe house first. Then he'd figure out what this mission really was.

LILY

As soon as her feet hit the ground, Lily scanned her surroundings. No terminals. No security lines. No arrival gate. No baggage claim. Just open air and a stretch of quiet asphalt.

This was how the other half traveled.

She'd flown commercial to Singapore once, crammed between two armrest hogs. But this? No crowds. No chaos. It felt surreal. Unbelievable, even.

Plus, it was her first time in the United States.

"This way." Kyle gestured to the left.

His voice snapped her back. She quickened her pace to catch up. If they weren't going to the hotel, where were they headed?

Dylan and Tommy were already piling into a waiting black SUV. A couple of waves, a cheerful goodbye, and they were gone.

She followed Kyle across the lot toward a parked car he pointed out. They were just feet away when an engine whirred behind them.

A second vehicle sped toward them and skidded to a stop.

Two men in suits jumped out, flashing badges.

"We're taking over escort duty," the taller one announced.

Kyle's body tensed. She felt it even before he moved.

He stepped in front of her. "Hold on. Let me see your creds."

They held out their IDs, official-looking, but something felt... off.

"We're under direct instruction from the senator," the tall one insisted. "Time's tight. Let's move."

The shorter one tried to step around Kyle, hand reaching toward her.

Kyle shoved her back. "Don't touch her!" he snapped. "I'll call to verify."

Her pulse spiked. Something wasn't right. Hadn't he just called to report? They would have mentioned the change of plans, wouldn't they?

A second car rolled up and stopped next to them.

The cabin attendant stepped out. She still wore her uniform, and a key fob dangled from her fingers.

"Sorry for the delay, Agent Peters. Took me a while to finish up with the plane. This is the vehicle you requested."

Uncertainty tightened Kyle's face. His gaze flicked from the men to the woman.

The attendant dropped the fob into his hand.

That decided it.

Kyle shoved Lily into the passenger seat, then sprinted for the driver's side.

"Hey—!" The shorter man started to follow. A sharp cry cut him off.

Lily turned in time to see him double over, clutching his side. Her breath caught.

Then the taller one reached under his jacket, a gun.

Her heart jumped into her throat.

This wasn't supposed to happen. This kind of thing only happened in movies.

He really was pulling a gun.

Kyle hit the gas. The car surged forward, tires squealing as they left the chaos.

She twisted in her seat, expecting the impossible—bullets, maybe glass shattering, something cinematic and terrible. But nothing came. Just the blur of pavement and buildings as they sped away.

"What just happened?" She pressed a hand to her throat, breathless.

"I wish I knew." He checked the rearview, one hand fumbling for his phone.

He dialed. No answer.

"I'll get you to the safe house. Then I'll try again."

CHAPTER 22

SAFE HOUSE, FLORIDA, USA

KYLE

That woman wasn't a cabin attendant.

Kyle tightened his grip on the steering wheel. That had been obvious the moment she handed him the key fob. Her posture was too crisp, her timing too perfect. Was she Roth's backup agent? If so, why hadn't anyone told him? Why couldn't he get through?

Had he dialed wrong?

No. He'd memorized the senator's number. He was certain.

"Take the next left. Your destination is on the right," said the robotic GPS voice.

They arrived at a duplex tucked into a quiet residential street. Kyle parked at the curb and scanned the perimeter—habit, protocol, instinct. Once satisfied, he led Lily to the left-hand unit and keyed in the door code.

The lock disengaged with a soft click, and he followed her into a modest space. Neutral paint. Cheap wood laminate floors. Drawn curtains.

"If you're hungry, check the fridge." He pulled out his phone. "There might be something edible."

As she moved into the kitchen, he tried the number again. A signal this time. Relief surged. He gave a clipped report on the safe landing, near-abduction attempt, and evasive maneuver.

But the response was garbled. Static.

He couldn't make out a word.

The doorbell rang. Three sharp knocks followed.

Lily stepped out of the bathroom, towel in hand. He hadn't even seen her slip away.

He pressed a finger to his lips, signaling for silence, and gestured for her to stay back. Something was wrong. He checked his phone. No signal bars.

A peek through the curtain confirmed it. Two men. Suits. Military haircuts.

"FBI. Open up!" one ordered from outside.

Kyle's spine stiffened. "Special Agent Kyle Peters. Who are you?"

"FBI Special Agents Park and Lee."

The names meant nothing to him.

Besides, Roth claimed this mission was off the books. He'd "borrowed" Kyle from the Bureau. No one else was supposed to know.

"Let me see your credentials!" Kyle slung his backpack over one shoulder and signaled Lily to grab hers.

She obeyed.

They moved to the back door.

"We're going," he whispered. If those men were legit, he'd take the heat later. Right now, he wasn't betting Lily's life on it.

They stepped onto the back porch as the front door exploded open.

"To the car!" Kyle ordered.

He didn't bother with stealth. Gun drawn, he ran after her, the car already unlocked and waiting in the driveway.

"Why are they yelling in Mandarin?" Lily asked as they sprinted.

He jumped into the driver's seat. "Because they're not real agents. What are they saying?"

"To take me alive and"—she slid into the passenger seat, breathless—"um…"

"Kill me." He slammed the gearshift into drive.

A glance in the rearview left no doubt. Their pursuers were regrouping. Armed.

"Holy macaroni! They have their guns out!" Lily cried.

He snorted. He hadn't heard that expression since grade school. He shoved her head down. "Stay down!"

If their orders were to take her alive, they might hold fire. But he wasn't counting on that.

In the mirror, he saw them pile into their vehicle and peel out after him.

Orlando traffic was already thickening. Lane by lane, Kyle weaved and surged forward, doing his best to widen the gap.

Then a car from the opposite direction clipped the pursuing vehicle. Tires screeched. Metal crunched. The black sedan spun out and slammed into a parked car.

"They're not going anywhere soon."

Ten minutes later, he spoke again. "You can sit up now."

She peeked over the dash. "This is like one of those TV shows I watch. Do you do this every day?"

He gave a dry laugh. "No."

Another call attempt. Still no answer.

"Where do we go now?" Her head swiveled from side to side.

He didn't answer right away. Roth had said not to contact him directly. Just call the number. But that hadn't worked. The line had either been jammed… or burned.

"It's just us now." She fiddled with her seat belt. "Please take me to the senator. I need to see him."

He glanced over at her. "You know you're supposed to meet him?"

She nodded. "Didn't he send you to escort me to him?"

"Yes, but the instructions weren't specific."

"Do you know where he is?"

"No. Not exactly."

"Doesn't he have an office?"

"Yeah, but he might not be there. He could be anywhere— DC, Tallahassee, Miami. I was told to call in for further directions."

She sighed. "So call."

"I did." He held up the phone. "No signal. Again."

She slumped in her seat. "So what now?"

He tightened his grip on the wheel. "I'll get you to another safe house. It's not far."

Three locations were listed in his file. Surely, one of them was still secure.

CHAPTER 23

THE ROTH RESIDENCE, FLORIDA, USA

PHOENIX

Thank goodness I was there.

If Phoenix hadn't stepped in, the young agent might've lost control of the situation, and it would've ended in blood. Kyle Peters was green, but he'd impressed her. He'd shielded the girl without hesitation and reacted fast when she dropped the key fob into his hand. He hadn't second-guessed. He'd moved.

She gave him credit for that.

Once the two imposters were neutralized, she made the call. Burns would take it from there. He wouldn't be happy about it, but he'd do it. Always.

After leaving the scene, she'd tracked Kyle and Lily to the first safe house. Just in case. A part of her wanted to believe the worst was behind them.

Then she saw the car.

It was parked across the street, out of place. Two men in suits. Too polished. Too still. They weren't Feds.

She stayed in motion, circling the block. Watching. Waiting.

When she spotted Kyle and Lily slipping out the back door, everything clicked. They were being hunted. Again.

Phoenix positioned her vehicle at the end of the street, engine idling. As soon as the black sedan gave chase, she turned the wheel and timed it just right, clipping the rear corner hard enough to spin them out into a parked car.

Minimal damage. Maximum disruption.

She didn't stay to explain.

Once the black sedan spun into the parked car, she'd rounded the corner and disappeared.

Time to report in. She opened the encrypted line.

"Phoenix. Authorization alpha nine two seven."

A moment of silence. Then Burns's voice crackled in. "Go ahead."

"Intercept complete. Two false flag agents down. Dispatch cleanup. Coordinates sent."

She disconnected, no further words exchanged. The channel would self-wipe in sixty seconds.

She tucked the phone away, pulled up the tracker again, and exhaled.

Kyle had gotten Lily out. The safe house was still holding.

Phoenix leaned back in her seat, the pressure in her chest easing by a fraction.

The easy part was over.

Now came the part she'd been avoiding.

Simon.

She'd put it off long enough, but he deserved to know. About the traitor. About Lily.

Now, there was one thing left to do.

Face Simon Roth.

ROTH'S OFFICE, FLORIDA, USA

SIMON

He had a daughter.

And Olivia was alive.

That single truth had haunted Simon since last night's visit with Burns. He hadn't slept. Couldn't. Not after everything he thought he knew collapsed in the span of minutes.

Lily.

His daughter.

And no one had told him.

He'd gone back to Roger's house afterward, needing something, confirmation, maybe. Closure.

The retired senator's poker face hadn't hidden much. Roger had known. Of course he had.

"It was for your own good."

Same words Burns had used.

For his own good?

Was that what it was called now? Years of silence, of lies?

He'd left the house in a fury, barely managing to keep from slamming the door.

Now, the only thing that mattered was getting Lily to him. Safely.

Too many pieces were still in motion, too many enemies, too many eyes, but that came later. First, the girl.

His secured phone buzzed on the desk.

PACKAGE LANDED.

Simon exhaled and rubbed his jaw. Good. Kyle had done his part. The next set of instructions should be en route, rerouting them to the task force office for debrief.

He tried to focus. Turned back to the documents in front of

him. Security briefings. Risk maps. None of it registered. His mind kept circling back to a girl who didn't know who she really was.

Not yet.

He checked the clock. They wouldn't arrive for a little while still.

He rose from his chair, already reaching for his jacket.

He might as well be there when she walked in.

PHOENIX

The house sat nestled in a gated, tree-lined enclave, quiet, polished, safe. The kind of place where power wore loafers instead of boots.

Phoenix stayed in her car, watching from beyond the entrance. He'd joined the State Department all those years ago, back when they met in Hong Kong. He hadn't dreamed of politics then.

He'd once told her he wanted to work for a nonprofit, maybe help underprivileged kids. Do some good. Life had a way of changing one's dreams.

She pulled on a sun hat and sunglasses, just another woman in an SUV outside a gated community. But she didn't drive in.

Instead, she parked and walked, taking the long route, cutting through the backyards of two neighboring homes. The senator's house was near the gate. No motion alarms in the yards, but plenty of doorbell cams and private security signs. She kept her face angled low.

Now, she stood on his driveway, just feet from the door. And hesitated.

Would he even see her? Would he shut the door in her face?

It didn't matter. He needed to know.

There was a traitor in his orbit. Someone too close to ignore. And if she had to face him to deliver that message, so be it.

Again and again, she'd thought about calling. But he might not pick up. And even if he did, would he believe her?

She rang the doorbell.

Nothing.

Minutes passed. Still nothing.

Probably the housekeeper was gone for the day. He didn't keep live-in help, never liked the idea of strangers in his space. Just a part-timer, mornings only.

Of course he's not home. It's morning, you idiot. He's at work.

She rubbed her forehead hard. She never missed details like that. Lately, her mind had been cluttered. Too many variables. Too much emotion.

She couldn't leave. She wouldn't. She'd waited long enough.

One way or another, she was getting inside.

He had a decent home security system, expensive, layered, but not impenetrable. With an associate's help, she bypassed it.

CHAPTER 24

THE ROTH RESIDENCE, FLORIDA, USA

SIMON

Simon was halfway to the task force office when the security company called.

Possible break-in. Sensors tripped. No forced entry.

Under normal circumstances, the system would've flagged local law enforcement, but he'd asked for alerts to go straight to him. Still, the whole thing sounded like a false alarm.

Probably nothing.

But he couldn't take the chance.

When he pulled into the driveway, everything looked normal. The front lawn was undisturbed. No squad cars. No police tape. No sign of anything.

Had they come and gone already?

And if it was a false alarm, why hadn't anyone called to confirm?

He didn't pull into the garage. Better to stay mobile. Just in case.

He stepped out, approached the front door, and entered the code to unlock it.

Inside, he paused. His finger hovered over the keypad, waiting for the system to prompt him to disarm the alarm.

But it didn't.

No beeping. No countdown.

Someone had already shut it off.

He scanned the room, instinct kicking in. The great room ahead was quiet, flooded with morning light through the floor-to-ceiling window. The stairway to the right was clear. So were the short hallways leading to the guest bath and the master suite.

Nothing out of place.

Except—

He took one more step.

And saw her.

A woman sat at the kitchen island, perfectly still. Watching him.

When she stood and stepped around the counter, his breath caught.

It couldn't be.

But it was.

Olivia.

She looked almost exactly as he remembered. Her dark hair was shorter now, cut close to her jaw in a clean, modern style. Maybe a strand or two of gray near her temples, but barely noticeable. Her face was smooth, composed. Calm.

She hadn't aged so much as… sharpened.

There was something in her eyes now. Something deeper. Wiser. More guarded.

But it was her.

The same Olivia who once held his heart.

For a second, he forgot how to breathe.

How many times had he asked himself, *What if?*

What if she hadn't disappeared?

What if he'd gone after her?

What if she were still alive?

Now she was here. Alive. Whole. Real.

He couldn't move. Couldn't speak.

All he wanted—*needed*—was to reach out, pull her into his arms, and confirm this wasn't some elaborate dream.

PHOENIX

Phoenix froze the moment she saw him.

All the years dissolved, two decades of silence, of masks, of becoming someone else. Now he was standing in front of her, very real, very close. And all she could think about were fragments of memories: Their first meeting. Their first kiss. The rush of falling in love in a world that had no room for it.

She'd kept tabs on him from a distance. Surveillance, secondhand updates, glimpses through photos, videos, and social media. But she hadn't seen him in person since Hong Kong.

The years hadn't touched her feelings for him.

Simon looked almost the same, just a few silver strands, faint lines at his eyes. No potbelly, no softness. Still disciplined. Still him.

His blue eyes locked onto hers, direct, searching. She no longer wore the mask. Not the skintight synthetic one she'd lived behind for years, nor the emotional one she used to survive. In a way, she felt exposed.

But he had to see her. The real her.

The woman he once loved.

She didn't know how long they stood in silence before he crossed the room and wrapped his arms around her.

She let him.

Her head rested against his shoulder, and then she was twenty again. Back in Hong Kong. Back when things were simple.

He was still five ten. She was still seven inches shorter. And for one fragile moment, everything felt whole.

He pulled back, but not far. One hand still on her shoulder. "I want to make sure I'm not dreaming. We need to talk."

She nodded. "I came to warn you. There's a traitor close to you. His code name is King."

Simon stiffened. "You don't know who he is?"

"No. We only use codes. But he's close. I'd bet he's been with you since your state days. You're good, Simon. But don't tell me you think your meteoric rise was pure luck."

His brow furrowed.

"Someone's been helping you along the way," she continued. "Guiding you. Grooming you."

"Why would they want to help me?"

"To put you where you are now. A US senator? That's power. Now imagine if they could control you."

"That's not going to happen."

She scoffed. "What if they threatened someone you love? What would you do, then? Do you know how many men in power have been compromised for less?"

He stayed silent, so she pressed on.

"If you were politically ambitious, what would you do to bury the scandal of a love child? And with a foreign national, no less. From a country the public sees as hostile. That's the kind of leverage they love."

"Hong Kong isn't China."

She arched a brow. "Technically, it is. And it's getting less independent by the day. But to Americans? It's all the same. It's about perception. And I thought politicians were good at that."

He sighed. "That's what I hate most about politics, image over substance."

"For what it's worth, I'm a US citizen now. Jay made that happen years ago."

He smiled. "I figured. You'd have to be, to work for the Company."

They stood in silence for a beat. Then she gripped his hand on her shoulder, squeezed it. "I'm sorry. Jay promised he'd tell you once they were sure you weren't working for the Ghost's people."

"I spoke to him last night. Not everything, but enough. I need to hear it from you. You're Phoenix?"

She nodded once.

His expression tightened. "He said it was for everyone's protection. But why not tell me about Lily?"

"That was the deal." Her voice caught. "The Ghost's people tried to kill me and the baby. I still don't know how they found out about the pregnancy. As far as we can tell, they saw us—me and the child—as a threat to their plan for you. Jay and Patty got me out. We had to make a choice. To protect her, we had to make it look like she never existed. If they'd known you had a child, they would've used her to control you."

"And you trusted him to decide that?"

"He wasn't working alone. His superiors wanted you right where you were. Close to the Ghost's network, but not compromised. Just like Jay wanted me to rise in their ranks."

Simon touched the side of her face, tilted up her chin, his fingertips gentle. "You've been deep cover that long?"

She looked away. "Yes. But not always with the same role or assignment. The world thought I was dead. That made it easier. I could be anyone."

He gestured toward the synthetic mask still on the kitchen island. "Is that how you did it?"

She lifted it. "You're on the Intelligence Committee. This shouldn't surprise you."

"I've heard rumors." His lips quirked. "Didn't expect to see one on my kitchen counter."

He pulled out his phone. "They're supposed to alert you when Lily arrives at the task force office. I'm meeting her there. You—"

"Wait." Her voice sharpened. "There's something else you need to know."

CHAPTER 25

ON THE RUN, FLORIDA, USA

LILY

Lily gripped the grab bar so tightly her knuckles hurt.

Her heart pounded like a warning bell, loud enough, surely, for Kyle to hear it. Maybe they'd made a mistake choosing her. What did she know about carrying intel? About dodging bullets?

And yet, part of her—some irrational, reckless part—had never felt more alive. Adrenaline still buzzed under her skin.

Would they get to the senator in time?

"Are we close?" She drummed her fingers on the console. She needed to go straight to the senator. Why wouldn't he just call the office? Find out where he was? But no. "I have orders," she mimicked in her mind, resisting the urge to roll her eyes.

"Yes. Right around this corner."

He veered into a driveway and told her to stay in the car. Then he walked to the front door, scanned the area—

And he turned and ran back.

"What's wrong?" she asked as he jumped in.

He didn't answer. Just started the car.

"What are you doing? Why are we leaving?"

Still nothing.

She twisted to look back, and her breath caught. A man had stepped out of the house. Gun raised. Aimed.

Not again!

The bullet didn't come. They rounded the corner just in time.

But a black car shot onto the road behind them. A man jumped in, and the chase began.

"They're following us!"

"I see that." Kyle tossed her his phone. "Press redial. See if anyone picks up."

She did. "It says the number is no longer in service."

Buildings blurred. Shops. Trees. More trees. Did Kyle even know where they were? *Please, God, get us out of this!*

Then pop.

"Get down!" Kyle shoved her head down.

More gunfire.

The car jolted, tilted, then groaned to a halt.

"What happened?" She gasped.

"They shot the tires." He yanked his door open. "Out. Now."

He ran around to her side, grabbed her hand, and hauled her out. His longer stride outpaced hers, but he slowed, tugged her forward.

She dared to look back.

Three men, not the Chinese goons from before. Gweilos this time. Armed and chasing.

They sprinted straight into a crowd of shoppers. The men didn't care, still coming. Still gunning.

Lily's lungs burned. Where were they going?

Then an idea.

A group of big guys headed their way, flanked by smaller teammates. A sports team. Some had lacrosse sticks slung over their shoulders.

She let go of Kyle's hand, bumped into one of them. "Sorry." She gasped. "They're trying to rob us!"

When she cried out, several dropped their bags and stepped forward, brandishing the sticks like weapons, ready to throw down.

Kyle grabbed her hand again and yanked her toward a side path as the goons hit a wall of unexpected defenders. "Smart move."

"It'll buy us time." She panted. "But not much."

They rounded a corner. Two motels came into view, low-end, peeling walls, bad vibes. Definitely not the Marino Hotel.

Gunfire cracked again. A window behind them exploded. Where did that come from?

Kyle shoved her behind a tree, drew his weapon, and returned fire from cover. "I think one went around the group."

She was sweating. Shaking. But she held her ground.

More pops. Sounded like more shooters—the other two men? Then silence. Sirens in the distance, getting closer.

"Kyle!" She turned—just in time to see him drop.

Blood darkened his pant leg.

He gritted his teeth. "I'll live. We need to move. Orders said no police."

Of course. Orders again. But she agreed. She couldn't afford to be detained. Not with what she had to deliver.

He leaned on her as they slipped toward the motel.

"Wait here." He handed her his wallet. "Go to the store we passed. First aid kit."

She hesitated. "Will you be okay?"

He nodded. "Go."

She ran to the store, paid in cash, and hurried back. Together, they approached the motel entrance.

The guy behind the counter didn't even look up from his phone. Just pushed a clipboard forward. "Two-hour minimum. Daily rate's on the wall."

Two hours? Oh. One of those motels.

Lily swallowed. She only had a few Hong Kong dollars. Kyle slid his wallet toward her again.

She scribbled a fake name, a coworker's, and handed over the cash.

The guy tossed a room key across the counter.

"Room 110. Down the hall to the left."

CHAPTER 26

MOTEL, FLORIDA, USA

KYLE

The room was even worse than he'd expected.

One bed. One window. Peeling paint. No chairs, no table. No coffee maker. No sense of dignity.

But at least they were alive. And for now, unseen.

"Hand me the first aid kit." He lowered himself to the edge of the bed. His leg was on fire, his throat dry. And the adrenaline propping him up ebbed away.

She held onto the kit, then cracked it open to inspect the contents. "You need to take your pants off."

He blinked. "Excuse me?"

She gave him a flat look. "I need to clean the wound. Don't worry. I passed First Aid with flying colors."

Of course she had.

The girl kept surprising him. The way she'd weaponized a bunch of lacrosse bros? Genius.

Maybe one of those thugs had limped away with a bullet in his leg, or the cops had scattered them.

His fingers went to his pocket for his phone, but all he pulled out were shards.

He swore under his breath.

The screen was spiderwebbed, the casing bent. Useless.

But then, if the phone hadn't been there, the bullet might've hit the femoral artery. He dangled the phone between two fingers. "Guess this might've saved my life."

"Come on." She snapped her fingers. "Unless you want me to take them off for you."

Seriously? Kyle shot her *a look*. "You sound like my mom."

She snorted. "That's comforting."

Grumbling, he unzipped and eased his pants off. She didn't flinch or look away. Her focus stayed on the injury. He appreciated that.

Now that he could see it clearly, the damage wasn't as bad as it had felt. The bullet had grazed him, slicing flesh, not punching through.

She worked in silence, wiped away the blood with surprising gentleness, then wrapped it with gauze and tape.

Efficient. Focused. Calm.

He watched her hands.

"Thank you."

She nodded and stood, digging through his backpack. Then she handed him a clean T-shirt and gray sweatpants. "You should change. Your pants are toast."

Outside, a car passed slowly. Too slowly.

Kyle didn't move.

LILY

Lily avoided Kyle's eyes while she treated his wound.

Thank goodness the hotel had required first aid certification when they promoted her. She'd grumbled about it back then. Now, it might've just saved his life.

Her heartbeat was slowing. Sort of.

Had he noticed how her fingers trembled while she cleaned the wound? She'd tried to act calm, focused, despite her frayed nerves.

And when he'd started pulling down his pants?

Her heart had slammed against her ribs. Loud enough for him to hear, for sure.

She'd smoothed her expression, forced her hands to keep moving, her thoughts to stay where they belonged. He was hurt. He needed help. She had a job to do. That's all this was.

Still, she couldn't stay in the room while he changed.

"I saw a couple vending machines outside." She grabbed the first excuse she could. "I'll get us some snacks and drinks. Can I borrow money?"

He barely looked up. "Take my wallet. Don't worry about it."

As she turned toward the door, something outside caught her eye.

A shadow, just past the vending machines. Still. Watching.

Something was going on with Lily.

She hadn't looked at him once while tending to his wound. No small talk. No nervous jokes. Just efficient silence. And the second she was done, she'd all but sprinted to dig through his backpack.

Now, while she was out hunting snacks, he changed. The pain in his leg had dulled to a throb, but when he scooped the shattered phone off the floor, his stomach twisted.

How was he supposed to contact anyone now?

The lock clicked.

"What's wrong?" She stepped in. "I heard you grumbling."

Before he could answer, she waved over her shoulder. "I thought I saw someone out there near the vending machines, but it was just a guy smoking."

He held up the broken phone. "No way to call in."

"Oh." She handed him a water bottle, aspirin, and a protein bar, then sat on the edge of the bed to sip her soda.

The room felt even smaller than before, a cramped, off-white box of peeling paint. Kyle perched on the foot of the creaky bed.

The silence stretched.

"Don't worry. I'll figure something out. We'll slip away before they find us." But even he didn't believe his pseudoconfidence.

And she wasn't listening anyway.

Her silence wasn't fear. It was something else.

"Lily, are you okay?"

"Huh?" She blinked like she hadn't heard him.

"Are you all right?"

"Oh, um, yes. May I ask you something?"

"Of course."

Her arms slipped around her middle. "Suppose… you were adopted. And you grew up believing your biological parents were dead. But then, you found out they were alive, and people had been lying to you all along. If your birth parents wanted to meet you, would you let them?"

Kyle shifted, twisting on the bed to kick his good leg up and face her. Up until now, he'd assumed she was focused on reaching the senator. On getting out alive.

But this?

This was different.

"When my parents separated, I blamed my dad. He was always gone. Classified missions, foreign assignments, we never knew where. Asia, the Middle East… it didn't matter. He missed birthdays, holidays… everything."

He paused, surprised at how easily it came out. "I was angry.

Shut him out for years. But he didn't give up. Eventually, I let him back in."

"I'm sorry."

"We're good now." He shrugged. "Took time, but we got there. It's not the same story, I know."

She smiled. "It helps."

His heart skipped. That smile, soft, grateful, made him forget the pain. Made him forget they were being hunted.

"Anytime. Why?"

She didn't answer, just sighed, and stared past him.

"You weren't speaking hypothetically, were you?"

Her hold on herself slipped loose. She latched her fingers together and focused on them. "Kind of. It's complicated."

The senator's words… *Keep her safe.*

And Lily—dark hair, mixed features, fluent in Cantonese, but undeniably Caucasian—

Could it be?

He touched her hand. The contact was electric. He wanted to hug her, tell her she wasn't alone.

But he didn't.

Instead, he met her eyes. "If you ever want to talk, I'm right here."

She leaned forward as if she might say something, or maybe just breathe. But then—

"They can't be far!"

CHAPTER 27

MOTEL, FLORIDA, USA

SIMON

"This is your last mission?" Simon needed to be sure he'd heard her right.

"Yes." Her voice caught, low, trembling, but steady. "Patty tried to talk me out of it, but I can't do it anymore. They killed Andrew. My brother."

He froze.

Andrew.

He remembered the name from Lily's file, listed as her uncle. Died in a car accident. That's what the report said.

Simon pulled her into his arms again. "I should've known." He pressed his cheek against her silky hair. "When I read that file, I should've realized he was your brother. I thought it was just… an accident."

Olivia shook her head. "It wasn't. The Ghost's people did it, and the people in her pocket covered it up. Andrew and Elsie were good parents. They loved Lily like their own."

She shuddered. "Elsie had cancer young. It went into remission, but it left them unable to have children. Lily was their entire world."

"You've been keeping tabs on her?"

"Of course." She eased away, grabbed a bottle of water from the counter, and drank half of it like she hadn't had a moment to breathe.

"Let's sit." Simon gestured toward the light-gray velvet sectional.

They talked for a while longer. About Lily. About what might come next.

Then she said, "You never married."

It wasn't a question.

"No. I came close a couple times. But each time, something fell apart before it got serious."

He met her eyes. *No one could replace you.*

"You?"

She snorted. "In my line of work? No one's even seen my real face since the day I 'died.'" A half smile tipped her lips. "You're the first."

Simon studied that face. Not the one she wore in the field. Her real one. Still familiar. Still beautiful.

Her last mission. And now she was here. Was God giving them a second chance?

Before he could follow the thought, his phone rang.

"Finally." He swiped to answer.

"Sir, we've had a development."

Never good words.

Olivia leaned in, listening.

"They're not at the safe house. Someone broke in. There's no sign they ever stayed there."

"They were there," Olivia whispered. "I saw them arrive."

He relayed it to the agent. "I got word from an operative that they were there. He never checked in?"

"The only time he checked in was when he landed."

She began tapping on her phone. Seconds later, she showed him the screen, a blinking dot on a map.

She mouthed, "Car."

He nodded and gave the location over the phone. "Relay this to all units. Report back as soon as they're located."

"Yes, sir."

As the call ended, Olivia stood and began pacing. "I should've stayed. I never should've left them alone. But I had to warn you."

"Olivia." He stood too. "It's not your fault. We'll find them."

She stopped cold. "What if Kyle's one of them? How thoroughly did you vet him?"

He pulled up Ron's number and hit call.

"Have you heard from Kyle?" Simon asked once Ron picked up.

"No. I thought you sent him to retrieve the package."

"I did. He called when they landed, but nothing since."

"I'll try him now."

A few seconds passed. Ron came back. "Straight to voicemail."

Silence fell.

Heavy. Dread-filled.

Simon's gaze met hers. For the first time in years, they were afraid for the same person.

RON

Ron hung up. He wouldn't sit around waiting for answers.

Kyle's phone wasn't just off. It was dead. And that didn't sit right.

He strode into the squad room.

"Hernandez, ping this number." He rattled off Kyle's digits.

Within seconds, a map lit up on the screen. A blinking dot appeared.

"Right here." Hernandez pointed to the dot.

Ron leaned over his shoulder, narrowed his eyes. "Got it. Thanks."

A pat confirmed his sidearm was in place. He turned to go. "I'll be back."

Tanner rose, grabbing his backpack. "Where are we going, boss?"

Ron didn't break stride. "Stay. I need to check something."

And he was gone.

CHAPTER 28

ON THE RUN, FLORIDA, USA

LILY

"They can't be far!"

The shout came from outside, too close.

Lily's breath caught. Her heart pounded. Kyle's phone was broken, his leg wounded, and they were out of time. *Lord, help!*

Kyle gritted his teeth and forced himself upright. He limped to the window and peeled back the curtain. "They're checking the other motel. Let's move. Where's your phone?"

She dug it out of her bag. "I—I don't know if—"

"Just call. They might charge more, but it doesn't matter. It's 011 for international, right?"

He reached for it.

But she held it close. "Who are you calling?"

"My dad. If I can remember his number."

She blinked. "You don't know it by heart?"

"It's saved on my phone. Do you know your godmother's number?"

She didn't. Not anymore. She used to know all her contacts by memory. Now? Her phone was her brain.

Then it hit her. "Wait. I have Dylan's number. He said to call if we needed help."

Kyle glanced through the curtain again. "Good. Text him. I don't want anyone hearing your voice."

She thumbed a quick message.

> We r in danger. Need to get away from bad guys. Need help.

"Let's go!"

They slipped out the rear exit, cutting around the far side past the dimly lit pharmacy. He moved as fast as his leg allowed, uneven but determined.

Up ahead, someone was leaving an apartment building. Lily lunged forward and caught the door just before it closed. They slipped inside.

The hallway, narrow and dark with yellowed walls, smelled of old food. He leaned against the inner door, keeping watch through a crescent-shaped glass pane.

> How can I help? What do u need?

> Pick us up. Need to see Senator Simon Roth.

Then she sent the location via Maps.

"Anything?" she whispered.

"Black SUV. Just turned onto the street."

Lily moved beside him. Through the window, she saw it, creeping along the curb outside the motel.

The SUV slowed.

Her pulse hammered in her ears.

No one got out.

Then the passenger-side window lowered just enough to suggest they were watching.

Her phone buzzed.

On my way. Stay hidden. Don't move.

Through the glass, the SUV's brake lights flared.
They were stopping.

DYLAN

Dylan had just finished a sandwich when his phone buzzed.

We r in danger. Need to get away from bad
guys. Need help.

He froze, rereading the message. Danger? Not again. He'd promised himself he was done with that. But this wasn't about him.

How can I help? What do u need?

While waiting, his mind spun. Lily was supposed to be safe. With Kyle. Had they been spotted? Tracked?

A second message came through with an address and a request.

Pick us up. Need to see Senator Simon Roth.

He grabbed his keys. He didn't even change shoes.

From his car, he called his office and asked for Jeff, some kind of executive something. He didn't remember the guy's actual title, just that Jeff made things happen.

"Dylan," Jeff answered, cheerful. "How was Hong Kong?"

"Good. Hey, I'm kind of in a hurry, need a favor. Can you find out where Senator Roth is right now?"

A pause. "He has an office in town."

"Yeah, but can you check if he's there? Or find out where he *can* be reached?"

"They'll want to know why we're asking."

He made a turn. "My grandmother wants to get in touch with him."

"Ah. That'll do it. I'll call his staff."

"Thanks, Jeff. You're the best."

"Flattery noted."

GPS took him to the location Lily had texted. He missed the building on the first pass and had to turn around. When he pulled up, Kyle was limping badly.

"What happened?" Dylan asked as Kyle climbed into the back and Lily slid into the front seat.

"Drive!" Kyle settled in.

"He got hit." Lily buckled in. "Those guys have guns."

"Do you need a hospital?"

"No. Drive!"

Dylan didn't argue. Tires screeched.

"Did you find out where the senator is?" she asked.

"Home. Jeff texted me the address. GPS says about an hour."

"No!" She pointed at the mirror on the side. "That SUV. He was one of them!"

Dylan checked the rearview mirror. A black vehicle was weaving through traffic.

"Step on it!" Kyle snapped. "Aren't you, what—a millionaire? A billionaire? Why aren't you driving a sports car with some juice?"

"Hey, first off, I'm not either of those things. That's my grandmother. I work for a living."

"Still, you could buy something faster."

"Sure. But then I'd stress about scratching it or curbing a rim. This car's from my grandma. A gift. I like not worrying about it."

"So buy two. Keep one for emergency getaways."

"Great plan, except I don't even know how to drive a stick."

Kyle groaned. "Of course you don't."

"Hey, I grew up driving a beat-up sedan held together with duct tape. I'm just happy this one has A/C and doesn't stall on left turns."

"We're being chased, Dylan. You could've sprung for horsepower."

"You're welcome for rescuing you," Dylan muttered.

"Guys," Lily cut in. "Can we argue about cars after we outrun the ones with guns?"

The SUV moved closer.

"Turn left. Now!" Kyle ordered.

Dylan obeyed, taking a side street.

"Next right. Then another left."

They zigzagged for blocks, shaking the tail. Everyone exhaled.

Dylan eased off the gas and let GPS reroute. "You wanna tell me what's going on? Thought you two were safe."

"Classified."

"Of course it is." Dylan rolled his eyes. "You sound just like your dad."

Lily shifted sideways in the passenger seat. "We don't know exactly. I think they're after me."

"Great."

They hit a stretch of empty road, just two lanes and scattered strip malls. Dylan started to relax. Then he checked his mirror.

A dark dot was growing fast.

"Hey, guys? They're back."

Headlights flared. The SUV was gunning straight for them.

CHAPTER 29

MOTEL, FLORIDA, USA

RON

Ron leaned across the check-in counter, jaw tight. "You haven't lifted your head. Take a good look."

The place stank. He held up the phone. Kyle's photo lit the screen. "He's with a young woman. Have you seen them?"

"Told you. I don't look at customers. Not my business what they do in their rooms."

"This isn't Vice. I don't care about that. Just him and the woman."

The clerk shrugged, glancing at the screen. "There was a girl earlier. Didn't catch her face." He tossed a clipboard on the counter. "She signed in."

Winnie Tang. The name wasn't Lily's, but it had been in the file. One of her close friends at work. An alias. Smart move. "What room?"

"Room 110. But don't waste your time, they're gone."

"Checked out?"

He snorted. "This look like the Hilton? Nah. I heard yelling and saw them slip out the back. Right around when those SOBs were out there flashing guns."

"Where are they now?"

The clerk nodded toward the apartment across the street. "They went there first, then took off. Don't know where. What'd the girl do?"

Ron headed for the exit. He barely made it around the building when a familiar voice stopped him.

"Fancy seeing you here."

Ana Ruiz. She'd vanished years ago under suspicious circumstances. Now here she was, calm as ever.

"Ana, what are you doing here?"

"Working. Can't talk about it."

"So, CIA now?"

She gave a coy smile. "Why would you think that?"

Before he could answer, someone shouted, "*¡Ayúdame! ¡Policía!*"

A woman was waving her arms from the other motel's lot. An older woman lay on the pavement beside her.

Ana bolted toward them, Ron on her heels. "*¿Qué pasa?*" she asked.

The woman responded in rapid Spanish.

"She says a guy with a gun shoved her grandmother into a car bumper. Knocked her out," Ana translated. "They're guests at the motel." She was already texting. "Ambulance is en route. Local cops will take it from here."

Ron stepped closer to the younger woman. "Ask her something for me." He showed photos of Kyle and Lily. "Has she seen either of them?"

Ana paused. "Should've guessed. He's your son."

"Yeah. You know him?"

"No." She hesitated. "But I tracked blood from a disabled car a few blocks away. Tires were shot out. I've been following the trail here."

"Orders from Senator Roth?"

"No comment."

"Taking that as a yes. We're looking for the same people. Let's combine efforts."

She weighed it. "Fine. What've you got?"

"Ask first. I'll brief you after."

Ana turned to the witness. More Spanish.

"She saw them come out of that apartment building and get into a car."

"What kind?"

More questions. The woman pointed to a sedan across the lot.

"Like that. But silver."

"Did they go willingly?"

"Yes. She said they knew the driver."

Probably Dylan. "How long ago?"

Before Ana could ask, the woman launched into another burst of Spanish, gesturing animatedly.

Ana translated. "The guy who shoved the old woman saw them getting in the sedan. He pushed her to get to his car. His partner was already behind the wheel. They followed the sedan."

Sirens howled in the distance, getting closer.

"One last thing. Ask what the pursuers were driving."

"Black SUV," Ana confirmed after a quick exchange.

Ron nodded. "They went that way. I'm going after them."

"I'm coming with. Let's check in with the officer first."

After a rapid debrief with the responding cop, they headed for Ron's car.

They were behind, but not out. But, in a chase like this, even a five-minute lead could be the difference between rescue and regret.

"Pull traffic cam footage," Ron told his team through the car's Bluetooth. "Black SUV. Stolen plates. Start five minutes before we got here. Cross-check movement."

Beside him, Ana just finished her update with the senator.

He tapped a button on the steering wheel. "Call Dylan Roche."

The car's system chimed. The line rang once, then dumped to voicemail.

Too easy. Always was.

Then Hernandez patched in. "Kyle's phone isn't pinging, no signal. But we got a location on Dylan's. Stationary. Out on a stretch of two-lane road."

Ron frowned. "Not a lot out that way."

He hung up. There were a dozen reasons Kyle's phone might not be working—dead battery, signal drop, maybe even intentionally destroyed. But the fact that Dylan's was stationary in the middle of nowhere?

That didn't sit right.

"Two-lane road. Wonder where they're headed. But we're heading in the right direction."

Ana's voice jolted him. He'd almost forgotten about her. Ron glanced at her. "So, are you a spook?"

She smirked. "Didn't you say the CIA doesn't operate stateside?"

"NSA, then? DIA?"

She reached into her coat and flipped open her credentials. Defense Intelligence Agency. "I've worked with the senator on a few ops. He wanted trusted people on this, so here I am."

"Then why aren't you assigned to the task force?"

"Because the task force is focused on the Ghost. I'm focused on making sure the package"—she gave him a meaningful look —"gets delivered to the senator."

Lily.

Lights flashing and sirens cut through the rural stillness.

Ron pushed the accelerator. "We'll be there in twenty."

The next minutes passed in bursts of conversation, catching

up between gulps of silence. Careers. Transfers. Losses. Lives that never quite returned to normal.

Then Ana leaned forward. "What's going on up there?"

About a hundred yards up the road, flashing lights bathed the scene in red and blue. A squad car. An ambulance. And a banged-up silver Accord.

Ron's chest tightened.

"I don't know. Let's find out."

But his gut already knew the answer.

CHAPTER 30

THE ROTH RESIDENCE, FLORIDA, USA

SIMON

Code name King. A traitor. Someone close. Someone with influence.

Simon couldn't stop thinking about it, not since Olivia told him a traitor was in his circle. Only two men fit that description, but neither could be capable of betrayal. Right?

Still, right now, Lily mattered more.

While Olivia paced, Simon stood at the window overlooking the backyard, staring out at nothing, hands clasped behind his back, praying.

"What's taking them so long to find the car?" Olivia snapped.

His phone rang. Finally.

He turned away from the window and answered. "Report."

Ana Ruiz gave a brisk update. She and Ron were in pursuit, but he'd put his team on locating any surveillance footage of the SUV's route. They'd track it from there if they lost visual contact.

He ended the call and moved to the kitchen counter. "You heard that?"

Olivia was already typing on her phone. "I'm trying to ping Lily's phone."

He wanted to ask how, but thought better of it. Instead, his mind circled back to King.

"What are you thinking?" she asked, not looking up.

"I was thinking about King. I only have two suspects, but I can't believe either of them would work for the Ghost."

"Tell me."

"Stop pacing." He flinched every time she pivoted toward him. "There's nothing we can do until we hear back. Come sit."

She slid onto the stool next to him. "I'm listening."

"Roger. You might've met him. Senator Rifkin. Retired now."

Her expression shifted. "I remember him. I met him once, maybe twice."

"When?"

"In Hong Kong. I came to tell you I was pregnant. He was at your place. Told me you'd been transferred."

Simon nodded. "I was staying with him. He's always treated me like a son. I've known him for years. I can't imagine him betraying his country."

"You'd be surprised how often operatives earn trust by playing mentor. If he was in the Ghost's pocket, his job would've been to influence you. Guide your decisions. Maybe even groom you to take over."

The thought chilled him.

"That's how I got good intel. I got close to people."

He studied her face. Who had she become in the years apart? How much of Olivia was still Olivia, and how much was Phoenix now?

But this wasn't the time for that.

"Did you tell Roger you were pregnant?"

"Of course not."

He still remembered the conversation like it had just happened. He'd told Roger he was thinking of proposing, said he'd figure things out with Olivia once he settled in Singapore. Instead of supporting him, Roger shut it down.

"This is a great career move. You want to throw it away over a girl? You could have any woman you want in Singapore."

At the time, Simon had assumed Roger was just being blunt, looking out for his future. Now? He wasn't so sure.

"I tried calling you so many times," Olivia said. "No answer. Then the number was disconnected. I wrote too. Never got a reply. I thought… maybe you were angry. That you just left."

"I went to Hong Kong on leave to find you. I remembered your best friend, Marie. I tracked down her convent. They said she was in the US but wouldn't give me any contact info."

"She was finishing her studies here."

"Roger had someone help me search. They found an obituary. I still have it. No mention of your brother. Or your parents."

"My handlers left it vague. They didn't want anyone connecting dots. They claimed my brother and his wife adopted a child, so I could disappear without questions." She fidgeted with her phone. "Let's set Roger aside. Who's the second name?"

He checked his phone. No updates. "Harrison Burke, my campaign manager. Used to work for Roger, his campaign manager and chief of staff. After a few years in lobbying, Roger brought him in when I ran for office."

"Did you even want to run?"

He rubbed his temples. "I don't know. I thought about going private. Roger said I had more to offer. That he had connections. Next thing I knew, I was in front of cameras, shaking hands, being paraded around."

"And now you're up for reelection?"

He nodded. "They've already got me doing the fundraising

circuit, the talks, the events. And because my platform is pro-life and pro-family, they keep saying I need a wife. A family."

She smirked. "They got you elected without one. Why the concern now?"

"What I asked."

She braced an elbow on the counter, rocked the stool side to side. "So, Rifkin has the pull. Still connected. Any strange votes on his record? Classified briefings he might've attended?"

"No odd votes. But yes, he had access to plenty of sensitive material."

"And Harrison?"

"Not directly. Only through—"

His phone rang. Sharp. Sudden.

Simon glanced at the screen. Unknown Caller.

CHAPTER 31

TWO-LANE ROAD, FLORIDA, USA

KYLE

"Idiot! Look what you did! You'd better hope you didn't kill her."

"Nah, I stood on the brake at the end. If I hadn't, they'd be toast. And how else was I supposed to stop them?"

"You could have cut them off! Now, let's get moving."

The voices felt far away. Muffled. Disconnected.

Kyle's head lolled forward. His vision was foggy, eyes swimming with light. Everything ached. His thigh burned. He blinked. Was that blood soaking through his pants?

He tried to lift his head. Immediate vertigo. The world tilted.

Road. Car. Dylan. They'd been driving.

Flying, he'd felt like he was flying. Hadn't Dylan said something? What was it?

Lily!

Where was Lily? Were they still… going somewhere?

"Leave them."

Darkness swept in again.

"Can you hear me, Kyle?"

Someone new. Not one of the earlier voices. Firm hands moved around him. He tried to nod.

"Yeah," he whispered, though it barely came out.

Pressure on his leg. The sticky warmth of blood. He was being moved. A stretcher. Then lifted.

Paramedics. Ambulance doors clanged shut behind him.

"Oh, good. You're okay. He's okay, right?" Dylan's voice, urgent.

"Please stay put," a paramedic said. "We'll be leaving soon."

"I'm fine. You patched me up. Vitals look good. My chest doesn't even hurt anymore."

"Probably bruised ribs. The seat belt and airbags did their job, but you were knocked out. Could be a concussion."

"I passed your test. You know, the finger thing. And the questions. I'm good. How is he?"

"Lucky. No head trauma, no spinal damage. But that leg? It's a gunshot wound. And he wasn't wearing a seat belt."

"He was in the back," Dylan muttered.

"We have to report it. And he's carrying a gun."

"I told you. He's an agent."

Kyle tried to speak. "Dylan."

Nothing. He forced it again, louder. "Dylan."

"Yeah, what do you need? You okay?"

"Credential pack."

Dylan patted him down, ignoring the paramedic's scowl. "Must've fallen out. Check the car!"

A beat passed, then—

"Found it!" someone called.

Kyle exhaled. But only for a second.

There was still one voice he hadn't heard.

"Lily?"

Silence. Then Dylan, quiet now. "I think they took her. She's not here."

No. No. No.

She'd been right there. They were so close.

He'd failed her.

And before the guilt could settle, a sound tore through the air—

Screeching tires. Fast. Approaching.

He braced. Instinct more than thought.

RON

Ron's stomach clenched as the wreck came into view, twisted metal, acrid smoke, the kind of scene that never stopped hitting too close to home. He slammed the brakes, stopping just short of the crumpled sedan.

The car was still in one piece, barely. The rear was crushed in, the trunk accordioned. The acrid scent of scorched rubber and leaking fluids filled his nose, airbags, maybe. Or something worse.

Not as bad as he'd imagined, but not what he'd hoped to see either.

Ana reached out and placed a hand on his arm. "Ron, let me check. He might not have been in the car."

"No. I need to do this."

He was already moving. The paramedics were about to shut the rear doors. He rushed forward.

"Hey! You can't be here!" the officer shouted.

"Federal agents." Ana flashed her credentials. "Ruiz and Peters. This is our case. What do you know?"

Ron didn't wait for the answer. He banged on the ambulance door.

"Federal agents! Open up!"

A paramedic popped his head out. "You've got one minute.

We need to move."

"Agent Peters!" Dylan's voice cut through the noise. "I knew it was you. I told them to stop. Kyle's bleeding. He got shot. Sorry, I'm rambling." He mimed zipping his lips.

Ron vaulted in, brushing past the paramedic. Kyle lay on the gurney, pale and clammy, but conscious. His eyelids fluttered open.

"You're gonna be okay." Ron bent over him.

Kyle blinked. "Dad… I'm sorry. I messed up. Lily's gone. I let her down. I let everyone down."

Ron's chest tightened. He didn't have time for reassurances, but Kyle's guilt was a gut punch. He wasn't just his agent. He was his son. "Nonsense. Let them take care of you. I'll talk to Dylan." He turned to the paramedic. "I'm riding with him."

The paramedic nodded. Ron leaned out the open door and motioned to Ana. "I'm going with Kyle."

"Go. I'll catch up." She pivoted toward the police.

The ambulance sped forward.

Ron touched Dylan's arm. "What happened? Where's Lily?"

Dylan shuddered out a breath, hollowed out. "She called me. Said they needed help. Kyle had already been shot. We had a tail. Kyle gave me directions to lose them. I did—er, I *thought* I did. But they found us. Slammed into us hard."

Ron narrowed his eyes. "What is it?"

"It's weird. They were coming full speed. I thought they were going to ram us head-on. But at the last second, they braked. Hard. Just enough to wreck the car but not kill us."

"Like they were following orders to cause maximum damage, but not casualties?"

"I guess." Dylan shrugged.

"They took Lily?"

"I didn't see them. But I heard them. Two voices, one yelling about not killing her. I think they knocked her out. I heard her moan, then dragging sounds. They didn't touch me. Just said,

'Leave them.' Next thing I knew, they were gone. I couldn't move… Airbag had me pinned."

Ron exhaled. "You did the right thing. If you'd tried anything, it might've gotten worse. What about before she called you? Any idea what happened?"

Dylan shook his head. "They didn't say."

From the gurney, Kyle spoke up. "They knew about the safe houses. Two guys posing as agents tried to get into the first one." Kyle paused, gulped, continued. "We went to another one on the senator's list. More guys were waiting. We escaped, but they chased us to a market. That's where they shot out the tires."

How? How had they known about the safe houses?

Deep pockets? Moles?

But that didn't explain how they'd known about Lily.

"After we landed, two men tried to intercept us. But the flight attendant stepped in, clearly not a real attendant. Must've been backup. We didn't see her again, but we left in her car."

Ron dipped his head. As far as he knew, Simon hadn't sent anyone else, but that could've been on a need-to-know basis, like Ana Ruiz had been.

They arrived at the hospital.

As Kyle was wheeled in, Ron stayed with Dylan to go over everything again. "And you need to get checked too."

"I'm fine."

"I want a doctor to confirm that. I'm not explaining this to your grandmother if you pass out in front of her."

Dylan sighed. "All right, fine. The car was her gift, you know."

"I'm sure she'll care more about you than the car. And she'll get you another one."

The hospital smelled like antiseptic and overheated plastic. Monitors beeped in the background, a reminder that Kyle was stable. For now.

After seeing to it that Dylan followed a nurse to an exam room, Ron was about to call Ana.

But she walked through the ER doors, a backpack slung over her shoulder. She nodded toward the corridor to the room. "How is he?"

"He'll live. Superficial gunshot wound, bruises, cuts. They're running tests. What'd you get?"

She pulled out her phone. "Not much. A passing motorist called it in, but didn't stick around. Said they were run off. Tire tracks show the SUV tried to stop. Makes you wonder what they were planning."

"I don't think they wanted Lily dead." Ron rubbed his neck, cracked the tension side to side. "Kyle and Dylan? Maybe. Or maybe not. The whole thing feels… off."

"I had the car towed to your office." She widened her stance. "We need to process it under the radar. But I grabbed Kyle's backpack. Lily's phone, purse, anything else, they took with her."

He started texting Tanner, then jerked his head up. "Wait. You said they took her phone?"

Ana bopped her head.

"Maybe we can ping it."

"I like your optimism."

Ron called Hernandez. "Try to ping Lily's cell."

A pause. "Let me know." Ron ended the call. "It's not a US number. It'll take longer."

He tapped his chin. "Let's trace the call from the passing motorist. Maybe they saw something."

"Already did," Ana said. "Burner phone."

They locked eyes.

"You thinking what I'm thinking?" she asked.

"One of the kidnappers." He rubbed his jaw, frowning. "But why call it in? They didn't kill the guys. They even braked. And then they called it in?"

"None of it adds up."

Her phone buzzed.

She checked the screen. "It's the senator." She swiped to answer. "Sir, you've got me and Ron here."

Simon's voice crackled through, low, flat, and dangerous. "They have Lily."

CHAPTER 32

THE ROTH RESIDENCE, FLORIDA, USA

OLIVIA

"This is all my fault. I should've stayed with them."

Olivia didn't even know how many times she'd said it—four, five? The guilt looped through her chest like a taut wire. She paced along the living room where the soft rug muffled her steps. The floor-to-ceiling windows overlooked a sun-drenched lawn, the beauty outside jarringly disconnected from the darkness blurring her vision.

"Pacing around and blaming yourself won't help." Simon tapped the kitchen island beside his phone like he hadn't decided who to call to get this over and done. "Those two agents are the best. I can bring in more people if—"

"No." She stopped, pivoting to face him. "We can't risk it. The Ghost has eyes and ears everywhere. Bringing in more people could make things worse."

He held her gaze from across the room. The early afternoon light filtered through the blinds, casting lines across his face, lines that hadn't been there years ago. "But they'll need help locating her."

"I know. But more hands don't always mean better odds. Especially not with someone like her."

Simon leaned back against the counter. His suit jacket was slung over a chair, his dress shirt rolled at the sleeves. The house was quiet except for the refrigerator humming. The contrast between the stillness here and the chaos out there made the air itself feel too thin.

"They knew when we landed." She pressed cold fingers to her burning eyes. "That wasn't public information. They were waiting at the safe house. Kyle never had a chance. First, they tried deception. Then they came in guns blazing. That's not coincidence. There's a leak."

Simon's shoulders tensed. "I'm not sure where it could've come from."

"I'm not blaming you." She softened her tone. "But someone close is feeding them information. Someone who knows Lily and everything surrounding this plan."

He wiped a hand over his face as if trying to brush away all his troubles. "I kept the circle small. The task force doesn't even know about this layer. Only Ron. Ana's operating independently. Ron didn't even know she was involved until recently."

"And the logistics? The flight, the safe houses. Who managed all that?"

"I coordinated with an intel officer overseas. Locally, it was need to know only. They secured the safe houses but weren't told what or who they were for."

She took a deep breath, absorbing the details. Her gaze drifted toward the dining room where a vase of white lilies graced the table. Her stomach twisted. "What did the caller say, exactly?"

Simon's brow furrowed. "He said they have Lily. That he'd call back with instructions. Then he hung up. I didn't even get a chance to respond."

Olivia crossed the room and placed her hands on the counter, bracing on cool marble. "When he calls again, put him on speaker."

The house might have been still, the room filled with sunlight, but a shadow settled deeper around both of them.

CHAPTER 33

HOSPITAL, FLORIDA, USA

KYLE

After another round of checking his vitals, the doctor signed off on Kyle's discharge papers. The nurse walked him through the instructions on how to care for his leg wound, when to take the painkillers, and what signs of infection to watch for.

He nodded through most of it, ready to be gone. They all kept saying how lucky he was the bullet didn't hit an artery. He didn't feel lucky.

Dad came in with Dylan, who looked freshly bandaged but alert. A neat white strip crossed his forehead, and his bruises were already fading.

"They're letting you go?" Dad asked.

"Yeah, I'm fine." Kyle glanced at Dylan. "You?"

"Good as new." Dylan tapped his chest. "They said the seat belt did its job. Just bruises and a knock to the head."

"You're lucky."

"We both are."

"Okay to come in?" a female voice called from the hall.

Dad stepped aside. "Come on in."

A woman entered, Latina, maybe in her forties, with dark hair pulled back and sharp eyes that scanned the room in one sweep. Definitely law enforcement.

"Ana Ruiz," Dad said. "Ana, this is my son, Kyle."

"I'm glad you're okay." She offered her hand.

He shook it. "Thanks. Any news?"

Ana and Dad exchanged a look.

Then Dad clamped a hand on Dylan's shoulder. "Need a ride home? I can get a patrol car to take you. Or if you want to leave in style, I can call Max."

Dylan gave a tight laugh. "Funny you should say that. I already called him. Used the nurse's phone while they were finishing up with me." He held up empty hands. "Didn't get to keep it, just made the calls. Also rang Jeff to send me a new phone."

Kyle arched an eyebrow. "You knew they'd shut you out?"

"I figured it was fifty-fifty." Dylan shrugged. "Still wanted to try."

Dad folded his arms. "You'll be safer at the estate. And I promise you'll be the first to know when we have news."

"That's not good enough."

At Dylan's sharp tone, Dad rocked back on his heels. "It's all I've got."

Dylan raised a hand to Kyle. "Come on. Tell him I can tag along."

Kyle didn't say anything. Then he shook his head and winced. "Sorry, bud. He's the boss."

Dylan deflated. "Okay. I get it."

A while later, all of them made their way to the hospital lobby. Dylan stood near the sliding doors, eyes scanning every vehicle that slowed.

Moments later, a black Range Rover rolled up to the curb, windows tinted to regulation's edge, polished but not flashy, the kind of vehicle Max would send when Dylan didn't want attention. The driver stepped out to open the door for him.

Dylan turned to them. "You know how to reach me."

"We do," Dad said.

Dylan hesitated. "Get her back."

"We will."

Without another word, he climbed into the SUV. The door shut, and the vehicle drove into traffic.

Back at Dad's car, Kyle was handed a bundle of clothes from the trunk.

"My change of clothes," Dad said. "Might be a little big."

"Better than scrubs." Kyle slid into the back seat to change.

Dad settled into the driver's seat while Ana took the front passenger seat.

"Okay." Kyle scooted forward, dressed and decent. "What's going on?"

Dad started the engine and glanced at him in the mirror. "Buckle up, and you already know." He backed out of the parking spot. "They took Lily. The senator got a call. The guy said he'd call back with proof of life."

Kyle's heart sank. "A kidnapping? That doesn't make sense. Nobody knows about her connection to the senator."

"What connection?" Ana shifted to face him.

Kyle muttered a curse. "Never mind."

"No—what connection?"

"I thought you knew. Don't you have clearance? Wouldn't the senator have told you?"

Dad and Ana exchanged a look.

Kyle groaned. "Great. I wasn't supposed to say anything." He slouched back and buckled in. "So… where are we going?"

CHAPTER 34

UNKNOWN CABIN, FLORIDA, USA

LILY

The low hum of the air-conditioning unit was the first thing Lily heard. Had she dozed off on the plane? But no, the ceiling above her wasn't the cabin's sleek white paneling.

She tried to sit up but gave up. Other than the metal door and a dim bulb, the room only offered the narrow bed beneath her and a shuttered window set high on the wall. No curtains. No furniture. No sense of where or when she was.

Her mind scrambled. The cabin attendant… Something had felt off. And Kyle was with her. So was Dylan. It all felt distant now, like pieces of a dream scattered across her memory.

Maybe she should close her eyes for a bit.

The next time she surfaced, the haze had lifted a little.

They'd been in a car. Yes. Driving. Heading to Senator Roth's house.

Then came the impact. The jolt. The crash.

Her head throbbed, dull and heavy, not like a regular headache. More like something had hit her. Her chest ached too, deep and sore. She slid her hand down the same clothes, wrinkled and slightly bloodied.

This wasn't a hospital. That was… good? Maybe?

She sat up and swung her legs over the side of the bed. Stocking feet. She found her shoes and slipped them on.

The floor was hardwood. Cold. No rug. The shuttered window had bars.

Bars.

Panic edged in. She stood and rushed to the door. The knob didn't turn. She twisted harder. Nothing. Locked.

Her heart pounded. Sweat bloomed across her palms.

She scanned the room again for anything—a phone, a purse, a bag. Nothing.

This couldn't be happening.

She pressed her fingers to her temple, willing the fragments into a full picture. A black SUV. Kyle in the sedan's back seat. A blur of headlights. The slam of metal against metal.

Then darkness.

Lily's breath caught.

They'd taken her.

She backed up, trying not to cry, not to scream. Her hand went to her abdomen. She traced the area where she'd placed the fake mole.

Still there.

That meant hope.

But for how long?

She turned back to the door. There had to be a way out. There had to be.

She just had to find it before they came back.

CHAPTER 35

THE ROTH RESIDENCE, FLORIDA, USA

SIMON

"I need to know she's okay. Put her on the phone." Simon strained to keep his voice level.

The reply came in a voice warped by audio scramblers, cold and mechanical. "You're not in charge. Two million. Unmarked bills. Twenty-four hours. We'll call back with instructions. If you want to see her alive again, have the money ready."

The line went dead.

Simon didn't move, just stared at the phone on the island as if the caller might reappear. Then he exhaled and stepped back, tension tightening his jaw.

"Kidnapped for ransom?" Olivia frowned. "That doesn't make sense. I thought you only confirmed she was your daughter yesterday."

"I did. I had this strange inkling a week ago when I first saw her photo. But I didn't get confirmation until yesterday. I mean…" His voice caught as he exhaled. "I thought you were dead. I had no reason to believe I had a daughter."

She stepped closer. Her expression gentler, she rested a hand against his chest. "But your heart wanted to believe it. The question is, did you tell anyone? Even hint at it?"

Simon stiffened, narrowed his eyes in thought. Secrecy was second nature after a lifetime of security updates, classified briefings, and political maneuvering. But this hadn't been a mission. It was a hunch, an ache in his gut he hadn't dared trust.

"Simon?"

"I don't think so. The only person I would've said anything to was Roger. But even then, I was careful." He massaged his temples, searching his memory. "I asked about your death. I never mentioned Lily. That, I'm certain of."

But something tugged at his mind. A memory surfaced—him and Roger sharing a bottle of chardonnay in the library, talking about family and legacy. "I might have said something like, 'There's this girl. Her eyes reminded me of you.' I mean, Olivia to him.'"

"And what did he say?"

"He brushed it off. Told me you were ancient history, stop thinking about the past, look to the future."

His phone chirped again.

He checked the screen. His pulse quickened. "We have company."

KYLE

Kyle leaned forward in his seat as they drove past manicured lawns and sculpted hedges. The whole neighborhood screamed wealth, but the house they pulled up to, while big, didn't flaunt it.

Three-bay garage, a stately front porch, not a single pillar trying too hard. Still, compared to the homes he'd grown up in, it was the most luxurious place he'd ever seen.

"Nice place," he muttered more to himself than anyone.

The front door opened before they reached it.

During the drive over, Dad had checked in with his task force. Dylan's car had been recovered and was being processed, though he doubted they'd find much. Agents were already canvassing the crime scene, combing for traffic or private security cameras. One witness had described the SUV, and preliminary tire-track photos matched the make and model.

"Come on in," said the man at the door, Senator Simon Roth himself.

They stepped into a modest entryway flanked by side halls, with a straight staircase climbing along one wall. Cool marble-look tile stretched beneath their feet, gleaming under the soft recessed lighting. A rust-colored runner lined the stairs, muffling every footfall. Kyle was still absorbing the space when a woman stepped into view.

She stood at the foyer's far end, calm, poised, unmistakably composed. And familiar.

Then it hit him.

She was an older version of Lily, more angular, full Chinese, but the resemblance was clear.

The senator moved to stand beside her. "Allow me to introduce you. This is Olivia Tso, Lily's mother. She's also with the Clandestine Service."

Kyle didn't try to hide his shock. "But I thought you were dead. The file—"

"I thought so too." The senator laid his hand on her arm. "We'll get to that later. Right now, we have more urgent matters."

Beside him, Dad and Ana exchanged a glance. Then Ana gasped. "You... you're Phoenix?"

A smile tugged at Olivia's lips. "Guilty."

Ana stepped forward, offering her hand like she was meeting a celebrity. "You're real? I thought Phoenix was a myth!"

A flicker ignited in Dad's eyes. The gears turning. Connecting dots.

Dad faced the senator. "Simon, is Lily your daughter?"

Kyle blinked. They were on a first-name basis?

"Yes, but this can't go beyond this room."

Ana and Dad agreed.

The group updated each other. Once the basics were out, Dad asked, "Simon, do you have access to the two million? We might be able to requisition Bureau funds—"

"No." The senator held up a hand. "I'm not using government money. We don't negotiate with kidnappers."

Everyone gave a look.

Olivia rolled her eyes. "We all know that's not entirely true."

"Still, I'm not using taxpayer funds."

"Then can you raise it?" Dad pressed.

"Not from liquid assets. But I believe I have a legal way to secure it." He didn't elaborate.

Ana's and Dad's phones buzzed. Ana checked hers first. "BOLO got a hit. A sheriff's deputy spotted the SUV."

Simon started to rise. "Let's go."

But Olivia stepped forward. "No. Ron, Ana, follow that lead. Simon, secure the funds in case this is just a kidnapping."

Kyle frowned. *Just* a kidnapping?

"I agree." Dad then turned to Olivia. "And what will you be doing?"

"I'm staying here to follow a separate lead. Research. My specialty."

Kyle cleared his throat. "I'll go with them."

Dad eyed his leg. "Why don't you stay here?"

Olivia offered another warm smile. "I'd love the company."

Kyle paused. He'd rather be in the field, but he wouldn't argue. "Sure. I'll stay."

Olivia nodded once. "Simon, when they call back, stall them. Get proof of life."

"And I'll have the team trace the call," Dad added, already stepping away to make it happen.

CHAPTER 36

UNKNOWN CABIN, FLORIDA, USA

LILY

Lily had searched every inch of the room—under the bed, inside the foam mattress, even beneath the window bars—but found nothing sharp enough to unscrew a hinge, no matter how many crime shows had taught her otherwise.

Now, she had her ear pressed to the door.

Two voices.

One gruff and irritated: "This setup's ridiculous. No tools, no backup. What do they think we're supposed to do with her?"

The other voice, cooler, more resigned: "Orders are orders."

A pause.

"Why'd the boss send two of us just to grab one little girl?"

Little girl? If they'd said that to her face, she would've kicked them in the shins and shown them how *not* little she was. But the reminder of her size gave her an idea.

"She's probably hungry. I'll bring her something. Might cooperate better."

Footsteps thudded closer.

She scrambled back to the bed and curled up, feigning fear.

She let the aches in her ribs and the pounding in her skull pull tears to her eyes. Not hard to do.

The door opened. A man stepped in—stocky and average height, but from her vantage point, he looked huge. Muscular, solid. No wonder they thought she was little.

"I'm sure you're hungry." He set a tray with its sandwich and plastic bottle of water on the bed. "I'm not gonna hurt you."

She shrank back further.

"I just want to check for other injuries. You took a hit in the crash. Might not show yet."

From outside the door, Gruff Voice called, "Maybe she doesn't speak English."

"She was with those guys. She understands." The tall man lowered his voice as if trying to coax her. "Come on. I know you understand. Just eat something."

He reached into his back pocket and pulled out a folded copy of the *New York Times* and laid it beside her. "I need to take a photo. Look up, just for a second. Don't make this harder."

She kept her gaze down. Silent. Unmoving.

Then a sudden bang.

She flinched, head snapping up. A phone clicked.

Outside, the gruff one cackled. "Knew that'd work."

The man inside grunted and slid the phone into his pocket. "Eat up."

He shut the door behind him with a final *click* of the lock.

She stared at the sandwich.

They still thought she was weak.

That was her advantage.

CHAPTER 37

THE ROTH RESIDENCE, FLORIDA, USA

SIMON

"You should be getting the photo of her now. Remember, we want two million in unmarked bills. The clock starts ticking now. We'll text you the drop-off instructions," the robotic voice said.

"I need more time to arrange for that amount of cash." Simon gripped the phone tighter.

"Come now, we both know you have access to that kind of cash if you ask the right person." A click signaled the disconnection.

Olivia got Ron on a video call and cast it up to the TV mounted across from the kitchen. The open-concept space flowed with understated elegance, kitchen to the left with a marble island, and a small round table tucked beside a bay window, acting as a casual breakfast nook. Kyle had claimed that table, posture tense.

The staircase hugged the wall near the entry, rising in a straight line. A wide velvet sectional faced the TV, centered around a clean-lined coffee table.

On-screen, Ron shook his head. "The call wasn't long enough to trace. Send me the picture. I'll forward it to the task force. They might be able to find something."

Simon forwarded the image but kept staring at it long after. The grainy photo showed a girl curled up on a bed, her face pale and frightened. His daughter. He had only just learned she existed, but the protective urge surged in his chest like fire. *Keep her safe, Lord. Please.*

"Let me see that." Olivia enlarged the image on his phone. "I don't think she's hurt, no fresh wounds, at least. Some bruises and cuts, likely from the crash. Nothing else obvious. That's a good sign."

Ron's voice cut back in. "What did he mean, 'You have access to that kind of cash if you ask the right person'? Sounded… pointed."

Simon hesitated. He felt their eyes on him. "I don't know," he lied.

A long beat of silence passed.

"All right," Ron said. "Stay in touch, everyone." The screen blinked dark.

Olivia already had her laptop open, her fingers flying over the keyboard. She didn't look up as she asked Kyle, "You have your laptop with you?"

"Yeah." He rummaged through his backpack and pulled it out. The casing was cracked. "Not sure if it'll work after the accident."

She gave it a glance. "Simon, do you have a spare he can use?"

"Sure." Simon headed into his study and returned with his personal laptop. "Nothing sensitive on here. Let me log in."

As he typed, Olivia spoke to Kyle again. "Assuming you're cleared for financials, I want you to comb through the money trails. Start with everyone in Simon's office. Harrison Burke and former Senator Rifkin are priorities."

Kyle nodded. "On it."

Then Olivia touched Simon's arm, her voice softer now. "I know you'll tell me when you're ready. But right now, you should do what you need to secure the funds."

Simon met her eyes. She knew. Not the details, but enough.

"Of course," he said.

He wouldn't loop in Ron, not yet. Only a handful of people knew the truth about his background. That he'd lost his parents young and, with no family able to take him in, had been placed in a private Catholic orphanage. It wasn't a story he shared often. He'd finished school there, guided by nuns and volunteers who gave him a foundation and a future.

But the kidnapper knew. That voice on the phone hadn't been guessing.

So who was it? And how close had they once been?

Later

Mirror Estate

The sign still stood—Mirror Estate etched into the stone, weathered but resolute. Simon eased to a stop before the gate and rolled down the window, his hand steady despite the weight behind this visit.

"Simon Roth. Here to see Mrs. Marino." He held his ID up to the camera, aware of the absurdity. He'd once been a nameless boy in the system, and now he had titles, influence, tailored suits. Still, in this place, the past loomed larger than any résumé.

A mechanical groan broke the stillness as the iron gate creaked open. He inhaled. Time to be humble.

He guided the car up the winding path, the tires whispering over the pristine drive. The mansion came into view like a memory made real, stately, serene, and unflinching. He hadn't been this close since he was a teenager. Even now, with the sun casting its warm gold over the façade, the place gave him pause. Not fear, reverence. The kind bred from knowing you owe everything to people who never owed you a thing.

The front door opened before he'd even shut the engine off.

"It's been a long time, Simon," said a familiar voice.

Max. The same calm presence, still trim and dignified, the kind of man who never seemed to age.

"Max." Simon stepped out, extending a hand, then froze when the man pulled him into a one-armed hug.

"I hear you're a senator now."

"Guess word travels." He managed a smile, grateful for the warmth in the older man's voice.

"Come in. Ms. Carol will be glad to see you."

They stepped into cool, polished air. The marble beneath his feet was flawless, gleaming like it hadn't aged a day. He felt underdressed, no matter how expensive his suit. This wasn't just a house. It was a curated legacy. The architecture whispered of power passed down, not seized.

"She's in the sunroom." Max led him through the great room. The hallway was wide and light-filled, but Simon couldn't shake the memory of standing outside those walls as a boy, waiting for someone to make decisions that would shape his life.

"Ms. Carol, the senator is here," Max announced.

She turned from the window with the quiet poise he remembered, but age had softened her edges. Not weakened, softened, like weathered stone.

"Mrs. Marino." He stepped forward and offered his hand.

She clasped it with unexpected strength. "It's good to see you again, Simon. Sit. Let's catch up."

He did, settling across from her in a chair that probably cost more than his first car. And yet, she looked at him not like a benefactor but like someone welcoming back family.

They eased into conversation without pretense.

"Have you located the young woman?"

Simon blinked. "You know?"

"Dylan told me. He said the girl was abducted while they were en route to see you. I assume there's a ransom."

"There is."

"How much?"

Before he could answer, a new voice entered the room.

"I heard Senator Roth was here." Dylan stood in the doorway, calm but alert. Simon hadn't met him, but heard about the newfound heir.

"Yes, come in, Dylan. I was just asking about your friend."

"She's alive. We received a photo. That's all for now."

"How much is the ransom?" Carol's voice remained even.

"Two million."

Dylan exhaled. "That's… a lot of money."

"We'll help," Carol offered without as much as a pause. "Do they want digital or cash?"

Simon hesitated, the directness catching him off guard. "Cash. Unmarked bills."

She peered back, unfazed, as though he'd told her the time. "We can do that."

"You don't have to—"

"But I want to." She held up a hand, fingers aged, but devoid of rings. "Consider this a gesture of redemption for our family's past transgressions."

Low and hoarse, Simon's voice roughed its way up his throat. "Thank you. Truly. We hope we won't need to pay. But if we do—"

"Then you'll be ready. Now, please accept our help and thank us by bringing her home safely."

"I will." He meant it with every fiber of his being. His hands curled in his lap, the tension given somewhere to go. "I really don't know how to thank you."

"You've been repaying me ever since you graduated. With your life's work. It's a shame the orphanage closed. You'd have made a fine poster child."

He let out a breath of humor. "It meant everything to me. The nuns, the volunteers. The faith, the discipline, they instilled in us. That mattered."

Her eyes gleamed, and she pressed that hand to her chest, visibly moved. "By the way, Fr. Bob passed, but Deacon Phil—he's Fr. Phil now. Still at the chapel."

"I plan to visit."

She rose, her gaze steady. "Dylan, will you take him to the vault?"

"Of course," Dylan said.

Simon stood as well. "Thank you again, Mrs. Marino."

"Don't be a stranger. And next time, bring the girl with you."

He nodded, the words striking something deep.

Not just a polite farewell. A charge. A vow.

I will. Whatever it takes.

CHAPTER 38

THE ROTH RESIDENCE, FLORIDA, USA

KYLE

There were a hundred ways Kyle preferred to find dirt on someone. Spreadsheets weren't one of them. Not what he signed up for when he joined law enforcement. But Senator Roth hadn't countermanded Olivia's directive, and she didn't invite second-guessing.

So here he was, at Simon Roth's kitchen table, sleeves shoved up, elbow-deep in spreadsheets and banking records, surrounded by the scent of dark roast coffee and the faint citrus polish that clung to the countertops. His laptop hummed, its advanced cooling system working to keep pace with his rapid commands.

He didn't belong in this world of numbers and nested corporations. Surveillance? Fine. Interviews? He liked talking to people. Takedowns? Bring it on. But this?

This felt like detention. With homework.

He rubbed his eyes. The lines on the screen blurred, half from exhaustion and half from a growing headache behind his right temple.

Across from him, Olivia pressed against the island, legs crossed at the ankle, laptop glowing beside her like a control tower. She made it look easy, like the data talked to her.

"Anything on Rifkin?" she asked, her tone clipped, but not unkind.

Kyle clicked a new tab, waiting for the slow load. "It's weird," he admitted. "He doesn't have much saved. Modest lifestyle, considering. Big house, but it's paid off. Regular payment to someone named Rosa. Just one car, also paid off. No vacation properties, no luxury rentals. I thought retired senators were supposed to be rolling in dough."

Olivia stepped closer, peering over his shoulder. "Yes, it is rather strange. Dig deeper. Hidden accounts, crypto, maybe a trust in someone else's name."

"Crypto. Of course." He resisted the urge to grumble louder. He didn't hate computers. He just hated feeling like an idiot. Olivia had walked him through the red flags on irregular transfers, sudden asset jumps, obscure shell corporations. But knowing what to look for wasn't the same as knowing where to look.

Every few minutes, he flicked his gaze toward Olivia's phone resting on the counter, hoping, expecting a call or text from his dad. Nothing. His own phone shattered with the bullet. He needed a new one, but he hadn't exactly had time for errands.

He leaned back, working out a kink in his neck. "Why would a guy like Rifkin hide money? He's already out of the game."

"Power doesn't retire." Olivia scrolled on her screen. "It just changes shape."

She stood and stretched before walking over to his side, glancing at his laptop. Her brows furrowed. "Wait. That payment to Rosa. It's labeled housekeeping wages?"

"Yeah. What's weird about that?"

"He always paid her under the table."

Kyle blinked. "You knew that?"

She didn't answer, just braced a hand beside the laptop, bending closer. "Check the registration for the company he's paying."

That, at least, he could do without a tutorial. He located the business registry and typed. "It's a shell. No staff. No real address. Just a mailbox in Delaware."

She picked up her laptop, set it on the table, and scooted out a chair beside him. The click of her keyboard was sharp, focused. "Keep going. That account may be linked to an offshore bank or laundering route."

The pieces started to align. He didn't like it. "You think it's blackmail?"

"Textbook Ghost. Pressure points and dirty money."

He dragged a hand through his hair. "Shouldn't we follow up now? Call it in?"

"We will. But this isn't just about Rifkin. If he's paying off someone without knowing who they're connected to, he's scared. And I want to know who has him spooked."

She stopped typing. "Now. Walk me through what happened after I left this morning."

He opened his mouth. "We..." His eyes wide, he looked at her in a different light. "You're the cabin attendant!"

She offered a dry smile but didn't deny it.

"You looked *completely* different. Were you wearing a—?"

"Focus, Kyle."

He huffed, then grinned. "Okay. So, after *you* left, we drove to the first safe house...."

He launched into the story, piecing it together aloud while Olivia listened, occasionally asking for clarification. Her attention was absolute, the kind that made you feel like your words mattered.

"They spoke Mandarin?"

"That's what Lily said."

"And they said they wouldn't hurt her?"

"Yeah, according to her."

"And you—what did you hear? I mean, at the crash."

"I was in and out, but yeah. One guy kept yelling something about not hurting the girl. Sounded like it wasn't part of the plan."

Her gaze sharpened. "And Dylan?"

"Said the ambulance showed up too fast. Thought it was OnStar, but Ana said a random motorist called it in."

Olivia straightened. "From a burner phone, according to your dad." She grabbed her jacket and swung it over her shoulders.

He rose. "Where are we going?"

"To visit a former senator. Time to ask some better questions."

CHAPTER 39

CONVENIENCE STORE, FLORIDA, USA

RON

R on didn't like working cases too close to home, and this one crossed lines faster than he could redraw them.

Beside him, Ana was still googly-eyed. "I can't believe I met Phoenix. I always thought she was a myth. In case you didn't know, she's famous in Spooksville."

"I figured." He kept his focus on the approaching gas station.

Deputy Baker sat in his cruiser, windows rolled down, the engine humming in the background. The SUV in question was parked near the dumpster, far from where most customers would choose to stop.

Ron had already called Tanner to arrange for a tow. They couldn't leave anything unchecked, no matter how unlikely it was they'd find a lead.

Baker stepped out as they approached. His handlebar mustache and mirrored sunglasses belonged in a different decade. His uniform was tidy, but the sweat around his collar showed the Florida heat wasn't giving him a break.

"You the Feds?" He extended a hand.

"Agents Ruiz and Peters." Ana took the lead. "What can you tell us?"

Baker shrugged. "Not much. I stopped in to use the restroom before grabbing a coffee. When I came out, I saw that SUV tucked in back. Weird spot to park, so I ran the plate. BOLO matched."

"You didn't see anyone get in or out?"

"Nah, I figure they'd already taken off. Didn't hear anything either."

A camera mounted over the entrance was pointed too far forward to catch much of the back lot. Ron thanked the deputy and walked toward the SUV. After doubling back to his vehicle, he popped the trunk and retrieved a slim jim from his kit.

The SUV door popped open easily.

"There's no blood or obvious signs of a struggle." One hand braced on the SUV's roof, Ana craned, checking the interior.

He lifted the hatch. "Trunk's clean too."

They headed inside the store, where the clerk blinked at their badges and led them to the security monitor. The grainy footage offered a lousy angle. It showed the SUV pulling in behind the store... then another SUV leaving a few minutes later.

"I'm sending this to Deanna. She might be able to clean it up." His thumbs worked on the phone keypad.

"You think we can get the plate? Driver, maybe?" Ana asked.

He lifted his shoulders. "Depends on how bad the glare is."

Ana huffed. "Maybe Phoenix and Kyle had better luck."

Ron was about to reply when his phone buzzed. "Tanner." He held up a finger before answering. "Yeah?"

"Boss, Deanna worked fast. She cleaned up the image—got a partial plate, blurry face. Cross-referenced it with military records and facial rec. Got a hit right away. The guy's in the system."

"Name?"

"Randall Hall. Ex-army. Dishonorable discharge. Multiple assault charges. Definitely not your neighborhood carpool guy."

The mugshot came through, close-cropped hair, hard stare, busted lip. A match for the grainy footage. "Start pulling his known associates. See if he's tied to any local crews, militias, or weird fringe types."

"Already in motion. I'll update you if anything jumps."

Ron waved the phone, gesturing Ana back toward the car, and following her. "We've got a name. Let's make sure it doesn't turn into a headline."

"And that's not all," Tanner added as they walked. "We flagged a car going the opposite way when the accident happened. Stopped for a second, didn't get out. We tracked it. Stolen plate again. About half a mile west, the driver tossed something."

Ron slid into the driver's seat. "What'd they toss?"

"A burner phone. Lab got a partial print."

His fingers curled around the steering wheel. "Tanner… what's on that print?"

"You're gonna want to see for yourself." Tanner's tone shifted, quieter, grimmer.

Ana's gaze flicked to the phone screen as the image loaded. "Oh, boy."

Ron exhaled through his nose, already dreading the politics ahead. The face staring back at him didn't belong to a low-level thug.

"Guess we know where we're going now."

CHAPTER 40

MIRROR ESTATE, FLORIDA, USA

SIMON

Security cameras tracked them from hidden corners as Simon stepped onto the estate grounds.

The path to the chapel cut through trimmed hedges and sun-warmed stone, but all he felt was a slow, tightening dread.

"You really went to school here?" Dylan waved to the old stone building ahead.

Simon nodded. "Yes. Back when the place had more nuns than guards."

They'd chosen to walk outdoors rather than take the tunnel. The fresh air felt cleaner somehow, less suffocating.

"Did you know Mickey Roche? He was in one of the last classes here."

Simon slowed, turning to get a better look at the young man beside him. There it was—the eyes, the jawline, something in the way he carried himself.

Of course.

"You look like him. Mickey was a few years behind me. I

didn't know him well." He hesitated. "I didn't know about him and your mother."

"Most didn't. Cop's son, Marinos' daughter. Not ideal for the old guard."

Simon understood the forbidden dynamic. Olivia's family didn't like her dating Westerners. She and Simon had barely met when they were forced to keep things quiet.

"What happened to him, your dad?" He slowed his pace. "If you don't mind."

"I don't. He died when I was two. I've been trying to piece it together, him, my mom, the whole hidden family."

"You didn't know what your family was involved in?"

Dylan gave a dry laugh. "Didn't even know they existed. My mom said they were all dead."

Simon said nothing. What could he say? "You're handling it well."

Dylan shrugged as they approached the chapel steps. "I fake it okay."

The building loomed ahead, familiar yet changed. Clean brick. Reinforced doors. The stained glass shone like polished secrets.

Simon paused, one foot on the top step. "I'll visit the priest. You start on the cash?"

"On it. I'll grab one of the guards on my way back." Dylan tapped his phone and headed off.

Simon turned to the chapel. The door creaked open with a push.

Inside, it was cool and dim. Lemon polish masked the age beneath. Gone were the peeling paint and creaking floors. But the silence—it was the same.

He moved down the aisle, past pews that had once held restless boys. The shadows stretched long. His gaze flicked to the old confessional, and then the years peeled away....

The chair outside Fr. Bob's office was still too small for him. Back straight, hands damp, he waited. The walls seemed to close in.

The door creaked open.

"Simon Roth?" Deacon Phil stood there, a file in one hand.

Simon rose. "Good afternoon, Deacon."

"Come in."

He stepped into the office, heart hammering. Incense clung to the bookshelves. His stomach twisted.

Deacon Phil sat behind the desk. "You're an A student. So I wasn't surprised you aced the exam."

Simon remained quiet.

"But another student—same test, same answers. Especially the essays."

Panic crawled up his neck.

"When someone like you cheats, there's a reason."

He swallowed. "He needed a scholarship. We wanted to go to college together. I tried to help him study. He wouldn't listen."

"Maybe he didn't want to go. Some don't."

That hit harder than it should've.

"He told me it was all his idea." The deacon folded his hands on the desk. "Said you had no choice."

"Not exactly." Simon ducked his head, squirmed as Deacon Phil studied him.

"Do you still want to go to college?"

"Yes. More than anything."

"We could suspend you."

Simon's chest seized. "Please. I'm sorry. I won't do it again."

"Okay. It won't go in your file. But you'll go to confession, and you'll tutor these two." He slid a note across the desk. "Fr. Bob named you his top pick for the Marino scholarship. Don't disappoint him."

The memory snapped like a rubber band. Simon blinked.

He was standing alone in the upgraded hallway. The office door was open. Empty.

No incense now. Just the faint buzz of a camera overhead.

"May I help you?" Fr. Phil stepped into the doorway—older now, gray at the temples, a bit softer, but with the same measured calm.

Simon extended a hand. "Fr. Phil, Simon Roth."

Recognition sparked. "Senator Roth, it's been years." They shook hands. "Come in."

Simon entered the office. Memories surged again, but he shoved them back. "I used to dread this room. Never liked going to the principal's office."

Fr. Phil smiled. "Fr. Bob handed out penance with gusto. Optimistic to the end. Believed God would keep the orphanage running."

Simon nodded, sobered. "I'm here because I think the man who kidnapped my daughter might be connected to my past."

"Ms. Carol asked me to pray for Lily. I have been."

"Do you keep tabs on alumni?"

"We try. Some update us. Others disappear. Most lead decent lives. A few have drug charges, but nothing like kidnapping."

Simon hesitated. "Do you remember Dan?"

"Of course. You and he… had a falling out?"

"He thought I got off easy. Didn't get a recommendation, so he resented me."

The priest sighed. "I doubt that was the real reason he resented you. And he had more than one incident."

That was news to him. "Do you know what happened to him?"

"He died in prison. Fight over contraband, I think. The state notified us. His brother was quite upset."

Simon's breath caught. "He had a brother?"

Fr. Phil nodded. "Half brother. Much younger. Idolized him.

When his mother was incarcerated, the boy ended up here before the orphanage closed. Then child services took him."

Simon palmed the tension in his neck. "I didn't even know he had a brother."

"You might've thought Dan was your best friend, but I'm not sure he saw it that way. You came from a good home. You only ended up here because your parents died and your last living relative was too old to take you in. Dan's story was different. He was in and out of juvenile detention before he set foot here. He learned to use people. You weren't the first student he pulled into trouble."

Simon leaned back, absorbing that. His chest tightened. If Dan was dead, who…

"Do you know what happened to the brother?"

Fr. Phil cocked his head. "Last I heard, he works for you."

CHAPTER 41

UNKNOWN CABIN, FLORIDA, USA

LILY

No footsteps. No voices. Just silence.

The door hadn't opened since the photo. That silence pressed in like a storm front.

Not because she missed the guards but because it meant something was about to change.

At first, she'd resisted eating. Drinking. But hunger had won. If she had to fight or run, she needed strength. Dehydration wouldn't help anyone.

The room still looked the same, no matter how many times she paced it, scouring corners for something, anything, useful.

Since waking up, she'd been replaying the last couple of days. Everything felt surreal. All her life, she'd dreamed of leaving Hong Kong. She loved the city but hated what her future there might become.

Her uncle used to say, *"Don't worry, Lily. We have American passports. We can leave anytime. One day, we will."*

But that day never came.

When she'd left, it had been sudden. Dangerous. But exciting too. The idea of meeting her father, maybe even her mother, had made it worth it.

Now, though, a small part of her longed for the stability of her hotel job. The guests, the schedule. Predictable. Safe.

But survival came first. That was her new mission. She had to get the intel to her father before it was too late.

She imagined him, tried out her name with his surname. Lily Roth. She'd carried her mother's name like a weight, a reminder she'd been born out of wedlock. But now, her father's name gave her strength.

Still, she missed her godmother's voice. *"Have faith. The Holy Spirit will guide and protect you."*

Lily closed her eyes and whispered a prayer. Then she stretched her arms, flexed her fingers. She couldn't let her fear win.

Her kung fu training wasn't advanced, but it was enough. A gun was just a faster knife, her instructor's words. If she moved fast, if she stayed sharp, she could escape.

No one was watching, so she practiced the moves that came from muscle memory. She dropped low. Jab. Turn. Palm strike. Her body needed to remember how to fight.

The air was still. Her breath loud in her ears.

If they came in now, she'd be ready, or as ready as she'd ever be.

The doorknob jiggled.

She darted back to the bed.

The door stayed closed.

She crept to the door, bare feet silent on the floor. Voices, sharp, muffled, bled through the wood.

"…changed," said someone new.

"That wasn't the order," replied the nicer-sounding man. The one who'd brought her water.

"Forget the order. I'm in charge now. Tell him to bring the money. Only him. No cops."

"I thought you said—"

"Just do it!" the voice ordered.

A pause. Then the nicer voice spoke again. "We'll text directions to the exchange site… not you. Dylan Roche brings the money. No cops. Or you won't see her again. Clock is ticking."

Her breath caught. Dylan?

She'd assumed her father would make the exchange. Why Dylan?

"Good. Keep her here until it's time. I need to make some preparations. I'll be back shortly."

Footsteps faded.

"I don't like this," Nice Guy muttered. "Who does he think he is?"

"We're getting another fifty K. I'm not complaining," said Gruff Voice.

"I'm checking with him." Another pause. "Yeah, it's me. Call me back, okay?"

"Why do you care? Money is money."

"Do you know who Dylan Roche is? He's the Ghost's nephew."

The ghost? What did that even mean? Some kind of code name?

"So?"

"I'm not messing with this. She gave strict orders. No one touches the kid."

The ghost was a she? Lily froze. Who gave these people orders?

Dylan had never mentioned an aunt. Or a "ghost."

"What do we do?" Gruff Voice asked.

Even the gruff one sounded afraid.

And if the monsters were afraid… she didn't stand a chance.

CHAPTER 42

MIRROR ESTATE, FLORIDA, USA

SIMON

His pulse still pounded from the conversation with Fr. Phil, but Simon didn't slow down. He called Olivia before the door even closed behind him.

"Olivia," he said the moment she answered. "I think it's Harrison. Dig into his financials."

"You got me and Kyle. But why Harrison? We're heading to Rifkin's house."

Before he could respond, a second call buzzed in.

"He's calling again," Simon muttered. "Gotta go."

He tapped Record, then swiped to answer.

"Yes?"

The same distorted voice came through. Flat. Mechanical.

"We'll be texting directions to the exchange site."

His grip tightened. "Okay. I'll have it ready."

"Not you. Dylan Roche brings the money. No cops. Or you won't see her again. Clock is ticking."

Click.

The line went dead.

Simon stared at the screen. The words echoed.

Dylan?

"Did I hear my name?" Dylan strolled toward him with two duffel bags slung over his shoulders, flanked by two guards. Calm. Unaware.

Simon's blood ran cold.

They wanted *him*.

CHAPTER 43

THE RIFKIN RESIDENCE, FLORIDA, USA

OLIVIA/PHOENIX

This wasn't a random kidnapping. Too many details pointed back to the Ghost's network and maybe someone higher. Someone like Rifkin.

Olivia didn't know yet how the money played into it, but the abductors must be tied to the Ghost's organization. The real question was: Who was King?

From the day she met Rifkin, she hadn't liked the retired senator.

Now, with what Kyle uncovered, she was convinced he was moving money through back channels. His housekeeper was undocumented, paid under the table through a fake cleaning company. That service was a front. Was Rifkin being blackmailed? Laundering money? Paying off someone like the Ghost?

Only one way to find out.

She parked in front of his house, another overbuilt monument in a high-end neighborhood. Kyle sat beside her, checking his notes. Young, green, but quick on his feet. He hadn't said a word about the bullet graze earlier, though even a glancing hit from a high-caliber round could send someone reeling. Something she knew all too well.

As they stepped out, another vehicle pulled up. Ron and Ana emerged, just as surprised to see them.

All four spoke over each other with versions of the same question: "What are you doing here?"

Ana answered first. "We found a burner phone near the accident scene. The fingerprint matched Rifkin."

"We followed the money," Olivia said.

"It all fits!" Kyle grinned.

They approached the front door—ahem, the *ajar* front door.

Ron raised a hand, motioning for Ana to circle to the back. Olivia and Kyle moved to flank the entrance while Ron drew his weapon. The others followed suit.

"FBI!" He pushed the door open.

Silence.

They moved in, sweeping room by room. Ana entered through the patio.

"Clear," Ron called.

"Clear," Kyle echoed a moment later.

Olivia stepped into the study and stopped cold. That smell. Sharp. Metallic. Familiar.

"In here," she called.

Rifkin lay face down by a liquor cabinet. A glass had shattered on the floor, bourbon still wet in a spreading puddle. The cabinet door was open. One bottle out, one full glass poured, and a second glass waiting. He'd been about to serve a guest.

No second vehicle outside. Whoever had come to visit walked in through the front—someone he trusted.

She crouched and examined the body. Shot in the back. No struggle.

Ron and Kyle entered. From elsewhere in the house came Ana's voice, "Body!"

"He knew the killer." Olivia pointed to the glass. "He was about to pour a drink."

Ron slid out his phone. "We'll have to call it in. Retired senator or not, FBI's got jurisdiction."

If this had been a Company matter, the cleanup crew might have been deployed. But this was bigger now.

Olivia pulled on gloves and began searching the room. She needed to know if Rifkin had been King. And if he wasn't, then who was? And if he ordered Lily's abduction, what was the endgame now?

Ana walked in. "Latina woman. I'm guessing the house-keeper. Shot near her bedroom door. Looks like she heard something and stepped out to check. Body's still warm. Maybe a few hours ago."

"Same here." Ron squatted by the body. "We'll coordinate with local jurisdiction. We can make the argument that her death is tied to his."

Good assessment. The time frame fit.

"This raises a lot of questions." Ana brought out her phone to take pictures.

Ron and Ana began photographing and examining the study. Kyle lingered near the doorway, visibly pale. "With him dead, how are we supposed to find Lily?"

Olivia softened. "First body?"

He nodded, sheepish. "That obvious?"

"I threw up my first time. You're doing fine."

Kyle gave a faint smile, raised a shaky hand to his temples. "I didn't think spies dealt with this kind of thing. I figured it was surveillance and tech stuff."

"There are different kinds of operatives."

She picked up the phone near the body. It was still warm.

Pressing Rifkin's thumb to the sensor, she unlocked it. "Maybe his phone can tell us something."

A notification blinked. One voicemail.

"Let's hear it." Ana peered over her shoulder.

Olivia played the message.

"Uh, yes, it's me. Call me back, okay?"

A man's voice. Anxious.

"Can we get a trace on the number?"

Ron was already working his phone. "Burner. They're trying to ping it now. Might take a bit."

She scrolled through recent messages. Her pulse quickened.

"We found who ordered the kidnapping." She held up the phone for the others to see.

> We got her. What do you want us to do?

> Hold her there.

> How long?

> Shouldn't be long. Remember not to hurt her.

Another thread, separate number:

> I don't think he's lying. He doesn't have the cash. Assets need to be liquidated.

> Don't worry. He'll get it. Someone will back him.

> You should have asked for more.

> I don't need more.

"Give me that number." Ron held out his hand. "We'll get it traced."

"Okay, Rifkin ordered the kidnapping." Kyle frowned. "But he didn't have the money. So who killed him?"

"Simon mentioned Harrison Burke as another suspect."

Olivia secured the phone in an evidence bag. "We were going to dig into him next. The task force might want to pick that up."

Ron agreed. "Now that it's officially our case, we will."

She gestured to the laptop on the desk. "Mind if I take a look before you bag it?"

"Help yourself, but it's going back with us."

She opened the laptop. No password.

Typical.

She searched. Nothing helpful. But she didn't stop there. From her pocket, she removed a lipstick tube. Inside, a disguised flash drive. She mirrored the hard drive.

As the transfer completed, she scrolled through the text messages again. She held the bagged phone up. "This last message. I believe it's from the killer. And if we find him, we find Lily."

"Sounds like Rifkin got double-crossed," Ana said. "They were going to split the ransom. His partner decided to keep it all."

"Plausible." Ron caught Olivia's eye. "Olivia, can I speak to you?"

She followed him into the hallway, sensing the curious glances behind them.

"What is it?"

"Do you know if Lily has the intel on her person?"

"Yes. She does. I'm sure of it."

"We've been monitoring for suspicious illnesses. At all major ports. So far, nothing. But if your intel is right…"

"It is. Once we have the notebook and the antidote, it can be contained. From what we've seen, the virus is one hundred percent fatal. But those exposed can survive if they receive the antidote within forty-eight hours."

She paused. Her voice was steady, but the images flashed back anyway. The screams. The skin blistering. The way one of them clawed at the wall before collapsing.

"The video," she whispered. "I couldn't finish it. It was horrific. The subjects… what it did to them."

Ron was quiet. Then he clamped a hand on her shoulder. "We'll stop it."

She gave a curt nod. "We have to. And remember, we still don't know if this was the full-strength virus or a prototype."

"I'm not taking chances. I'm alerting the CDC and putting their teams on standby."

Her phone vibrated. She checked the screen.

Simon.

She stared at his name a beat longer than necessary.

"Telling him about Rifkin isn't going to be easy."

KYLE

Flashing lights cast long shadows across Senator Rifkin's driveway by the time Kyle stepped back. Local police were arriving fast, but Dad intercepted them, flashing his badge and waving them off. The moment he claimed jurisdiction, they didn't argue.

Two bodies, including the senator's. The local officers looked relieved not to have to own it.

Kyle didn't blame them. Moments later, Dad's team arrived. Kyle stayed out of their way, still processing.

He'd only glimpsed the housekeeper's body before Dad pulled him aside and ordered everyone back to Senator Roth's estate. But that glimpse stuck with him, slippers on her feet, like she'd been heading to the kitchen or the laundry. One moment alive. The next—

Collateral damage.

Dad had left Agent Tanner in charge of the scene. Olivia and Ana headed out first. Kyle waited to ride back with Dad.

Lily was still out there. If they didn't act fast, she might be next.

As Kyle stepped into the Roth house, Dylan's voice met him, urgent and defiant. "I want to help. They asked for me."

Kyle followed Dad toward the living room. Dylan stood in the middle, his posture braced. The senator faced him, tension carved into his jaw.

"No," Senator Roth said.

"Too dangerous," Dad added.

Ana and Olivia walked in behind them. Quick intros followed before the tension resumed.

Dylan blinked, startled. "Wait. You're Lily's mom? She said you were dead."

"Story for another time." Olivia's tone stayed dry.

"And you're a spy?"

"An intelligence operative."

"Semantics."

"Dylan," Dad said, "you don't understand what you're walking into. We don't know if this is about money, revenge, or something bigger. If this man is connected to someone like the Ghost, he's dangerous. We can't let you make contact."

Dylan's jaw clenched. "If this guy's working with my aunt, then I need to step up. I'm not going to sit this out while someone else risks their life for Lily. They asked for me. What else do you need?"

Kyle took a breath, then stepped forward. "I'll go. I'll take his place."

All eyes shifted to him.

His dad frowned. "You're still healing. That leg—"

"It's fine." Kyle kept his voice level. "And he's right. We're close in age. Same height. Similar build. I'm trained, and they don't know my face."

His leg still throbbed beneath his jeans, but he forced himself not to limp. He couldn't stand by while Dylan volunteered to walk into danger, especially when he, Kyle, had the tools to do something.

"Kyle, I appreciate that." Olivia rubbed her temple. "But if the kidnappers did any recon, they might have pictures of Dylan."

"I don't have any social media," Dylan said. "That was the first thing Agent Peters made me cut. Online presence is a liability."

"No press releases?" Senator Roth asked. "Nothing when you joined the company?"

"No. I told my grandmother I wasn't ready to step into anything public. She agreed. I've been training under the radar. Well, they did send out internal memos, but there was no picture."

"He's telling the truth," Dad confirmed. "We had his online profile scrubbed clean. Any old photos are outdated. His look has changed. Kyle could pass if we adjust a few things."

Olivia studied them both. "I've done disguise work. With minor tweaks, it could work."

Senator Roth gave a nod. "Let's do it."

Ana leaned against the wall, head tilted, eyes bright.

Kyle cuffed Dylan's arm. "We'll get her back."

"I'll hold you to that."

With the decision made, the room shifted. Everyone moved with purpose. Dad started issuing orders. Olivia didn't look up from her screen.

Kyle stepped closer to the counter where she worked, her attention on her laptop, hands flying across the keyboard. He couldn't see what she was doing, but her expression didn't change—tight jaw, narrowed eyes, focused.

She wasn't waiting. She was hunting.

Probably trying to find Harrison Burke. If their theory was right, Harrison had killed Rifkin. If they could find him, maybe they could find Lily too.

Dad broke the silence. "Dylan, I'll have an agent take you back to the estate."

"No need. Duke drove me. He's waiting in the backyard."

Kyle blinked. Duke? Must be the family chauffeur.

Then it hit him. He'd just volunteered to walk into a trap.

CHAPTER 44

UNKNOWN CABIN, FLORIDA, USA

LILY

Lily pressed her ear to the door. No footsteps. No voices. Just the ticking panic in her head.

The third guy hadn't come back.

Her hand rested on the doorknob. Thank goodness Nice Guy forgot to lock the door last time he came in and out. She debated whether an unexpected attack was better or if she should wait for one to come to her.

She cracked the door open, just a sliver.

Gruff Voice was riffling through the fridge. Nice Guy paced. Neither held a weapon, but two handguns were on the table. Her bag was there, too—phone, everything.

She could wait. Maybe the third guy would return, and they'd argue again. Maybe she could slip out in the chaos.

No. Too risky. He might not come back at all.

Two were better than three. She needed the element of surprise.

It was now or never.

They were under orders not to harm her, weren't they? She

had to take advantage of that. She made the sign of the cross. *Be with me, Lord.*

She opened the door—quiet, deliberate.

And moved.

In a single motion, she spun into a roundhouse kick, catching Gruff Voice off-balance. Before he could recover, she delivered a sharp upward kick to his groin.

He dropped hard, groaning.

The other man lunged for a gun.

Lily struck his wrist with a knife-hand blow, just as she'd practiced. The weapon hit the floor.

She grabbed her bag and ran. She didn't know where she was going, only that she had to go.

Trees blurred past her as she tore through the woods, the forest thick and endless. Branches scratched her arms, her legs burned, but adrenaline pushed her forward. She heard them behind her. Shouts. Crashing footsteps.

No cover. No trail. Just trees.

Then an idea.

She threw her bag over one shoulder and scrambled up a thick tree, using the notched bark like a ladder. Higher. Higher. Until she found the last perch strong enough to hold her.

She crouched behind a cluster of leaves, clutching a branch, calming her breathing.

Please don't look up. Please don't look up.

Her heart thundered.

Below, voices closed in.

"Where did she go?" Gruff Voice—nearby, winded.

"I thought she came this way," said the other. Farther away.

"I don't see her. What do we do?"

"Let's go back. King said not to hurt her."

"Yeah, but the dude—"

She didn't catch the rest. Their voices faded.

She didn't move. Not yet.

Only when the forest fell still did she exhale, slow, controlled.

Fifteen minutes passed before she dared shift. She pulled out her phone and dialed 999.

The line clicked, then came an automated voice. "Sorry, the number you've dialed cannot be connected. Please check your number and dial again."

She swore under her breath, heart sinking.

She wasn't staying in a tree all night. She climbed down and ran toward the only thing she'd seen from above, a cabin in the clearing.

Whatever was inside, she'd face it. Hiding wasn't an option anymore.

CHAPTER 45

ON THE ROAD, FLORIDA, USA

DYLAN

"They're not letting me help." Dylan leaned against the armrest on the rear passenger door, the city whirling by beyond the window. "They should."

They wouldn't let him do the exchange, even though the kidnapper had asked for him. That alone raised red flags. Why him? How did Lily's captors even know who he was?

And if he had been the target all along, they'd had their chance. They could've killed him at the accident scene. But they hadn't. They'd taken Lily. Not him.

He tapped the armrest. The only reason he could think of was her, his aunt. The Ghost. Even in federal custody, she had reach. Contacts. A network. He wouldn't put it past her to pull strings from behind bars.

But why Lily?

His stomach twisted. Maybe this had all been a trap for him. Lily was just the bait.

His phone dinged.

I need help. I don't know where I am.

His pulse shot up.

A voice in his head screamed at him to call Agent Peters, to forward the message, to be smart. But another voice, stronger, said this was on him. Lily trusted him, reached out to him. Not the FBI. Not the senator. Him.

And if Peters got involved, they might shut him out again. They'd lock things down, call in a team, maybe delay too long.

His thumbs flew.

Tap the map. Text me a screenshot.

Battery low. Will try.

Seconds felt like hours until the image came through. It wasn't much. Just a rough pin—Cabin 6950. No coordinates. But it was enough.

Stay there.

Be safe. On my way.

The last message stayed unread. He sent another. And another. Nothing. Her phone had died.

"Duke, would you drop me off right there?" Dylan pointed ahead to a rental car company.

Duke glanced at him in the mirror. "Something wrong?"

"Just something I need to take care of."

He opened his phone again, thumb hovering over *Contacts*. He needed to let someone know, just in case.

Kyle. He should tell Kyle.

He started to text, only to freeze. Kyle's phone was damaged. He wasn't sure if Kyle got a new one yet. If he texted the agent, it could be days before the message would be read.

If he texted Agent Peters, the man would just say to go home. Let the professionals handle it.

No.

Dylan opened his messages and tapped out a text to Tommy.

Going to find Lily. Cabin 6950. Don't tell Grandma. If I don't check in by 8, let Kyle know. Map to follow.

He hit send, took a breath, and looked at Duke.

"What should I tell Ms. Carol?" Duke asked as he eased to a stop.

"Tell her I'm running an errand." But this wasn't going to be that simple, was it?

CHAPTER 46

UNKNOWN WOODS, FLORIDA, USA

LILY

The clearing opened up around her like a stage lit by fading light.

The number 6950 hung crooked on the mailbox post, the metal rusted, hardly visible beneath layers of peeling white paint. Lily skidded on the gravel footpath, her breath ragged, her pulse pounding in her ears.

Anyone—or anything—could be inside the cabin. But hiding in a tree had bought her time, not answers. That cabin was her only shot.

She charged up the porch steps and banged on the front door. "Hello? Please! Someone—I need help!"

Nothing.

No footsteps. No creak of wood. Just the whisper of wind threading through pine branches overhead and the faint thrum of distant insects.

The house, a rustic cabin with fading white paint and cracked shutters, gave no response. No flicker of light. Nothing.

She ran around back, dodging thorny shrubs, but found no

one. Just a rusting lawn chair half buried under weeds in the overgrown yard and a crooked shed near the trees. Her heart thudded. She could break into the house, but what if the owners returned? Or worse, what if someone dangerous was already inside?

She chose the shed.

The door creaked as she slipped in. Dust danced in the slivers of early evening sunlight spilling through warped wooden slats. The thick air hoarded a scent of oil, rust, and cut grass, and shelves held rows of tools she didn't recognize, jagged, heavy, unfamiliar.

She sifted through a few, lifting them for weight and balance.

A wrench—too heavy.

A clawed thing—too sharp to carry.

Then she found a lantern. Battery powered. She tested the switch. It worked. Into her bag it went.

She spotted a riding mower, the kind she'd seen in movies set in American suburbs, like the sitcom her uncle used to watch. She crouched behind it, trying to steady her breath, heart still racing.

Safe, for now.

She unzipped her bag and pulled out her phone. Emergency services still wouldn't connect, but she could send one more text. Her hands trembled as she typed.

> I need help. I don't know where I am.

She glanced at the screen, praying—*Please, God, let Dylan be okay. Please let him respond.* The reply came.

Her chest sagged. He was alive. She tapped out the number —Cabin 6950. Seconds later, her screen dimmed. Battery gone. She had a charger, but without a converter, it was useless.

She clutched the phone, whispering another prayer. For Dylan. For Kyle. For herself.

Kyle. She hadn't seen him since the crash. He'd been bleeding from the leg. She winced. What if he hadn't made it? No, she wouldn't go there. Dylan was alive. That meant Kyle probably was too.

Please, God. Let them be okay.

She shifted against the cold metal mower and touched the fake mole still adhered to her abdomen. That tiny capsule could save lives if she got it to her father in time.

Her father.

The thought came as a whisper, then grew louder.

Would he recognize her? Want to know her? Would he even believe she was his?

She imagined his face, sharp-featured like hers? Kind eyes? Disbelief? Relief?

What would she say when they met?

"Hi, I'm Lily. I think, I mean, I know you're my father."

Such clumsy words, foreign in her mind. Still, she practiced them, over and over, holding onto the hope that the moment would come.

She tightened her grip on her bag and drew in a shaky breath.

She didn't just need to survive. She needed to deliver the truth.

CHAPTER 47

THE ROTH RESIDENCE, FLORIDA, USA

KYLE

Kyle didn't need to ask if something was wrong. The silence in the kitchen told him everything.

Ever since Dylan left, Olivia had gone quiet, fingers flying across her keyboard, expression unreadable. Senator Roth hadn't touched his coffee. He just sat there at the island, staring at the wall like it might offer answers.

Kyle leaned on his elbows, and the hard edge of the stool dug into his ribs. The air inside the house had taken on that sterile, heavy stillness, like a waiting room before bad news. He couldn't imagine what the senator was going through. A daughter he hadn't known existed was gone. A trusted mentor had orchestrated it. Now, a friend might be a traitor.

The screen in front of them pinged to life. Agent Tanner.

"Sitrep," Dad ordered.

"One neighbor was home," the agent replied, "but didn't hear or see anything. We're checking door cams. I sent you footage. White sedan pulls in at 2:56 p.m., leaves at 3:04. Can't make out the plate. Bad angle. It's a man, but the face is obscured."

Kyle sat up straighter. His dad beat him to it.

"Hold up. Simon, come take a look."

The senator blinked like he'd just heard his name for the first time all day. He looked up, and Kyle caught Olivia watching him with quiet worry before she dropped her gaze back to her screen.

Senator Roth rose and crossed the room. "What is it?"

"Send it over." Ana tapped her phone. "Might be easier to see from this angle."

A moment later, she held her phone in front of the senator. "Recognize this guy?"

He studied it, jaw tight. "That's not Harrison's car. And I can't say it's him. Maybe. He dresses like that, but I can't tell from the angle."

Kyle crowded closer to the screen. The guy didn't look like the ones who'd chased them. Too lean. No military bulk.

"He's not one of the guys from the alley. Those guys had combat written all over them. This guy's built like a stick of gum."

Tanner's voice came through next. "We traced Harrison's phone. It was at the senator's office this afternoon."

"At least the phone was," Dad muttered. "Find out if anyone saw him. Check the logs."

"Already working it. Hernandez is digging into the laptop. Deanna's still processing the physicals."

"Good."

"We also followed up on Randall Hall," Tanner added. "Agents spoke to a few of his known associates. No one's seen him in the last two weeks, just dropped off the radar. Word is, he took some kind of job. No details. But given what we know now, I'd bet he's working for Rifkin."

He hesitated, then said, "And based on the footage, Hall's not acting alone. He's got a partner. Might explain the coordination. It's too clean for one guy."

Dad didn't reply right away. "What about the burner?"

"No luck. Either powered off, trashed, or something in between. But we've got the store, time, and payment method."

"Keep digging."

"I've got something!" Olivia hollered.

CHAPTER 48

UNKNOWN WOODS, FLORIDA, USA

DYLAN

What kind of place was this?

The road had vanished a mile ago, replaced by ruts and gravel, the kind that rattled every bolt in his rental's undercarriage. Dylan gripped the steering wheel tighter, his gaze darting between the GPS map and the thick woods crowding in on either side. Trees loomed like silent guards, their branches clawing at the last rays of daylight.

He should've rented an SUV. But he hadn't been thinking about terrain when he booked the car. He'd been thinking about Lily.

He passed one cabin, weather-beaten siding, no signs of life. Then, a few turns later, another came into view. Smaller. More recent tire tracks. This had to be it.

He cut the engine and sat still for a beat, the ticking of the cooling engine the only sound. Should he call her name? What if she came running? What if someone else heard?

Quiet. Fast. In and out.

He stepped out, shoes crunching against damp pine needles.

The air smelled of earth and old smoke. A slight breeze stirred the trees. He approached the front door and knocked gently. "Lily," he whispered.

No answer.

He tried the window, nothing but shadows inside. Rounding the back, he spotted a shed tucked against the tree line. The door sagged on its hinges.

"Lily," he tried again.

A sound. A rustle. Then the door creaked open.

There she was.

Her face was pale beneath streaks of dirt, her clothes smudged and torn, hair tangled, hands scraped and trembling. She looked like she hadn't slept in days. And yet, she was standing.

She all but collapsed into him. "Thank you... Dylan. You came."

"Of course I did."

She pulled back just enough to see his face. "How's Kyle? Is he okay?"

"He's fine, banged up, but the doctors cleared him. He's already out."

"You took him to the hospital?"

He nodded. "Ambulance came after the crash."

"Do you have his number?"

He hesitated. "We'll sort that out later. Right now, we need to move."

He led her around the house, toward the car. Then he froze mid-step. Two figures up ahead. He barely saw them through the trees, just enough.

Lily bumped into his back with a soft grunt.

He raised a finger to his lips and motioned her back.

She peered over his shoulder, then ducked down, and pointed toward the shed behind them.

Dylan groaned. Going back meant putting themselves in a

box with no exits. But the men were close, too close to risk the car.

A voice drifted toward them. "Look, this is a rental. Who in his right mind comes out here?"

"Probably tourists," another replied. "Airbnb rustic nonsense."

"I thought the guy said he set traps and cameras. Said not to worry, the girl'd trip something if she moved."

"Yeah, but what if she slipped past them? And he was supposed to check in, right? He said he'd be back."

One of the men snorted. "Place looks empty. No lights. No sounds."

"You want to knock?"

"No thank you. Let's check the shed. Then we're out."

CHAPTER 49

THE ROTH RESIDENCE, FLORIDA, USA

OLIVIA/PHOENIX

"I got something!"

The words had slipped out before Olivia realized she'd spoken them aloud.

But this, this was her specialty. She hadn't become Phoenix overnight. Back when she'd been recruited, Jay and Patty had kept her behind the screen, a ghost in the machine transmitting intel from cyberspace. It wasn't until later, after she'd earned their trust or proved her usefulness, depending on how you looked at it, that they'd sent her to the Farm.

No one had expected her to infiltrate the Ghost's network. Not even her.

The first time she'd met the Ghost, she hadn't even known it. Just a casual encounter at a company function her legend or her cover had been required to attend. She remembered it like it was yesterday because it was Lily's birthday.

She'd stepped onto the sixty-fifth-floor balcony, desperate for air. The view was spectacular, sweeping city lights, humming traffic far below. Any other night, she might've admired it. But that night, all she could see was one image playing over and over in her mind: Lily in the hospital bassinet, so small, surrounded by machines, tubes taped to her fragile skin. Jay had warned her —giving Lily up was the only way to keep her safe. The Ghost's network had already tried to kill the baby once. They wouldn't stop.

She'd wrapped her arms around herself, not for warmth but stability.

Then a voice behind her.

"You look glum."

She turned, startled. A woman stood a few feet away, holding a drink in a crystal tumbler. Her presence was polished and poised, like someone used to commanding attention without asking for it. Shoulder-length dark hair curled at the ends, expertly styled. Her olive-toned skin glowed under the ambient balcony lighting, as did the diamond pendant resting at her collarbone, offset by her sleek navy cocktail dress.

The woman smiled. "Reflecting?"

Olivia dipped her head. "Something like that."

"You're not drinking."

"I had a cocktail earlier." She smoothed her dress, a simple but well-fitted black number, professional, appropriate for the gathering, nothing flashy.

"Care to share your thoughts?"

She hesitated. What could she say? The truth was dangerous. "It's my daughter's birthday."

The woman's expression shifted. "Shouldn't you be with her?"

"She passed away." The lie slipped out with practiced calm, even as her throat tightened.

"I'm sorry. I lost my mother right after I was born," the woman said. "It's not the same, I know, but I understand grief."

There was something about her. Warm, attentive... too attentive, maybe.

"I'm Marge." The woman offered her free hand.

"Jade," Olivia replied.

"You're the IT analyst I've heard about."

She had nodded, giving a practiced, empty smile.

That night changed everything. They'd only spoken once in person. After that, it was all digital. Marge Beaumont, known to the world as the Ghost, began sending encrypted files. Harmless at first. Then came coded messages for her lieutenants, data transfers, logistics. Olivia became the Ghost's most trusted digital shadow.

Now, staring at her screens, Olivia blinked hard and pulled herself back to the present.

She tapped a few keys to connect her laptop to the big screen. "Simon. Kyle. Ron. Ana. You all need to see this."

The room shifted toward her. She enlarged the files.

"I know why Rifkin was being blackmailed. Kyle and I already flagged these payments, weekly deposits to a shell company, masked as wages to a housekeeper. But here's where it gets worse."

She clicked to another folder. "These are deleted image files. But they're not just photos. There's embedded data. I only opened a few, but every one I've checked holds classified material."

"Are you saying he was selling secrets?" Simon asked.

"I'm not sure he sold them. But he had them."

Kyle edged closer to the big screen, rubbing his jaw. "When we checked, he didn't seem to have many assets."

"Then why keep them?" Ron asked.

Ana shrugged. "Maybe he hadn't sold them yet?"

"No." Olivia shook her head. "He was passing them along. To the Ghost's network. I recognize the formatting. It's her style, her encryption patterns."

"Why pass classified info for free?" Ron asked. "No ideology, no money?"

Olivia's fingers stilled above the keyboard. "The Ghost doesn't always pay. Bribery, blackmail, seduction. Those are her tools. More officials have secrets than morals. She finds pressure points and pushes."

Simon held up a hand. "It happens. Affairs, escorts, gambling. Take your pick."

Ana crossed her arms. "So… seduction?"

"I don't know." Olivia drummed her index finger alongside the keys, something she couldn't quite tap into yet. "But if Rifkin wasn't doing it for money or belief, she had something on him."

"Then who blackmailed him?" Ron asked.

"Harrison." Simon turned over the hand he'd raised as if offering something. "He's the only one close enough."

Ron's phone buzzed. He checked it. "Update from Tanner."

Moments later, Tanner appeared on the screen. "Harrison was at the senator's office all afternoon. Three witnesses confirm it."

"We're missing something," Ron muttered.

"What about the morning?" Ana unfolded her arms. "Was he there all day?"

"No. He went to lunch. Then came back."

"How long?" Ron asked.

"About an hour and a half. He met with a reporter." Tanner tapped his screen. "Here's footage."

On-screen, Harrison walked into a restaurant. Ninety minutes later, he walked out.

"He could've hired someone during lunch," Ron suggested.

"I hate to say it," Kyle cut in, "but this doesn't get us closer to finding Lily."

"We know." Olivia maintained her calm, despite the ache in her chest. "But if we find the killer, we should find her. Ron, can your team bring Harrison in? I want to see his reaction when you show him the photo of the man from the footage."

"Glad you brought that up," Tanner responded. "We've been trying to reach him. He left the office around six. Didn't answer calls. Phone's off. Staff said he hasn't been home either."

"Check his house," Ron ordered. "If he's not there, issue a BOLO. Find him."

Tanner gave a tight nod. "Yeah, boss."

CHAPTER 50

UNKNOWN CABIN, FLORIDA, USA

LILY

The voices were getting close.

Lily's spine tingled as she glanced back at the cabin. No time. She pointed toward the shed. Dylan met her eyes and nodded.

They ran, quiet as they could, shoes thudding on pine needles. The shed loomed ahead, squat and shadowed, its door hanging ajar.

Dylan eased it open with a faint groan. They slipped inside.

Darkness swallowed them whole. Ah, the scent again—gasoline, old dirt, something rotting! Her nose burned. She ducked behind the rusting lawnmower while Dylan crouched near a stack of rank-smelling bags.

Footsteps outside.

"It's dark in here," came a voice, low, rough, too casual.

"Turn on your flashlight," a second voice ordered.

She froze, hands clenched against her sides. The flashlight beam danced across the walls. She pressed back as far as she could, praying it wouldn't catch on metal or skin.

A thud. Then another. Boots. Getting closer.

"I don't see anything."

"Me neither. Let's go."

The door creaked shut again.

Still, she didn't breathe. Not yet.

A whisper broke the silence. "Psst."

Dylan's voice.

She peeked over the mower. The door remained closed. He tiptoed toward it, opened it a crack, and checked outside. Then a thumbs-up.

She stood, wiping her palms against her jeans. Her knees ached. Her heart still thudded.

"No signal." Dylan checked his phone. "It's gonna be dark soon. We can't stay here."

"What do we do?"

He tucked his phone back in his pocket. "Let's wait until it's dark. Then we make a run for the car."

She agreed, but dread sat heavy in her stomach. "Let's hope they don't come back."

They slid down against the far wall. She braced her palms on the gritty floor and breathed in the scent of oil, old wood, and the faint sourness clinging to Dylan's shirt.

"Hey," he blurted out. "Your mom's alive."

She blinked. "What?"

"I met her. Olivia, right? She's… a spy or something. Intelligence."

Her mouth opened, but no sound came out. Warmth flooded her chest. "She's here?"

"Yeah. And your dad too. The senator. They didn't say anything outright, but the way they were looking at each other, trust me. Something's there. And they're seriously worried about you."

Her voice was a whisper. "They know about me?"

"Of course. They wouldn't tell me much—classified stuff. I

was the only one there without credentials. But Kyle's dad was there. Your parents. Another agent, some woman whose name I forgot."

She swallowed hard. All that time in the locked room, thinking no one cared. Thinking she was expendable. But they'd been searching for her. Fighting for her.

"What happened?" She gripped his arm. "Tell me everything."

He did. The story poured out—her father's visit to Dylan's grandmother, the priest, the hidden vault.

"My dad grew up in an orphanage?"

"I think he just went to the school." He frowned. "Or maybe he did for a bit anyway. You've got to visit the estate sometime. It's like Disney World for grown-ups. Or maybe that's just me."

She smiled for the first time since they landed. Was that this morning? Or yesterday? Time seemed to run together.

Then came the ransom part.

"Wait. You're saying your grandmother gave him two million dollars, just like that?"

He scratched his head. "She said something about redemption. Apparently, she helped your dad once. Told him, 'You've been repaying me ever since you graduated.' No clue what that meant, but she meant it."

She let the words settle. "Wow. And he really talked to a priest?"

"Yup. I didn't hear the convo, though. I was counting stacks of cash."

She elbowed him. "That sounds made up."

He snorted. "It's not." Then he sank back against the wall. "They made me do the drop. The kidnapper. I was supposed to bring the money."

"Why you?"

He rocked his head side to side on the wall. "I don't know."

"You do. I can tell."

He hesitated. "I'm hoping it has nothing to do with my evil aunt."

Her breath caught. "Wait, your aunt? The Ghost?"

He jolted upright where he sat. "How'd you know?"

"Those goons. They said something about the Ghost's nephew."

He groaned. "Figures. I knew this was connected to her. It's never-ending."

"What does that mean?"

"Trust me, explaining would take hours. Kyle volunteered to take my place at the exchange, and I was sent home."

Warmth spread through her chest, quickly chased by worry. She never expected him to risk himself like that. "He did that?"

"Yeah. Brave, stupid, or both." He checked his phone. "Seven forty-eight. Think it's dark enough?"

Shadows had swallowed most of the shed. The edges of his silhouette were barely visible. "I guess. I can hardly see you."

"It's eerie in here." He flicked on his phone light. "Come on. I'll light the way."

They slipped outside, careful not to make a sound. The ground was damp beneath her shoes. Leaves crunched as they skirted the cabin and approached the car.

Then Dylan stopped short. "No…"

All four tires on the car were flat. Slashed.

He muttered a curse. "Sorry. I didn't mean to say that."

The car had been gutted without a sound.

He checked his phone again. "I don't understand. You texted me earlier, but why don't I have a signal? Stupid network."

Darkness wrapped around them like a warning. No tires. No help.

And now, nowhere to run.

CHAPTER 51

THE ROTH RESIDENCE, FLORIDA, USA

KYLE

Kyle stood near the back of the room, his focus on the screen.

Tanner appeared on-screen again, this time inside a house. Beige walls, muted light, hardwood floors. Too quiet. Kyle didn't like it.

Dad stepped forward. "What you got?"

Tanner didn't waste words. "We found Harrison."

He turned the camera. The body lay just inside a doorway, one arm twisted under him, legs sprawled like he'd dropped midstep. Blood had soaked into the wood beneath his ribs.

Kyle's stomach tightened. Another one down. The second man linked to Lily's abduction. First Rifkin. Now Harrison. If these were hits, someone was scrubbing the operation clean.

"His car's in the garage," Tanner added. "No sign of forced entry. Looks like he opened the garage door and caught a bullet before he could step through."

A hit. Fast. Efficient.

The senator's eyebrows shot up. Olivia didn't try to hide her reaction—her arms folded, lips pinched tight. She was already running mental equations. Kyle could see it. He was doing the same.

Who was next?

"Same caliber as Rifkin?" Ana asked.

"Looks that way. But we'll let forensics confirm. This wasn't personal. He lived alone. It's clean. Professional. Like the other scene."

Dad nodded once. "Okay. These murders are connected to the Ghost somehow. We own this now. I want full victim backgrounds, financials, contact logs, comms, everything. Start canvassing. Get the physical evidence to Deanna quietly. Don't talk to the press. I'll handle the ME, and we'll regroup at the office."

"Yeah, boss," Tanner confirmed, then the screen went dark.

Dad clapped once. "Okay, guys. Let me know if you need anything here." His gaze locked on the senator, then Olivia. "We'll get her back."

Kyle believed him. At least, he wanted to.

The senator gave a distracted nod, already half absorbed in his phone. "The president has called for a meeting in the SCIF."

SCIF. Kyle had only been inside once. Thick walls, no windows, phones in a Faraday bag. A place for secrets that never saw daylight. If the White House was watching this closely, then things were even worse than they seemed.

Olivia stepped toward the senator, voice low. "You're not going to tell them about your relationship with Lily, are you?"

"Not until she's safe. I need to stay in the loop. But I'll update them on the rest."

Kyle shifted his weight, a chill prickling down his back. What "rest"? What else did they know that no one was saying?

Bodies were stacking up. Trails were being erased. And Lily was still waiting to be found.

If they didn't move fast, there might not be anyone left to talk.

CHAPTER 52

LILY'S APARTMENT, HONG KONG

SR. MARIE

Bleach and something metallic tainted the hallway. Sr. Marie paused at the stairwell. A strip of yellow tape fluttered near the door. Lily's door. Her stomach tightened.

The officer beside her cleared his throat. "Sister, sorry to have to call you away from the school, but you're listed as Miss Tso's emergency contact."

"I understand." She folded her hands, the knuckles pale. Lily should be in America by now.

The flat door stood ajar. Officer Chow motioned for her to enter.

She stepped inside and staggered. The disarray struck like a blow. The cushions had been slashed open, and upholstery stuffing lay scattered across the floor like torn feathers. The refrigerator door was ajar, puddles spreading across the tile. Books, photos, framed certificates, all tossed like garbage. In all three bedrooms, the mattresses and box springs were shredded.

She brought a hand to her mouth. "Oh my. What happened? A robbery?"

"We hoped you might help us." Officer Chow opened his notepad. "According to the neighbor across the hall, who's lucky to be alive, two men rushed out of this flat. He was coming out of his, and they stabbed him in the abdomen."

A cold dread settled on her chest. "Oh no."

"He's in surgery now. We're trying to piece together what they were looking for."

Sr. Marie's brows knitted together.

He flipped through to a previous page. "We haven't been able to reach her. Her phone goes straight to voicemail. Do you know where she might be?"

"She told me she was leaving for America, and as far as I know, she's there now. I haven't heard from her since." All technically true.

"If you hear anything, please let us know. And if you get ahold of her, have her contact us."

"I will. Of course."

Chow motioned again toward the flat. "We believe the men were looking for something. This doesn't look like a typical burglary. Is there anything valuable here? Something someone might come after?"

Olivia had warned them—dangerous people might follow. Sr. Marie swallowed her unease. "Not that I know of. Lily didn't mention anything like that. This flat was inherited from her uncle. She kept it neat. Simple. I've never known her to keep expensive items here."

He nodded. "Would you mind walking through? Just let us know if anything jumps out. Don't touch anything."

"Understood."

She moved through each room, pausing to observe but not disturb. Her heart ached at the mess, at the violation. She stopped before the empty shelf where Lily kept her books. Perhaps she'd packed those before leaving. The crucifix on her dresser was untouched. No sign of theft, just destruction.

She'd have to return for a few things. The photo albums. The letters. Anything Lily would want kept safe until she came back.

"No, I don't think anything's missing." She rejoined the officer. "Not that I can tell, anyway."

"All right." Chow handed her a card. "If you hear from her, pass along our request."

"I will."

Back at the convent, she headed straight to her office, closed the door behind her, heart still pounding. There were too many unknowns. Too many implications.

She picked up the phone, dialed the school office, and informed the assistant principal she'd be out the rest of the day.

Then, with a deep breath, she tried Lily's number.

Straight to voicemail.

She set the phone down and folded her hands. *Protect her, Lord. Keep her hidden from whoever seeks to harm her.*

This counted as an emergency. She opened her contacts and scrolled until she found a number saved under the innocuous name Chang's Watch & Jewelry Store.

She tapped the call icon and waited.

CHAPTER 53

THE ROTH RESIDENCE, FLORIDA, USA

OLIVIA/PHOENIX

Olivia's phone buzzed with a distinct chime, the one she reserved for emergencies.

She lifted it without hesitation, interrupting the conversation around her. "Excuse me." She stepped aside. "This might be important."

She tapped Accept. "Marie?"

"Olivia." The warm, familiar voice came through in Cantonese. "It's good to hear your voice. Are you here in Hong Kong?"

She shifted, lowering her voice. "I'm in America now."

"Is Lily with you?" Marie's voice warmed further. "She left the evening before last. Waved to me and left a hasty note."

How to respond? Olivia pushed out the careful words. "She's here, not with me, but yes. This is an emergency?"

"Her apartment has been ransacked. The police believe someone was searching for something. They asked if I knew what. I said I didn't. Which is... kind of true."

A cold knot tightened in Olivia's chest. The Ghost's network had found Lily's trail. And they thought she was the carrier.

"Thank you for telling me."

"They want Lily to call. I'll text you Officer Chow's number. Would you have her reach out when you can?"

"I will. I'll speak to the police myself. Thank you, Marie. Please keep praying for us."

"I always do. Take care now."

Olivia ended the call, lowered the phone, and broke into the group's discussion. "Lily's apartment was searched. That confirms it. Her kidnapping is tied to the intel."

Simon tensed. Ana muttered something under her breath. Kyle, though, frowned. Poor kid, trying to catch up.

"What intel?" he asked. "I'm missing something."

"Need to know," Ron said.

Simon spoke up. "Read him in. He's already in deep."

Olivia agreed. "The Ghost threatened to release a bioweapon. America was the first target. We intercepted and destroyed the final version, but a test batch was already distributed to her network. We don't know how potent it is, so we're not taking any chances."

Kyle paled. "There's an antidote?"

She nodded. "We recovered the scientists' notes. And that formula is the intel. Lily is carrying it."

The kid stood up straighter as understanding obviously clicked into place. "That's why she needed an escort. All those precautions. But… why not transfer it through official channels? You know, your spook ways."

She let out a laugh. "Because the Ghost has spies too. High-level ones. They know our operatives, our routes. Diplomatic pouches aren't safe. We needed someone off-grid. A fresh face."

"I see."

Olivia folded her arms. "Now that we're all on the same

page, I suggest we split up. Ron, Ana, you were going to see the ME?"

"Yes." Ron gestured Ana to the door. "Let's go."

"Simon, I assume you need to brief the president."

Simon stood. "I need to be at the SCIF in fifteen minutes. Leaving now. Keep me posted." He walked toward the garage door.

At the door, Ron pivoted. "Kyle, you can come—"

"I'd like him to stay," Olivia cut in. "I could use the help. Someone to bounce ideas off."

Ron gave her a look. "Fine. He's yours for now."

When the door clicked shut behind Ron and Ana, Olivia turned to Kyle. "Here's what you don't know. We only have a short window of time. If that test strain is in play and it's even partially viable, symptoms could show within hours of exposure. According to the scientists, we'd have maybe twenty-four hours left to act."

"To stop the spread?"

"To contain it. Or at least treat it. The formula Lily's carrying is the key."

Kyle leaned forward. "So we need to find her. Fast."

"I thought Harrison might lead us to her. But with him dead, we need to reanalyze everything."

He pulled Simon's laptop toward him. "Mind if I map this out? I'll project it onto the TV."

She gestured. "Go ahead."

The screen blinked to life, a digital reflection of his thought process. Clean. Organized. Methodical.

"The Ghost is in federal custody. That's a fact." She paced out her own thoughts. "Now we need to determine who knows about Lily's relationship with Simon. Who knew she had the intel? There's a leak close to Simon. Was it Rifkin? Was he King?"

Kyle typed as she spoke.

"King's a code name. I couldn't uncover the identity. Some believed Rifkin was King. He was close to Simon. A mentor. But Simon insists he always voted his conscience."

Kyle looked up. "Sounds like Senator Roth."

She exhaled. "The kidnapping was about the intel. But something changed. Dylan said the fake agents told the goons not to hurt her."

"No, Lily said they were speaking Mandarin and that's what she understood."

"And then there was that accident." Olivia reached the floor-to-ceiling window, pivoted back toward the kitchen, the carpet muffling her steps, but not her thoughts. "One of them was panicking, thought they killed her."

Kyle braced his chin in his hand, scowling over the open laptop. "And the motorist who reported the crash, Rifkin, we think he did it right away. That suggests he wanted help to get there."

"Exactly. Then came the ransom call, demanding Dylan."

He frowned. "If they wanted Dylan, they could've killed him at the crash site. They didn't. So what changed?"

"Up until that point, I believe Rifkin didn't want anyone hurt. He wanted the money, yes, but not bloodshed. He cared about Simon. That's why I doubt he planned for Lily to be harmed."

"But now Rifkin and Harrison are dead. Someone new is pulling strings."

"Someone who wants the intel." Olivia's steps tapped the kitchen tile. "A new player, likely inside the organization."

Kyle's voice lowered. "Before I became an agent, I remember Dad talking about how gangs fracture when a leader's taken out. The lieutenants scramble. It gets ugly."

"It's a good theory." She waved him off. "But taking over the Ghost's empire? That's a death sentence. Maybe in Europe, but not here. No one's tried it, at least not openly. She's ruthless. Some say she killed the woman who raised her."

"But is it possible someone's challenging her?"

"I don't know." She paused her pacing. "But it's worth exploring."

"How?"

"We ask the Ghost."

He blinked. "We're going to ask her?"

"Not *we*." She donned her mask of calm. "Jade will."

His brow furrowed. "Who's Jade?"

CHAPTER 54

UNKNOWN WOODS, FLORIDA, USA

DYLAN

All four tires were slashed.

Dylan stood there, blood thrumming through his head louder than his thoughts. No getaway. No signal. No time.

They had to move.

"We can't go back to the shed."

Lily gave him a skeptical look. "Why not? At least we know it's safe."

"For now, but they'll search it again. Eventually. We stay put—we get caught. We run—we've got a chance."

He didn't wait for her agreement. Just started walking toward the trees. After a moment, she followed.

They moved fast, at least, as fast as they could with roots underfoot and shadows thick as smoke. He tried to retrace his steps, orient himself by memory. But after twenty minutes, it all looked the same. Trees. Darkness. Silence. No lights. No people. Just endless woods.

Breathless and aching, he dropped against a thick tree trunk. He rubbed the back of his neck. "Let's stop here."

She sat beside him, hugging her knees, eyes scanning the darkness.

He checked his phone. One bar. Then none. His battery icon flashed red.

"Battery's dying," he muttered. "I'm gonna turn it off. We'll lose the light, though."

Lily dug through her bag and pulled out a lantern.

He blinked. "Where'd you get that?"

"I found it in the shed. Before you showed up. Figured I might need it."

"Smart girl. Seriously. That's thinking ahead."

"I'm not turning it on. I don't want those goons to track us."

"Good thinking." He ran a hand through his hair. The woods felt too quiet now. Like they were being watched.

"You know where we are?"

He let out a breath. "No clue. I've only lived here a few months. I thought we were heading toward the road, but... maybe I was turned around. Might've gone the wrong way."

She didn't reply for a moment. "It's weird. They slashed the tires, but didn't follow us. Why not?"

"Didn't one of the guys say something about another guy having a way to find us? Like surveillance or something?"

Her expression froze. "You think we triggered something?"

"Could've. Motion sensors. Trail cameras. Maybe one's hidden out here."

They sat in tense silence.

Then Lily stiffened. "Wait. You hear that?"

Dylan froze. His ears strained.

A rustling sound. Leaves shifting. Then crunching.

Footsteps.

He cocked his head. "Stay quiet—"

Too late.

A thud. Pain exploded across his skull. White light flashed, then nothing.

Somewhere in the dark, Lily screamed.

And the world went black.

CHAPTER 55
THE ROTH RESIDENCE, FLORIDA, USA

OLIVIA/PHOENIX

"I've got to take care of a few things before Jade can talk to the Ghost." Olivia powered down her laptop.

Kyle blinked. "I still don't know who Jade is."

She closed the screen and stood. "You don't need to be concerned about Jade." Then, gesturing toward the kitchen, she added, "I'm raiding the senator's fridge. You want anything?"

He shuffled foot to foot. "Uh, are we allowed to do that?"

She was already walking. "Trust me. If Simon were here, he'd offer. Besides, I'm not letting a full fridge go to waste."

The housekeeper had stocked it well. She found cold cuts, bottled juice, and neatly labeled containers in the freezer—Chicken Parm, Shrimp Scampi, Spaghetti Bolognese—each dated and arranged like a frozen meal service.

"Shrimp scampi for me." She slid it out. "What's your fancy?"

Kyle crowded in behind her. "Guess I'll go with the chicken."

"Good choice." She found plates in the cabinet, silverware in a drawer, and set about heating the meals.

As the microwave hummed, she stepped to the corner of the room, away from Kyle but not out of sight. She unlocked her secure phone, turned her back, and pressed her thumb to the biometric reader. A soft chime prompted her for her authorization.

She keyed it in: A927.

The line connected after a short encrypted handshake tone.

"Ops desk," a calm male voice answered. "Confirm status word."

"Phoenix One. Green."

"Copy. Stand by for Burns."

A soft click, then a few seconds of silence before Jay came on. "They know about Lily and the intel."

Jay didn't waste time. "How?"

"Her apartment in Hong Kong's been torn apart. She's been abducted."

"What? I thought you were shadowing her."

"I was. I tracked them to the safe house. She disappeared before I could get her out. We're working on it."

Behind her, Kyle opened the microwave, took her dinner out, and put his plate in. She lowered her voice, but not enough to be fully discreet.

"I need you to get in touch with someone local. An attorney who can handle things with the Hong Kong police. I'll text you the officer's name. Lily's going to need representation for the break-in."

"I can arrange that. What else?"

"Jade needs to speak with the Ghost."

A pause. She could feel Jay bristle on the other end. "No. We don't have jurisdiction here."

"You've bent the rules before."

"That was different. And don't forget, I warned you about involving Lily."

"I remember. I made that choice." She softened her tone. "We don't have time. Jade can go in as her attorney, private, no monitoring. It'll be fast."

Another pause. She caught Kyle trying not to look curious, but the name Jade must've landed.

"Fine. I'll arrange it. I'll text you where to pick up the package."

"One more thing. Do you know if Shadow Shot is in the country?"

"Why?" Jay's tone changed.

"As a precaution. If this goes sideways, I want options. My daughter's life is on the line."

"I'll check."

"Thank you."

She ended the call. Kyle was pretending he hadn't been listening, but failing.

"Was that your handler?"

She nodded. "Also, a friend."

"Jade's a spy too?" He crossed his arms and leaned against the counter. "And Shadow Shot, is that a person?"

She gave a half smile. "That's need to know."

Then her gaze drifted to her phone screen, Lily's photo, a moment frozen in time. Her fingers hovered over the image as if the contact could somehow be real.

We'll get you back, baby girl.

KYLE

The last bite of spaghetti lingered on Kyle's tongue when the garage door opened behind him. He froze, fork still in hand, like a kid caught raiding a candy jar.

Senator Roth had returned and beelined for Olivia. No words, just a wave of acknowledgment in Kyle's direction. Then the two of them stepped outside, voices low, shoulders tight. Whatever news he brought wasn't good.

Kyle stood to clear his plate, but Olivia's phone buzzed on the counter.

His dad's name lit up the screen.

His brows pinched. Her phone, not his. But still, if Dad was calling, it mattered.

He knocked on the glass door. "Sorry to interrupt." He kept his gaze on Olivia. "Dad's calling. On your phone."

She took it out of his hand. "Thanks. We should go back inside and get the updates from everybody."

"Yeah, let's go." Senator Roth sighed.

The call had already gone to voicemail, but Olivia didn't check it. She called back, connecting to a secure video line. Kyle leaned in as Dad's familiar image appeared, flanked by Ana, with Tanner moving in the background.

"ME's office just got Harrison Burke's body." Dad got right to it. "The death investigator didn't have much to add. TOD within the last four hours. It was a pro hit. No witnesses. Door cam was disabled. Hernandez is still checking the cameras around the area. So far, CSU reports no prints, no blood trail. Nothing to work with."

"However," Ana added, "earlier surveillance from across the street picked up a vehicle, same make and model as the one used at Rifkin's."

"The same killer?" Senator Roth asked.

"We think so." Ana fielded that one. "Deanna's enhancing the footage. With luck, we'll get a partial plate to compare. Still circumstantial until we can ID the driver."

"How did your meeting go?" Dad directed his question to the senator.

Simon cleared his throat, then rubbed his neck. "Not great. The boss wants the antidote. Now. He's under pressure to act, possibly do something reckless."

"Please don't tell me he's going to cave."

"Not there yet. We have twenty-four hours to find Lily. After that…" He let a shrug finish the sentence. "But there's a positive. We've been granted provisional access to NSA satellite coverage. That'll help us if we need to scan a remote location."

Olivia had returned to her laptop, her fingers gliding over the keys. Kyle's gaze flicked between her and the screen. She was multitasking. Fast.

Tanner stepped forward. "Kyle, someone named Tom Rivers called the field office asking for you. Message got routed here when they saw the last name."

Kyle frowned. "Tommy? Dylan's friend. Weird. I don't know why he'd call me."

"Call him back," Dad suggested. "Could be important."

Kyle patted his pocket. Right. His phone had been destroyed. Olivia passed him hers again.

He started. But Tommy's number wasn't in the contacts. "Does the system save Tommy Rivers's number?"

Tanner gave a nod. "Yeah. We logged it when he left the message. I can text it to Olivia's phone."

A moment later, the phone buzzed with the number.

> Hey, this is Kyle Peters. I heard you called the field office.

Almost as soon as it sent, the phone rang. He stepped away and swiped to answer.

"Kyle?"

"Yeah, Tommy."

"Thank goodness. I didn't have your number. Or your dad's. Dylan isn't answering, and I think something's wrong."

He walked back to the crowd and switched it to speaker. "Slow down. What are you talking about?"

"I was watching a movie, missed the message until maybe an hour ago. Dylan texted me. Said he was going to get Lily. I don't get it. He didn't explain. Just said to contact you if I didn't hear from him tonight. There was supposed to be a map, but it never came through. I've been trying to reach him, but it's straight to voicemail."

A heavy silence settled over the room.

Then Dad leaned in. "Tommy, this is Ron Peters. Are you saying Dylan left to go find Lily? Did she contact him?"

"I guess? I mean, something must've happened. Do you guys know what's going on?"

Olivia took the phone. "Hi, Tommy. I'm Lily's mom. Just so you know, this is my phone. You'll see my number on the call. Can you forward the text to me and Agent Peters? I'll text you his number."

"Lily's mom? I thought—wait, never mind. Sure. Sending it now." Tommy paused. "Hang on. This wouldn't have anything to do with his psycho aunt, would it?"

Olivia exchanged glances with the senator and Dad. "What do you know about his relationship with his aunt?"

"There's no relationship unless you mean the part where she tried to kill him. This is about her, isn't it?"

Nobody answered.

"Look," Tommy continued, "I don't need the secrets. But I want to help. He's my best friend. Let me help. I know him better than anyone else here does."

"He's got a point," Dad admitted.

Tommy huffed. "The guy nearly died a few months ago. And let's be honest, I'm not ready to lose a billionaire best friend. Perks are real."

A faint smirk twitched on Ana's lips.

"All right." Dad rubbed a hand over his face. "I'll send someone to bring you in tomorrow. If anything breaks tonight, we'll let you know."

The moment Tommy ended the call, the room erupted.

"She escaped?"

"Why didn't he call anyone else?"

"Hey," Dad called over the chaos. "One at a time!"

Ana raised a hand. "Did she escape? Why else would Dylan say he was going to get her?"

Olivia tapped the phone. "Reading it now. All Dylan said was he was going to get Lily. That's it. We don't know what she said or how she said it."

"Or if it was really her." Dad massaged his temple. "Could've been bait."

Olivia spoke without looking up. "I knew the Ghost had someone monitoring Dylan. Just didn't know why."

Dad exhaled. "Long story. Dylan's mom and the Ghost were twins. Right after they were born, Dylan's grandfather tried to go legit. His second-in-command, Charles Townsend Sr., tried to get on board, but Senior's daughter, Mel, took one of the twins. Raised her to be a weapon."

"How do you kidnap a baby from a hospital?" Kyle asked.

"Money. Power. The usual. Dylan's grandparents thought the baby died. As you all know, months ago, Ms. Carol found Dylan with the help of Charles Townsend Jr. She wants him back with the family. I'm thinking the Ghost saw him as a threat. But Dylan's parents had backup plans—buried evidence, ledgers, maybe even treasure. The Ghost didn't know where it was, so she waited for Dylan to uncover it."

Ana gawked. "That's messed up."

"You don't know the half of it," Olivia chimed in. "Word is, the Ghost killed the woman who raised her. Took over overseas branches. She's ruthless."

Kyle leaned closer. "Then if Lily escaped and contacted Dylan…"

"…he went after her without telling anyone—"

"Likely because he thought we'd tell him to stand down." Ana sighed.

Made sense. Kyle bobbed his head. The way Dylan wanted to be a part of this…

"Or maybe it wasn't her," Olivia countered. "Could've been a trap, like Ron suggested."

She opened another window on her laptop. "I forwarded Lily's last-known location. We can try to ping Dylan's phone. See if they're together."

His dad arched an eyebrow. "You had her location this whole time?"

"I couldn't connect earlier. Let's just say… it's better you don't know how I got it."

The senator said, "Exigent circumstances, Ron."

Ana frowned. "But if she escaped, why not call 911?"

"Maybe she did," the senator replied. "In Hong Kong, that's 999. It's instinct."

"And this was her first day here. She's scared," Olivia added. "She might've panicked."

Kyle could feel it, that desperate tug in everyone's voice. Not just strategy now. This was fear.

Ana went on. "Okay, say she got out, reached Dylan. Then why not call anyone else?"

"Maybe they did." Kyle swallowed a bitter taste in his mouth. "And something happened."

Dad nodded. "We need to assume they're together. But his phone's not pinging anymore."

"Could HRT search the area?" Senator Roth asked.

Dad shook his head. "The last ping was along the Beachline Expressway, an unpatrolled stretch. Could be heading to the coast or hiding in Tosohatchee. It's dense, not residential. Tough terrain."

Frustration zinged like static across the room.

"I'm staying." Ana crossed her arms, notched up her chin. "Just in case anyone wants to send me packing. By the way, you don't know what they might do now that they have Dylan. Wonder if they'd call it off."

"That depends on what they want." Olivia resumed pacing. "If they want intel, they don't need him."

A phone rang.

Everyone went still.

The senator checked the screen. His eyes widened.

"It's them."

CHAPTER 56

UNKNOWN CABIN, FLORIDA, USA

LILY

The slap echoed through the cabin like a gunshot.

Lily jolted in her chair as the goon smacked Dylan's face a second time. He didn't move, still slumped forward, head lolling, tied to a chair like her, wrists bound to the chair arms.

"Wakey-wakey," the man said in a singsong voice, drawing back for another hit.

Lily's stomach clenched. She'd already seen enough. The strike landed, tilting Dylan's head at an awkward angle.

Still no response.

The man doing the hitting was the third voice she heard earlier—Scar Face, she'd dubbed him. Tall. Blond. Cruel. A jagged scar sliced down the left side of his face like a tear in old leather. He radiated the kind of danger that made her skin crawl.

Behind him stood the two others. Gruff Voice, with muscles and not much else. And Nice Guy. He hadn't hit her. Yet.

"Sheesh, there was another dude in the car." Gruff Voice gripped his hips, rocked off his toes. "This one was driving, other one in the back."

Scar Face spun on him. "Then why didn't you finish them both?"

"Because that wasn't our order."

"Why'd you drug this one too?" Scar Face jerked his thumb at Dylan.

"You said to use the cloth on both!"

"He was already down, you idiot!"

Gruff Voice wasn't exactly the brains of the operation. Lily might have laughed if she weren't duct taped to a chair, the adhesive pulling at her skin.

Nice Guy leaned against the wall. Just watching.

Lily swallowed hard, her throat dry. They were back in the cabin, the one from before. She recognized the rough plank floor, the faint mildew smell, the sagging table with her backpack spilled across it. No one had bothered to clean up.

Dylan stirred with a groan.

Blood from his nose had dried in a line down his lip. She winced as he started to wake, slow, sluggish. One eyelid cracked open.

Scar Face stepped toward him again, raising his hand for another hit.

"Stop!" she shouted.

He froze mid-motion, then turned his mocking smirk on her. "Oh, you don't want your boyfriend getting roughed up?"

She didn't respond. Not to that.

He closed the distance and crouched in front of her chair. Something chemical scented his clothes—gasoline or maybe a cleaner.

He coaxed the words out like he was bribing a toddler. "All you have to do is tell me where it is. And I let you both go."

She narrowed her eyes. "Where *what* is?"

"You know what I'm talking about. It's not in your bag or your pockets. So… where?"

The fake mole. That's what he was after. The only thing she

had worth hiding. She fought the urge to look at her stomach. Didn't move a muscle. She'd watched enough TV to know even a glance could give her away.

"I don't know what you're talking about."

His eyes flicked lower. "Do you know what a drug mule is?"

She tensed, but remained quiet.

He smiled, slow and deliberate. "They swallow the stuff. Or hide it somewhere… creative."

His gaze drifted to her crotch.

Her chest tightened, breath catching in her throat.

"What say we check?"

"She gave it to me!" Dylan's voice rang out.

Lily whipped her head toward him and got the message.

"No! Stop it," she snapped. "I trusted you!"

"Sorry." Dylan shrugged with what little movement he could manage. "I don't want to die."

Scar Face advanced on him. "Smart choice."

"They're going to kill us either way!" she shouted.

"Shut her up."

Gruff Voice grabbed her hair from behind and shoved a sour cloth into her mouth.

She squirmed, fought it, but he was stronger. Her arms strained against the ties, useless.

"She gave it to me on the plane." Dylan notched his chin higher. "Said it was top priority. I was supposed to keep it safe until Senator Roth could retrieve it."

Lily blinked hard. Senator Roth? What was he doing?

"So…" Scar Face crouched before Dylan. His index finger scraped the blood from Dylan's lip. "Where is it?"

Dylan jerked his head away. "I put it in the vault at Mirror Estate, the safest place."

Scar Face licked the dried blood from his finger. "Who are you?"

"Dylan Roche. Check my wallet."

Gruff Voice dug into Dylan's pocket and opened the wallet. "Name's not Marino."

"Nope. Carol Marino is my grandmother."

"If this guy is Dylan Roche"—Nice Guy spoke for the first time—"then he's the Ghost's nephew. I wouldn't mess with him. She left strict instructions."

"Jackpot." A slow smile crinkled up Scar Face's scar. "Boss said to hold him. I don't need to wait for the exchange."

Still hunkered in front of him, he gripped Dylan's chin, raising his face. "How do you access the vault?"

"I can take you there."

Scar Face scoffed. "You'd alert security. No thanks. I want you to call someone who can get it and deliver it—with the senator."

Dylan didn't miss a beat. "You'll still need me to unlock the case. And Lily's biometrics."

"You're bluffing."

"Try me. Top secret intel doesn't come in sandwich bags."

Scar Face stood to fish his phone from his jeans pocket. "Number?"

"Call the Mirror Estate landline. Ask for Max."

He did. Dylan's voice stayed even.

"Max, it's Dylan. My phone's dead. I'm calling from a friend's. Please retrieve the item I put in the vault today. Senator Roth will pick it up. My authorization code is 225591. He'll need my voice and Lily's biometrics to unlock the case."

"Yes, sir," came the response.

Scar Face ended the call and yanked the cloth from Lily's mouth.

Then slapped her. Hard.

"Ow!" she cried.

Another slap. Her cheek burned.

"Stop it!" Dylan shouted. "I gave you everything!"

Scar Face didn't blink. "Watch them," he told the others. "I need to make a call."

And then he was gone.

Lily shivered. How long had they been there, silent, sore, and straining against the panic icing her chest?

Scar Face had come back, then left again. The remaining two were in the kitchen now, rummaging up food, probably. The fridge opened, drawers clattered, and a faucet ran. Then the distinct *shik-shik* of a knife rasped a cutting board.

Dylan's voice cut through the clatter. "I'll take the works."

"Shut it!" Gruff Voice hollered. "Nobody said this was for you."

"I'm just saying," Dylan replied. "We haven't eaten since lunch. And I'm thirsty."

"You think we're your butlers?" A mouthful muffed the guy's gruff voice.

From what little she knew of Dylan, he'd never acted entitled. He'd been... normal. Kind. Thoughtful.

Footsteps approached.

Nice Guy untied one of her arms. She froze, uncertain, until he set a sandwich on her lap and a water bottle by her feet.

"Thank you," she whispered.

He grunted.

Then he did the same for Dylan, warning, "Don't try anything."

"Ah, you softie," Gruff Voice jeered when he came back in. "Feeding the prisoners now?"

"They need to eat."

Maybe Nice Guy was the weak link.

If only she could get to him.

While Dylan ate, he shifted. One hand moved toward his waistband, subtle, deliberate. He slipped something into his tied hand.

She tried not to react. But her heart leapt.

He had a plan.

Now they just had to move before Scar Face came back.

CHAPTER 57

THE ROTH RESIDENCE, FLORIDA, USA

OLIVIA/PHOENIX

Olivia's pulse quickened when Simon's phone rang again.

"It's them." He swiped to answer. "Roth."

A flat, synthetic voice filled the room. "Change of plans. You will bring the money and intel to the exchange."

Her stomach dropped.

Simon's gaze locked with hers. "What are you talking about? What intel?"

"You know what I'm talking about. Go to the Mirror Estate to retrieve the item. It will be waiting for you. Bring it to the exchange. I'll text you the location. Remember, no cops. And in case the girl is not enough leverage, I now have Mr. Dylan Roche. The clock's ticking. To motivate you, have a listen."

A click.

Simon's screen flashed as an audio file landed. He tapped it.

Lily's screams reverberated through the room.

The sound was sharp, immediate. Olivia's lungs locked. Her fingers clenched around the table's edge, hard enough to sting.

Across from her, Simon's jaw tightened, his mouth downturned in a grim line of helpless fury.

"We will get her back," Ron said.

"Yes, we will," Ana added, her tone like steel wrapped in silk. "Think positive."

They exchanged glances, a current of determination passing between them. Kyle stood off to the side, fists clenched, the skin over his knuckles pale. He hadn't said a word, but his furious eyes said everything: He cared about Lily.

"Guess we know they've been caught again." Ana leaned against the wall.

"Or it was a trap." Ron checked his phone. "Hold on. Marino residence is calling."

He answered. "This is Agent Peters."

"This is Max Warner, the Marinos' majordomo," came the calm voice on speaker. "Dylan called from an unlisted number. He's in trouble."

"Did he say where he is?" Ron asked.

"No. But since his last ordeal, we've implemented new protocols. He used a code meant to signal he's being held at gunpoint or otherwise under duress. The message was short. I recorded it."

"Please forward it to me."

"Certainly."

"Can we hear it first, Max?" Simon asked.

"Is that you, Simon? You were my next call. Dylan said you were supposed to come by to retrieve an item. Do you know what he meant?"

Simon hesitated. "Yes, I do. But I won't be coming by."

"Understood. I'll play the recording now."

After a short pause, Dylan's voice came through, measured, like each word had been chosen carefully. It wasn't what he said —it was how he said it. Controlled. Performed. The kind of voice you used when you were trying not to die.

When the message ended, no one spoke for a beat. Ron thanked Max and assured him they'd do their best to bring Dylan back safe and sound. The call ended. He scanned their group. "Thoughts?"

"He made it sound real." Ana crossed her arms. "Smart. At least now they think he's their only shot at getting the intel."

Olivia drummed her fingers on her thigh. "Let's just hope the kidnapper doesn't call his bluff."

Simon reached for her hand and enclosed it with a gentle squeeze. "Like Ana said earlier, let's stay positive."

Ron checked his watch, then his phone. "Deanna might've left for the night. I'll check to see if anyone's still in the lab. Maybe we can work some magic and trace the call."

But his voice lacked conviction.

And Olivia knew he was thinking the same thing she was.

The clock wasn't just ticking.

It was already running out.

SIMON

Sleep didn't come easy, not when your daughter was missing, and the last thing you'd heard from her was a recorded scream sent by a monster.

Simon had tried to rest. Closed his eyes. Focused on Olivia's voice as they'd prayed together the night before. But each time his thoughts slipped into unconsciousness, visions of Lily—tied up, hurt, afraid—yanked him back.

Kyle had left for the task force office sometime after ten. Olivia had mentioned an errand and slipped out shortly after. She hadn't said where she was going, only, "Need to take care of something." No further explanation.

Simon hadn't asked. He trusted her. Still, part of him wondered.

She came back around midnight, tired but composed, and told him her contacts hadn't uncovered anything useful. Only that the Ghost had left strict instructions not to touch Dylan Roche.

"I doubt she wants to protect him," he had said.

Olivia's response stayed with him. *"It means she wants to deal with him personally. Whether to kill him or something else, she wants to be the one to do it."*

That had been enough to keep him awake the rest of the night.

Now, the smell of coffee guided him toward the kitchen where Olivia sat at the counter, laptop open and fingers flying across the keys.

He poured himself a cup. "Did you sleep at all?"

"A little. You've done well. I remember when you wanted to work in nonprofit, helping underprivileged kids."

A weary sigh slipped free. "Life has a way of diverting you. Lately, I've been wondering if I'm cut out for public life. I feel like a puppet, Rifkin pulling the strings."

She patted the stool beside her. "Sit."

He did.

"It's never too late." She swiveled hers his way and reached for his hand. "I gave over twenty years to this world. I'm grateful for what Jay and Patty did and the opportunities I've had. But I gave up something else. Our daughter."

His thumb rubbed the back of her hand, her skin soft. "Do you regret it?"

"I have plenty of regrets. But not Lily. And not you. That's the sacrifice I had to make to keep her and you safe."

As he gazed into her eyes, he saw not the polished operative, not the strategist. Just Olivia. The woman he'd once loved, still did.

Did she lean closer? He held his breath. But she turned away instead.

"Guest room's comfortable." She stood up.

The moment passed. Again.

"You could've—never mind."

She replenished her mug. "You're a real coffee connoisseur. This machine has more settings than some command centers."

"What can I say? My only vice."

Her laptop chimed. She tipped the screen toward him.

Mysterious Illness Surfaces in Small Ohio Town— Symptoms Resemble Ebola, Cholera, and Smallpox

The baffling illness has surfaced in Brea, a small town in Ohio, affecting two residents who presented symptoms similar to early-stage Ebola fever, cholera, and smallpox…

Simon scanned the article, the words blurring. Fever. Pus. Containment.

"How long before the panic spreads?" he asked.

As if in response, phones started buzzing and ringing in tandem.

"Didn't take long." Olivia checked hers.

He glanced at the screen. White House. Again. "Roth." He got up and stepped into the living room.

It was another summons.

When he returned, Olivia was off her call. "Ron's checking in. Their tech's analyzing the recording. They might get a lead soon. He also reminded me that those two fake agents at the first safe house spoke Mandarin. That lines up with my theory."

"You think they were Chinese operatives?"

"I think they were sent to recover the intel. Rifkin's men caused the crash, but those two? That's something else."

"I thought no one knew about Lily."

"There's a leak. Somewhere."

He dragged a hand down his face. "The big boss wants another update. What should I tell him?"

"Buy us time. Say we're closing in."

That hand stopped. Cold fingers splayed. He studied her through them. "Do you have something planned?"

"I'm going to see her."

"Her? Who—?"

"Jade is going to talk to the Ghost."

He frowned. "Who's Jade?"

She offered an almost apologetic smile. "It's my legend. I used it when I worked deep cover. She's the one the Ghost knows."

"And you think that'll work?"

"I don't need her to give me everything. I just need her to slip. See, Ron's doing what he does best. I'm gonna do what I do best."

"What makes you think it wasn't the Ghost?"

"Kyle gave me the idea. Add what Ron reminded me about the Mandarin-speaking agents. Rifkin wouldn't have hired them. And I doubt the Ghost ordered Lily's kidnapping. Someone inside the organization is trying to rise up. Someone who wants Dylan and the intel."

So much to process. "Rifkin didn't want Lily hurt. He called for help."

"Exactly, and now he's dead. So is Harrison. Hit man. Clean. Quick. Someone else is pulling strings. Someone who wants control."

He rubbed his forehead. "How did we get sucked into this?"

She stepped closer. "We'll get through it. We'll find her." She touched his hand again, then stepped back. "Now I have to go see the devil."

He pulled her into a quick hug. "Okay. I trust you, Olivia."

Her head rested against his shoulder for a beat. "Thank you. Also, you might want to give your housekeeper the day off. We don't need any more innocent bystanders. First Rifkin. Then Harrison. They probably won't come here, but… just in case."

"Good idea. I'll make the call."

He watched her go, then reached for his phone.

If they'd already reached Rifkin and Harrison…

Who was next?

CHAPTER 58

UNKNOWN CABIN, FLORIDA, USA

DYLAN

Dylan resisted sleep as long as he could, but his eyelids grew heavier with each blink. He dozed off, then jerked awake with a start.

Across from him, Lily was out cold. Her arms hung at her sides, her breathing steady but shallow. No doubt she'd also fought to stay awake. He could tell. But exhaustion had won.

The room was dim, the air stale. A faint gray glow pushed through the windowpane, the edge of dawn. The fire had long since gone out. No sounds from the hall. No movement. The scar-faced psycho wasn't in the room.

No clock in sight, but it must still be early. He hated how the light made him think someone might be coming. It was too soon for hope.

His back ached from the chair. His wrists throbbed. But the small pocketknife pressed into his palm gave him something else —possibility. He'd worked it free earlier, inch by inch, from the hidden pocket sewn into his waistband. Ever since he'd nearly been killed a few months ago, he carried a pocketknife everywhere and kept it somewhere no one else would think to look. Tommy called it neurotic. Dylan called it survival.

He didn't know why he'd blurted out that story about the vault and the intel. Maybe it had been instinct. Maybe it was the way the scar-faced psycho had looked at Lily, like she was something he could break apart and sell in pieces.

He'd had to give them something. Anything. Something that wasn't her.

Max would've picked up on the cues. Protocols were in place. If Dylan triggered the code, Max would've alerted someone. And Tommy, he should've received the map by now. Agent Peters would come. They had to.

A strand of hair had fallen across Lily's cheek. Her expression was peaceful.

She deserved better than this.

Then a flicker in the corner of his eye.

His muscles tensed.

A shadow moved, just behind him. Before he could twist to see it, a blade whispered through the air. The duct tape binding his right wrist to the chair arm split apart.

Then a voice, low, urgent: "Special Agent Dante Ortiz, undercover FDLE."

Dylan's breath caught. That voice, he recognized it. One of the men who'd been guarding them.

Ortiz crouched and sliced the tape at Dylan's ankles. Then moved to Lily.

She startled awake as the blade cut her free. He repeated the words to her, finger to lips.

Lily nodded, wide-eyed.

Ortiz pointed to their gear on the table, then to the door.

"Where's the other guy?" Lily whispered.

"Sleeping. Took hours to slip something in his drink. He was too busy watching porn to notice. But I don't know when Hans is coming back. Let's go."

Dylan grabbed his bag. He was trying not to hope, but it was there now, swelling behind his ribs.

The morning air outside hit like a slap—cool, damp, laced with pine. Mist curled around the trees like ghosts waiting to be named. If he weren't trying to outrun death, he might've admired the scenery.

Ortiz opened the truck. "Get in."

Dylan helped Lily up first. She moved fast, barely needing the assist.

"What's FD-something?" she asked once inside.

"Florida Department of Law Enforcement." Ortiz hopped into the driver's seat.

Dylan climbed in and slammed the door. "What's the plan?"

"Get out." Ortiz turned the key. "My assignment was Rifkin. I could've stopped the crash. The kidnapping. But the higher-ups wanted King. I had to keep my cover. I hoped you'd get her out of the safe house on your own. I left clues. Did everything I could from the inside. But Hans? He's not working for the Ghost. He's a freelancer. Trigger-happy. And when you showed up..." He paused. "I know what he'll do once he's got what he wants. You're expendable."

"I thought the Ghost ordered them not to hurt me."

"She did. But whoever Hans answers to now? Doesn't care. Probably has a death wish trying to take her place."

"This feels like a thriller movie," Lily said. "Except it's real."

Ortiz's gaze flicked to the mirror. "Good guys usually win in movies. Let's hope—get down!"

Dylan didn't ask. He grabbed Lily and dropped. Metal groaned around them. The truck lurched backward, then spun hard left.

"Is that Hans?" Dylan asked.

"Yes. Stay down!"

The engine howled. Then—hissing.

The truck shuddered.

"Tire's gone! Move!"

Doors flew open. Dylan leapt out, adrenaline roaring in his ears. He pivoted to help Lily, but she'd already jumped, running full speed across the gravel. He chased her, breath ragged.

Behind them, gunfire.

Ortiz was shooting. Covering them.

"Do you know how to fire a weapon?" Ortiz called.

"Me?" Dylan choked. "No."

Then—a scream.

Ortiz was down, blood spreading across his shirt. One hand clutched his stomach. The other held his weapon.

"Run!" he shouted.

Dylan couldn't move. Couldn't leave him.

But then, another shot. Ortiz fired. A body crumpled behind them.

Lily was already moving. "Help me get him behind a tree!"

Dylan ran to her side. Together, they dragged the wounded agent to cover.

"Take this." Ortiz shoved the pistol at Dylan. "Safety's here. Flip it. Point and shoot."

Dylan stared at it. He couldn't breathe. "No. You need it more than we do."

Ortiz shoved it harder. "Take it!"

"I don't want to shoot her or myself by mistake. Please keep it." Dylan pushed it back to Ortiz. "You stay alive."

Lily pulled a shirt from her bag and pressed it against the wound. "Hold pressure. Tight!"

Ortiz grunted and obeyed. "Thank you. Now go!"

"Phone?" she asked, hopeful.

"Gone. Lost it in the truck. Go!"

This man bleeding in front of him risked everything to get them out. Something twisted in Dylan's chest.

They couldn't save him. Not now.

Lily crossed herself and whispered, "He's right."

Dylan grabbed her hand.
They ran—
With a man bleeding behind them.
A killer hunting them.
And no idea if anyone would make it out alive.

CHAPTER 59

FEDERAL DETENTION CENTER, FLORIDA, USA

OLIVIA/PHOENIX

Olivia hated prisons. Her only other visit had been a tightly controlled tour in Hong Kong, clean, sterile, full of protocol. *This* was different. The thick air carried something metallic and stale, and the muted clatter of distant doors echoed like bones knocking together.

But today, she had a role to play.

She adjusted her wig and took a slow breath. The mask pulled at her cheeks. She closed her eyes, preparing herself to resume her cover identity. When she reopened her eyes, Olivia disappeared. Jade Lam stared back. And today, she'd be Jade Wong, criminal defense attorney.

Jay had come through. Her fake credentials had been waiting in the drop box, tucked inside a weathered manila envelope. Before sleeping last night, if pacing and replaying contingency plans counted as sleep, she'd memorized her cover's backstory. Ivy League degree, boutique law firm, just enough arrogance to get in the door.

The guards didn't pay much attention to her as she passed

through security. Her shoes clicked on linoleum that felt too slick, like a surface waiting for blood. In her hand, a slim leather briefcase. Inside, a file, a legal pad, and two printed screenshots.

She was led into the attorney-client room. Windowless. Fluorescent lighting. A thick table bolted to the floor. One chain on each side.

She sat, arranged her props, and waited. Her palms felt damp.

The first post:

Just in: A retired senator has been found dead at their home. Our thoughts go out to their family and loved ones during this difficult time. #RIP #RetiredSenator

The second:

Police are currently investigating. Cause of death unknown. More details as they emerge. #BreakingNews

She didn't glance up when the door opened. But she heard the cuffs. The rustle of fabric. The heavy boots.

Marge Beaumont, the Ghost, was led inside.

Olivia met her eyes.

Marge's gaze flickered over her face, resting just long enough. Recognition. But no reaction. No betrayal. Just the faintest twitch at the corner of her mouth, like she'd found something amusing.

"Knock when you're done. If she gives you any trouble—"

"I'll let you know," Olivia told the guard.

The door shut.

Only then did Marge speak. "What are you doing here, Jade? I thought you were in Hong Kong."

Olivia didn't blink. "King sent me the moment he heard about your arrest."

Marge's face stilled, but her fingers curled on the table. "Oh? Why? I told him I had a plan."

"He thinks someone's trying to take your place."

A scoff. "Nobody dares. Not unless they're suicidal."

"I'm just reporting what he said."

Marge tilted her head, scrutinizing her. "You're holding something back. What is it?"

Olivia slid the paper forward. "Rifkin is dead."

For the first time in all the years she'd known her, the Ghost lost her composure.

Marge's lips parted, but no words came. She blinked hard, once, twice, then drew in a slow, measured breath. "No. Not Roger."

Olivia's spine straightened. Not because she feared Marge. But because this was grief.

Real, personal grief.

"I'm sorry." Olivia frowned. "I didn't know you two were…"

"It's complicated." Marge sighed. "But it's been several years. Nobody knew." A beat. "How?"

"Shot in the back. No forced entry. I went to see him, saw the cops. Teased it out of a patrol officer." Olivia rotated the printout. "Yesterday. Same killer took out Harrison too. Nobody threatened to take over? A rival, maybe?"

Marge shook her head. "In Europe or Asia, maybe. Harrison was Roger's shadow." She looked up. "No break-in. That means someone with access. Someone King knew." A beat. "Bishop."

"Who's Bishop?"

"Ambitious. Cunning. I kept him on a short leash for a reason." Her nails tapped the metal tabletop. "He's the only one reckless enough to make a move. He's always wanted the top seat."

"What do you want me to do?"

"Tell him to come see me."

Olivia didn't flinch. "And then?"

"I'll take care of him."

"How do I find him?"

CHAPTER 60

TASK FORCE OFFICE, FLORIDA, USA

SIMON

Simon's position on the Intelligence Committee granted him access to sensitive intel, as it did every other member. After what Olivia had revealed, he couldn't help but eye the others differently. Were any of them compromised? The Ghost's reach might be deeper than they realized. He'd have to ask Ron for his take.

The morning air had been crisp when he'd grabbed coffee and pastries. A small gesture, but one he hoped would lift spirits. Sleep had evaded him last night, his thoughts looping between Lily and the virus.

How many years had it been since he prayed with sincerity? Last night, in quiet desperation, he and Olivia had prayed. Together, they surrendered the whole situation to God. Now, even in this pressure cooker of uncertainty, he believed there was still a path forward.

As he entered the task force office, the aroma of warm pastries trailed him.

"Good morning," he called out.

"Do I smell coffee?" Agent Tanner stirred from a chair, blinking sleep from bloodshot eyes. His shirt was rumpled, stubble heavy on his jaw, signs he'd never gone home.

"Yes, indeed." Simon placed the container on a central desk and opened the pastry box. "Help yourself. Hopefully, there are enough cups around here."

Tanner grabbed his mug, beelining for the coffee. "You're a lifesaver, Senator."

"I want the cream cheese one, Tanner." Ana appeared, her hair tied back, eyes alert.

Simon waved. "Morning. You look… fresh. Did you actually sleep?"

She grinned. "Trade secret."

Before he could respond, Ron stepped in with another agent, young, clean-cut.

"Senator, this is Agent Jose Hernandez," Ron introduced.

Simon shook his hand. "Nice to meet you. Hope you like Danishes."

"I like caffeine better." Hernandez's gaze was on the coffee.

As they settled in, a woman in a lab coat came from the back in a beeline for the pastries.

"Senator Roth, Deanna Swanson." Ron did the introduction. "She's been working since dawn."

She bit into a Danish, then waved it at Simon. "Senator, might have something for you soon."

He gave her a warm smile. "Appreciate you burning the early oil. No pressure."

Then he pivoted to Ron. "I've got a briefing in the SCIF. Any updates I can take to the big boss?"

Ron shrugged. "Not yet."

Simon looked around. "Where's Kyle?"

"Break room. Still asleep, I think. I told him to go home. He refused."

Over an hour later, Simon emerged from the SCIF. Thankfully, everyone agreed—no deal with the Ghost. Still, the president's patience wore thin. What chilled Simon was the question the president had asked: Did the carrier have to be alive for the intel to be recovered?

They all knew the answer. No.

The CDC had dispatched teams to Ohio. Results were still pending, but all signs pointed to confirmation of the virus's deadly potential. The president, under mounting pressure, had floated a military operation to storm the Tosohatchee region. Simon argued against it. There was no solid evidence Lily and Dylan were there. They could already be heading toward the coast.

Back at the office, Ron waved him over to the squad room. More agents had gathered, including a young man beside Kyle. Probably Tommy.

Ron confirmed it. "Kyle and Tommy are going to tour the facility while we brief. Kyle already got the full debrief."

They left. It was clearly a pretext to shield Tommy from sensitive intel.

Ron's lips flattened, and his brow tightened. He crossed his arms. "Okay, team. We traced the earlier calls to a burner phone bought downtown. But the last one? Satellite phone. Deanna pulled the call history."

Hernandez clicked the remote. A call log appeared on-screen.

"There's your call, right in the middle." Ron pointed.

Simon leaned closer. "Who's that number before and after?"

"We traced it." A satisfied glint flashed in Hernandez's eyes. "But there's more. Deanna found a traffic cam near Harrison's place, far angle, but she enhanced the image."

Click. A grainy photo appeared. A man's profile. Blurry, but familiar.

Simon's breath caught. "I've seen him. He was with Congressman Pearson at Roger's house the other night. They were leaving as I arrived."

Ron nodded. "Name's Hans Wagner. Interpol flagged him. Tanner and another agent are headed to bring him in. Oh, and that phone number? Belongs to Congressman Pearson."

Simon's gut clenched. "Pearson? No. That can't be right."

Ron's phone rang. "It's Tanner."

As Ron took the call, Ana snagged the last Danish. "Wagner killed Rifkin and Harrison. He called Pearson before and after your call. Looks like orders. Or check-ins."

Ron ended the call. "Wagner is in the wind. It's time to have a chat with the congressman."

CHAPTER 61

ON THE ROAD, FLORIDA, USA

OLIVIA/PHOENIX

The moment the prison gates clanked shut behind her, Olivia strode to her car with a phone in her hand, calling the task force office.

Bishop.

It had to be him.

The Ghost hadn't mentioned the virus. She'd only said she'd told King she had a plan. That omission told Olivia everything. Marge didn't know her plan had gone awry.

And if they didn't move fast, Lily would die.

She started the car. The call connected with a soft chime.

"Olivia, we're about to head out," Ron's voice came through, taut and alert.

"I know who's behind it."

There was a pause. "Congressman Pearson?"

That stopped her cold. "How'd you know? Did you find something?"

"We found an image of his henchman, Hans Wagner. He's in the wind. We also pulled the call history from the sat phone

Wagner used to call Simon. He contacted Pearson right before and after that call."

Her pulse surged. A political player. That explained the resources, the timing, the media silence.

"Ana and I are going to pay him a visit," Ron added.

Olivia gritted her teeth. "He'll hide behind lawyers."

"He might. But we've got enough to pressure him."

"Not fast enough."

Ron didn't answer.

"I need his number." She didn't ask again. She *said* it.

A beat of silence. Static crackled.

Ron exhaled. "Olivia…"

"Ron, I'm not asking you to like it. I'm asking you to trust me."

Another pause.

Then Ana came on the line. "Sending it now."

A vibration buzzed across the console. Olivia checked the screen. Number received. "Thanks. I owe you."

"Don't make us regret it," Ana warned before hanging up.

Olivia rested her phone on the dash and let the silence settle. The hum of traffic beyond her windshield felt muted, distant.

An idea had popped up during her talk with the Ghost. It had been percolating until now.

She hit redial. "Would you please wait until I get there? I need your help."

"What do you need?" he asked.

She stared ahead at the sun slicing through the windshield. Her reflection in the glass looked calm. Controlled.

"I need you to kill me."

CHAPTER 62

UNKNOWN WOODS, FLORIDA, USA

LILY

Branches clawed at Lily's arms as she followed Dylan through the trees, her breath coming in fast, painful bursts. Every few steps, a twig snapped beneath her shoes, far too loud in the silence. She didn't look back. Couldn't.

They had left Agent Ortiz possibly bleeding out.

She clenched her jaw, shoving the image from her mind. *"Let God take care of what you can't,"* her godmother always said. Maybe that meant Ortiz too.

Dylan moved in zigzags, avoiding anything resembling a trail. The woods pressed in, thicker, darker than anywhere she remembered. Had they ever gone this far before?

No gunfire. No voices. Just birdsong and their crashing through the undergrowth.

Did that mean Ortiz was still alive?

They stopped behind an outcropping of moss-covered stone. Dylan doubled over, hands on his knees, scanning the woods behind them. Lily pressed a hand to her pounding chest.

"Why aren't they after us?"

She bent beside him, catching her breath. "Now that you mention it… I kind of thought we'd be dead by now."

Dylan frowned, eyes narrowing. "Remember what we overheard last night? About waiting until we tripped over something? What if this is part of it? They let us run so we'll walk right into their trap. Again."

The air around her felt colder. She craned around, but the trees were just trees. Still, she couldn't shake the feeling something watched them. "Does your phone have a signal yet?"

He pulled it from his pocket. The screen stayed black. "Battery's dead."

"So, no phone. Great." She turned in a slow circle, scanning the thick canopy. "Do you have *any* idea where we are? Or how to get to civilization?"

"We're going away from the main road. Ortiz steered us back, away from where the truck was headed." Dylan gestured left. "If we keep following the slope, we might hit a creek or something."

"Yeah. Or a bear."

A voice cut through the woods, calm and close. "I can get you out."

Relief started to flood through her. She spun.

A man stood fifteen feet away, his eyes too calculating, too cold, a pistol raised, his suit jacket flapping in the breeze.

Not Hans. Not Ortiz.

This guy was smaller, softer-looking. Corporate. Like someone who handled expense reports, not fieldwork.

But the gun was steady.

"You!" Dylan's gaze went to the gun. "What are you doing here?"

The man shrugged. "Stopping you from escaping."

"But I thought you were one of the good guys."

"Money can work magic." The man smiled without warmth. "Now move. To your right."

Lily stared at him. "Who *is* this?"

"His name's Conway, with the State Department or CIA. Who knows? He brought Kyle to see me in Hong Kong."

"Enough talking," Conway snapped. "Walk."

She looked at Dylan. Their eyes locked. She gave the faintest headshake, then widened her eyes. *Wait. Let me lead.*

He dipped an almost imperceptible nod.

She stumbled forward, pretending to trip over a root. Her foot twisted, and she dropped hard to one knee, gasping.

Conway shifted.

That was all Dylan needed.

He lunged, grabbed Conway's gun arm, and drove it up. A shot cracked through the canopy. Birds exploded from the branches.

Dylan slammed his elbow into the man's face. Lily surged upward and kicked, hard, into Conway's groin. He crumpled with a strangled grunt.

Dylan ripped the gun free and elbowed him again, this time across the jaw. Conway dropped.

Dylan stood over him, panting. "I'd say he's down for the count." He held up his hand. "High five?"

Lily slapped it. "Let's go."

She slung her backpack over one shoulder, just in time to hear a *kruntch* behind her. She froze.

Leaves rustled. Then something heavy and fast snapped.

"Ow!" she cried as an arm seized her from behind.

She barely had time to scream before steel wrapped around her throat and a cold barrel pressed to her temple.

"Drop it!" a familiar voice ordered.

Dylan turned, gun up, eyes wide.

Hans.

Lily didn't dare move. The metal dug into her skin. His arm crushed her windpipe just enough to keep her frozen.

"You know I won't hesitate," Hans growled. "I'm sure there are other ways to decode whatever it is that needs decoding."

CHAPTER 63

TASK FORCE OFFICE, FLORIDA, USA

SIMON

"What? You can't be serious!" Simon's voice thundered from the dash.

Olivia didn't slow down. She weaved through midday traffic like the brake pedal was optional. The moment she'd stepped out of the prison, the plan had begun forming, bold, reckless, but airtight if executed properly.

She'd called Jay on the drive. Told him everything. That the virus was out. That the Ghost had set her sights on Congressman Pearson. And that the only way to walk away from all of it, for good, was to kill Jade.

Jay hadn't hesitated. "If you want out, this is your moment. But it has to look real. You ready for that?"

She was.

Now, she pulled into the nondescript lot and strode to the door. The hard part wasn't staging her death. It was getting Ron and Ana to go along with it.

She burst into the task force squad room, breath short but eyes clear.

"I hope you weren't serious earlier on the phone." Ron faced her, coffee in hand.

"I was. This is the only way."

Ana sidled up. "So, you want us to kill your legend? Publicly?"

"Yes." Olivia crossed her arms and notched up her chin. "Jade dies today."

"And your handler, or whoever you report to, okayed this?" Ron asked.

"He knows I'm out."

Ron looked at Ana, who shrugged, then back at Olivia. "Guess you'll let us know how we're supposed to kill you."

"Thank you!" Olivia then found Simon and led him down the hall, around the corner under a stairwell where they wouldn't be overheard. The fluorescent light buzzed above them.

"I want out, Simon. You know that. I'm done with the code names and the lies. But I can't just disappear. Not while the Ghost still thinks Jade's working for her."

He wiped a hand over his face. "You think this'll work?"

"It has to. We let the Ghost believe Jade went rogue. That she tried to take out the congressman in some twisted show of loyalty to King. Jade dies. I disappear. No blowback."

"So, what's the plan?"

"They're going to talk to Pearson. He'll lawyer up fast. I'm counting on it. Then Jade shows up. Instead of delivering a message from the Ghost, she tries to kill him. But Ron and Ana intervene just in time. They put her down."

"Dramatic."

"It has to be. Word gets back to the Ghost that Jade is dead. That she died trying to avenge King. A loose cannon. A tragic end. But I walk away clean."

He rubbed his jaw, his eyes closed. When he reopened them, his expression remained unreadable. "Are Ron and Ana on board?"

"All's ready." She rested her hand against his chest. "When Jade is gone, I'll be free."

He lowered his hand to cover hers, squeezed it. "Then we'd better make it convincing. Because if the Ghost doesn't believe it…"

KYLE

Kyle hated waiting.

He hated it more when he was injured and sidelined, left to play tour guide. His leg still throbbed with every step, a reminder of how far he was from 100 percent. And now that they didn't need him for the exchange, he was benched. Again.

He opened a door to yet another nondescript hallway and gestured for Tommy to follow.

"This is it?" Tommy rolled his eyes. "You guys are committed to the whole secret-government-bunker vibe, huh?"

Kyle gave a humorless smile. "Security protocol. This office isn't in a federal building, and it's supposed to stay anonymous."

"I figured as much. They blindfolded me in the car. I didn't even know we were here until they pulled it off."

Kyle shrugged. "Standard procedure."

He didn't bother apologizing. Tommy didn't need reassurance. He needed answers. And Kyle needed to feel useful again.

The elevator dinged. Deanna stepped out, balancing a tablet and two iced coffees.

"Good, you're here," she said, then caught sight of Tommy. "Oh. We have a visitor."

Kyle made the introductions. Tommy was respectful, eager but sharp.

"I sent the call history over to your dad earlier, Kyle." She tapped the tablet.

"Thank you, ma'am." He didn't need to look at it. He already remembered. One of those calls had gone to Congressman Pearson.

Tommy piped up. "Dylan said he texted me a map, but I haven't gotten it. Think you could, I don't know, retrieve something from cyberspace?"

"Legally?" Deanna quirked an eyebrow. "That would be a no, unless you want me to risk a subpoena."

"Just thought I'd ask."

But something clicked. Kyle held up a hand. "The map reminded me—didn't you ping Dylan's phone?"

"Dylan, yes. Not Lily."

"That's right. Olivia gave us the tower data. Cell signal hit near the Beachline Expressway… right around Tosohatchee."

"Protected land. Not much out there."

"But a few scattered cabins," Kyle added. It was thin, but it was something. He gripped Tommy's shoulder. "You want to do some research?"

Tommy's slouched posture straightened, his height gaining a lost inch or more. "What kind of research? Will it help find them?"

"I hope so." Kyle didn't wait for more questions. "We'll start with property records. Cabins near that ping zone. It's slow work, but it's legal, and you can help."

They thanked Deanna and made their way to an empty bullpen with two open desks and aging government-issue computers.

Kyle signed in and opened the property search databases. Tommy sat beside him, eager but visibly overwhelmed.

Thirty minutes in, Kyle's eyes were starting to glaze over when Tommy blurted, "Hey, see this!"

He shoved his phone toward Kyle.

A news alert was glowing on the screen.

Just in: Mysterious Illness

Two Ohio residents have been hospitalized with a mysterious illness, and health officials have no clue yet about the cause. The affected individuals are being closely monitored, and investigations are ongoing. #Ohio #mysteriousillness #healthconcerns

Kyle's stomach dropped. Another alert chimed in.

Update: Mysterious Illness

Two other Ohio residents have been found exhibiting similar symptoms to the two individuals who were hospitalized with a mysterious illness. Local health officials are urging residents to report any symptoms or potential sources of exposure as investigations continue. #Ohio #mysteriousillness #healthalert

"Let's get to work." Kyle handed the phone back to Tommy. They were running out of time.

CHAPTER 64

THE PEARSON RESIDENCE, FLORIDA, USA

OLIVIA/PHOENIX

Olivia adjusted the synthetic skin at her jawline and leaned into the mirror. Almost perfect. But from the wrong angle, under the wrong light, even the best disguise could fail.

Ana gaped. "Wow! That's amazing. Does it hurt?"

"You get used to it." Olivia didn't elaborate. *You also get used to silence. Secrets. And longing for a man you can't have.*

They'd reviewed the plan three times that morning. She drove the rental under Jade's name. Ron and Ana followed in his car, hanging back a block. The rest of the team, if needed, would descend fast and loud.

They'd timed it well. Mrs. Pearson was at the salon. The kids were at school. The congressman was home, alone.

As Olivia climbed the front steps, her nerves quieted. Jade was stepping into the role now, cool, lethal, untouchable.

The doorbell camera blinked. Good. Let him see her.

Then the door opened—the congressman himself?

"What took you so long?" Congressman Pearson didn't hesitate. Dressed in joggers and a half-zipped fleece, he looked more like a suburban dad than a corrupt politician. His tone was annoyed, not cautious. No sign of Hans. Odd.

"Excuse me?"

"My wife called the maid service an hour ago. You're late."

Hope you're paying attention and cancel the maid, Ron! She stepped forward. "I think you've mistaken me for someone else."

He scanned her again, frowning. "You're not from the maid service?"

Hardly dressed like a housekeeper, but undercover work made you versatile. "No. I'm here on the Ghost's behalf."

He froze.

Then glanced over her shoulder, toward the street, right away. The door slammed shut.

"What are you doing here? That's not protocol."

"She wants you to visit her."

His eyes narrowed. "She's in federal custody. How would you even—"

"I have my ways."

He stepped back. "Why would she want me to visit?"

"I believe you already know." Her gloved hand gripped the pistol in her coat pocket. "Did you know she and King were involved?"

His retreat was automatic. "No. So?"

"You know now. Your bodyguard murdered him. The Ghost knows it was on your orders."

His skin went sheet white. "I–I don't know what you're talking about. You need to leave."

Why so rattled? If he was planning to seize power, he shouldn't be showing fear. She filed that reaction away for later.

"Hans Wagner. Ring a bell?"

"What about him?"

"We can call him. If he says it was all a mistake, I'll report that."

"He's not here right now."

"You can call him."

"He… can't be reached."

"Few places a cell phone can't reach." She stared him down. "Call him!"

"You don't understand." A beat later, something shifted in his expression, and he stiffened. "You should go now."

She pulled the pistol with smooth precision and leveled it at his chest. "What should I tell the Ghost?"

His mouth opened, but no words came. Only a soft wheeze.

Then a knock on the door. Moments later, the doorbell.

His gaze darted toward the sound. That was all she needed.

She fired, just to the left of his head. Missed on purpose.

The door exploded inward.

"Federal agents!" Ron shouted, storming in.

Ana followed, both weapons drawn.

"She's trying to kill me!" Pearson ducked behind an armchair.

"Drop your weapon!" Ron commanded.

Olivia didn't move. Her feet stayed planted, gun still aimed, off to the side now, shaky.

"This is for King," she hollered. Her voice shook just enough to sound unhinged. She aimed her gun.

"Don't do it!" Ron and Ana shouted in unison.

Then came the shot.

Not hers.

Pain burst through her lower back, off-center. A hot punch. Controlled, but real enough.

Her legs gave out, the floor tilting beneath her.

She went down hard, gun clattering from her grip, vision tunneling fast.

Then darkness swallowed her whole.

⁕

RON

Ron had seen a lot of performances in his career, fake grief, fake innocence, but watching a man lie while shaking with real fear? That took talent.

"Are you sure you don't want the paramedics to check your vitals?" he asked.

Congressman Pearson sat at the dining room table, a white-knuckled grip on his tumbler of water. The scene had shifted, Crime Scene Unit now dusting the entryway, the ME team long gone, the "body" already transported. All of it precise. Professional.

And fake.

None of these people were the actual ME or CSU. For all Ron knew, they were contractors, trained to play the part. Olivia managed the arrangements with her handler.

He'd wanted to argue jurisdiction. Remind her the CIA had no business operating domestically. But word from upstairs was clear: Cooperate.

"I'm fine." Pearson's voice wavered. "Shaken, is all. She was —delusional."

Ana, seated across from him, didn't blink. "Can you tell us what happened? She mentioned King. Said something about avenging him for the Ghost. Any idea what she meant?"

Pearson's jaw twitched. "No. Like I said, she wasn't right in the head." Hands on the tabletop, he pushed back and stood. "If we're done here, I need to call my wife."

Ron rose too. "You can call her from our office."

Pearson hesitated. "Your office?"

"We came to invite you in for a chat."

He flattened his hands on the table, leaning over them. "What's this about?"

"We'd rather discuss it there." Ana gestured for him to move.

"No," he snapped. "You tell me now."

"All right." Ron shrugged. "It's about the deaths of retired Senator Roger Rifkin, his housekeeper, Rosa Torres, and his aide, Harrison Burke."

Pearson paled. "I'm not talking without counsel."

"Of course. You can call your attorney from the office."

What Ron didn't say was only vetted attorneys were allowed inside the task force building. And the net was closing.

CHAPTER 65

TASK FORCE OFFICE, FLORIDA, USA

OLIVIA/PHOENIX

When Olivia came to, the cool sting of antiseptic bit into her senses, and her body rocked with the faint sway of a vehicle in motion. She was in the ME's van, lying on a stretcher. Had they gone off script?

But then she saw the paramedic's familiar face, the real one, not part of the illusion.

It had gone as planned.

The dart she'd jabbed into her leg had knocked her out seconds after the gunfire. The impact packs had burst on cue when the dummy rounds struck, selling the hit. To any observer, including the congressman, it had been a clean kill.

The "medical examiner" had insisted on checking her vitals, just in case. Professional to the end. Apparently, even fake corpses needed real clearance.

Almost an hour later, out of the wig, mask, and blood-soaked blouse, Olivia had become herself again. Jade Lam was dead, mourned only by the media and, eventually, the Ghost.

The photos would leak soon. The press would devour them.

A Chinese woman gunned down after a violent break-in, caught on a doorbell cam. A public tragedy. A private message.

Inside the task force observation room, Simon was waiting. He didn't ask how she felt.

"I heard it went according to plan." He gestured toward the glass.

"It did." Olivia stepped beside him. "Has he said anything?"

"Nothing useful."

Beyond the one-way mirror, Congressman Pearson sat hunched beside his attorney in the interrogation room. Across from them, Ron and Ana held the high ground.

"Something's off." Olivia crossed her arms. "He was terrified. If he wanted to seize control of the Ghost's network, why be scared of Jade?"

Simon nodded. "Ana mentioned it. Let's see what shakes loose."

They stood shoulder to shoulder, listening.

"We need to talk to Hans Wagner. Where can we find him?" Ron asked.

"I don't know," Pearson focused on his hands.

"Try again." Ron flipped the folder open, turning a set of photos and phone records toward them. "Hans Wagner leaving Harrison Burke's house. Satellite phone logs. You'll recognize the highlighted numbers."

"If you have his number, you don't need my client," the attorney said.

Ron didn't blink. He dropped another page on the table. "Bank transfers. Fifty thousand dollars, routed through layers of accounts, traced back to Wagner. Want to explain that?"

The congressman faltered. His lawyer leaned in, whispered something. A beat passed.

The attorney said, "What would you offer if my client shared pertinent information?"

"That depends," Ron replied. "What kind of information?"

"I don't know where Wagner is now. I swear. But I had no choice," Pearson said.

Ron waited.

The attorney stepped in again. "He and his family would need protection. And an understanding about possible charges."

"We'll notify the US Attorney," Ana said. "If your intel leads to Wagner's arrest, we'll put in a good word. As for protection, we can arrange that. But why do you need protection?"

Pearson rubbed his face, his composure cracking. "Because they'll kill me. My family too. I didn't have a choice."

"Who's 'they'?" Ana asked.

"The Chinese. I think. I don't know if it was the government or the triads. Two guys in suits showed up. IDs, but I didn't catch what they said."

Simon exhaled beside her. Olivia stiffened. That tracked with Lily's statement, Mandarin speakers posing as federal agents.

"Blackmail?" Ron asked.

Pearson's head drooped in a nod. "Photos. Escorts. They said they'd leak everything."

Behind the glass, Simon whispered to Olivia, "He's up for reelection."

"And in exchange?" Ana asked. "Kill Rifkin? Harrison?"

"No! They wanted something from a girl. I didn't know who at first. Turned out Rifkin's men had her. Wagner was supposed to retrieve her, find out what she had. I had no idea he was going to kill them."

"So you didn't order the hits, but you knew who committed the crime—"

"Only after the fact," his attorney interjected.

"But you didn't report it."

Pearson looked down. Guilty silence.

"What was the plan once Wagner had the girl?" Ana asked.

"He was supposed to grab the item, whatever she's holding,

and drop both off at a pickup point. I don't know where. He didn't tell me."

"What did he say during your last conversation?"

"He said the plan had changed."

"Changed how?" Ron pressed.

Pearson hesitated. His lawyer nodded.

"I think Wagner is working for the Chinese too. Playing both sides."

Ron frowned. "What did he say?"

"He said he'd have the money and the item ready. Said he'd leave the girl in a secure place. That someone would pick her up."

"Someone Chinese?"

Pearson shrugged. "He didn't say."

"Where's the ransom money supposed to go?"

"I don't know. Wagner picks it up. Leaves it with the girl."

Ana leaned back. "You trust him that much?"

"He handles that kind of thing. I'm not… built for this."

"He doesn't tell you where the girl is?"

"No."

On the other side of the glass, Olivia widened her stance, rubbed at the pulse racing in her temples. "He doesn't know about Dylan. Something's still off."

"Think the exchange is still on?"

"Oh, definitely. But Wagner doesn't plan on splitting the prize."

So who was Wagner really working for? It sure wasn't Pearson.

And it sure wasn't over.

CHAPTER 66

UNIDENTIFIED HOUSE, FLORIDA, USA

LILY

The blindfold was gone, but the panic hadn't left.

Lily sat on the damp cellar's cold floor, wrists sore from the zip ties. The air smelled like mildew and old wood, thick with the kind of silence that warped time. How long had they been down here? Long enough for her shoulders to ache and her legs to go numb.

Conway, the traitor spy who'd pretended to help them by suggesting he could get them out, slouched in a chair a few feet away, glaring at her every so often and muttering curses under his breath. He was still mad she'd kicked him in the face. Good.

Hans had vanished, leaving Conway to babysit. He kept trying to get a signal on his phone, only to curse when it failed to connect. Then he stood and stomped up the stairs.

"Do I need to stay down here with them?" he shouted through the door. "They're not going anywhere!"

No answer.

"Hey, Hans!" he yelled again, louder.

Then came a single, terrible thud.

Lily flinched as Conway's body hit the stairs, once, twice, three times, before landing in a heap at the bottom. His limbs were twisted unnaturally. Something wet glistened beneath his head. A muted pop echoed faintly in her ears.

Her brain stalled.

"What…?" she whispered.

"Don't look!"

But she was already staring. The red pool. The stillness. And then her mind caught up, a gunshot.

Her scream broke loose before she could stop it.

Breath hitched. Chest tight. She was hyperventilating.

"Lily. Lily. Look at me!" Dylan's voice broke through.

She turned to him, gulping for air.

"Breathe in. Breathe out. That's right. Keep going."

Above them, Hans's voice filtered down. "Ciao! Nice chatting with you. Thanks to you, I'll be two million richer. Oh, and by the way, it's started. People are getting sick. Might not even need you."

His laughter followed, fading as the lock clicked into place.

Panic surged again. "He locked us in with a dead body! And people are dying!"

"Lily, breathe."

"How are you so calm?" she cried. "We're tied up. No phone. No signal. How are we going to get out?"

She couldn't stop the tears. Her nose was running. She couldn't even wipe her face. "I thought this was some great adventure. I left Hong Kong. I thought I was finally free. And now, I'm going to *die* here."

"This isn't the first time I've faced death." Dylan's voice was steady. "And I promised myself, if it happened again, I wouldn't be helpless."

He shifted his bound hands. "You are *not* going to die here. Not today. Your dad is a US senator. Your mom? Superspy. They *will* find you."

"They don't even know me," she whispered.

"They *do*. Your dad's probably moved heaven and earth by now. And your mom? I guarantee she's breaking all kinds of laws to track you down."

He gave her a crooked smile. "Besides, don't forget the agents. Kyle, his dad, the whole task force. They're not giving up."

She sniffled. "You think… they'll find us?"

"Of course. I never told you, but… I have a powerful family too. Not senator powerful, but old-school powerful. By now, my grandmother must know I'm missing. And trust me, she still has friends in places that matter. She'll call in every favor she's got."

"You said she was rich. How would that make her powerful?"

"She is rich. It's complicated. Long story."

"Well…" Lily wiped her cheek against her shoulder. "We've got nothing but time."

Dylan didn't answer. He looked focused now, shifting his shoulders. Then his hands slung free.

Her eyes widened. "How'd you do that?"

He grinned, holding up a small pocketknife. "Took forever to work it loose. Didn't want to try it with Hans around."

He stood, rubbing his wrists, then leaned down to cut her ties. "There. Better?"

She got up, rubbing her wrists. "Thanks. When did you even hide that?"

"Secret pocket. I've had it this whole time."

She glanced at the top of the stairs. "Hans wouldn't leave the door unlocked, would he?"

"Let's find out." He crept up the stairs and tested the door. It didn't budge. Then he scanned the side of the door. "Good, the hinges are on our side."

Then he knelt, flipped open the knife's screwdriver attachment, and began working the hinges. "It's not ideal, but I've seen worse."

Her heartbeat steadied. There was something in his calm... something she wanted to believe in.

"What Hans said... about people getting sick. What did he mean?" Dylan asked without looking back.

She hesitated. "It has something to do with what my mother gave me. I'm not sure what it is. But someone thinks it matters."

He paused, then nodded. "Moms and secrets. Mine kept the family legacy hidden for years. And the truth about something buried deep on our estate."

"Seriously?"

"Dead serious. I got out of that jam. We'll get out of this one too. Like Fr. Phil says, have faith."

"That's what my godmother says. I can hear her voice now. 'Trust the Lord. Have faith.'"

"Too bad Fr. Phil's a priest. We could set them up."

She laughed through her tears. "For your information, she's a nun. Sr. Marie Ramos."

"Well, there goes that match."

He gave the screwdriver attachment a final twist. "Let's have faith that this sucker... comes... off—"

Phop.

The top hinge pin popped loose, clinking onto the stair tread.

One hinge pin down. One to go. And maybe, just maybe, one way out.

Friday, 12:30 p.m.

CHAPTER 67

GARAGE, FLORIDA, USA

OLIVIA/PHOENIX

Olivia adjusted the comm in her ear and crouched low behind the elevator structure on the parking garage's south side. Level 4. Wide open. Minimal cover. Perfect for a controlled exchange and a clean shot, if needed.

She scanned the concrete expanse one last time.

No civilians. No movement. No mistakes.

Everyone was in position.

Hans Wagner had said "no cops," which meant Simon was walking into the exchange alone, vested, but still a target. The duffel bags were packed with cash, the flash drive loaded with decoy data.

Their agents were in position, two levels above, one level below, others in unmarked vehicles circling the perimeter. Ron had the area scouted and cleared hours ago. They were invisible.

"Phoenix, this must be important," a familiar voice came through in her earpiece.

She smiled. Shadow Shot. Always the same dry wit.

"It is," she whispered. "Thank you for coming."

"Of course. You knew I'd come. He's your Prince Charming, isn't he?"

She ignored the bait. Shadow Shot was the only person outside the Agency who had ever seen her face and the only one who'd never told a soul. Loyalty like that was rare.

"Target should be here any second. Do you have a visual?"

"Affirmative. East side only."

He was watching from the rooftop across the street, using the exposed gap between garage levels to track movement.

"Wound, not kill," she said.

"Copy that."

The garage was nearly empty. Two dusty sedans sat near the far wall, probably abandoned weeks ago. She'd already swept them. Nothing unusual.

A blue work truck rumbled up the ramp and parked by the exit. Wagner.

Simon arrived thirty seconds later in a black SUV, pulling up and stopping at a calculated distance. He stepped out, hands loose at his sides. Calm. Composed.

The two men met in the open.

Wagner looked different. The beard was gone. Hair bleached blond. Likely color contacts too. But Olivia didn't need facial recognition to spot the tension in his shoulders, the nervous energy. He wasn't here to play by the rules.

"That's far enough," Wagner called out, gun holstered, but hand near it.

"I don't see Lily," Simon said. They'd agreed, mention only Lily.

"You give me the money and the drive, and I'll let you know where to find her. She's secured."

"I need proof of life."

Wagner tapped his phone and turned the screen around. Through Simon's button cam, Olivia saw the image. Basement.

Concrete walls. A red smear of blood. A body—not Dylan or Lily. Two figures at the top of the staircase, just shoes visible.

"That doesn't prove anything," Simon said. "Where's her face? Where's the timestamp?"

"Blame them for cutting the restraints," Wagner snapped. "Now, enough. Slide the bags."

Simon did.

Wagner crouched, unzipped the bags, and examined the contents. Cash. Drive.

Then he drew a weapon.

"Now!" Olivia ordered.

Wagner's shoulder snapped back. Then his head jerked, and he crumpled to the ground.

Her stomach dropped. She sprinted toward Simon, yanked him toward the elevator shaft, all the while assessing angles, scanning the rooftops. Something wasn't right.

"Wasn't me," Shadow Shot said in her ear. "I hit his shoulder. Wound only. As you requested."

"I know."

Ron's voice came through on the comms. "Olivia, secure Simon. I saw movement in a building across the street. We may still have time to intercept."

"Already done!" Then to Simon, "You okay?"

"I'm fine. But what happened? I'm pretty sure his shoulder was hit first, then his head. Did the assassin miss?"

She hadn't told Simon about her plan. "I'm not sure. Stay here."

She darted back toward Wagner's body.

The shoulder wound, entry on the right, clean exit. The forehead shot was deeper, more forceful. Different angle. Different caliber.

A professional kill. Executed before Wagner could talk.

Their only lead—dead before they could ask a single question.

⟡

RON

Ron watched the footage from Simon's button cam. Everything had looked controlled. Until Hans Wagner reached for his gun.

As soon as he hollered for Olivia to secure Simon, he and Ana scanned the surrounding buildings. The sunlight was brutal, washing everything out, but Ron caught a flicker of movement across the street.

"There." Ana pointed to the same spot.

Exactly where he would've picked. The building was under heavy renovation. Multiple access points. Little oversight.

"Tanner, secure the scene," Ron ordered into his comm. Then he and Ana took off running.

They flashed their badges as they entered the building's lobby. The entire first floor had been stripped down to steel beams and dust. The air reeked of sawdust and varnish. Nail guns and hammers pounded away in the background.

Ron raised his voice over the noise. "Anyone see someone come down recently?"

A few hard-hatted workers shook their heads. "Just us."

"Is this the only way up?" He gestured to the stairs nearby.

"There's the elevator too," one of them offered.

"Shut it down," Ana ordered.

The foreman scowled. "We got guys up there, ten floors. You serious?"

"Now."

Grumbling, he waved at another worker to kill the power.

Ron was already bounding up the stairs. Ana stayed close behind.

At the fourth floor, they heard a voice.

"Coming through!" A man in dusty overalls came down,

hauling a toolbox and a couple of two-by-fours. His hair was messy, eyes shadowed with sweat.

Ana leaned aside to let him pass.

He grumbled along. "Why does the elevator have to stop working now?"

They kept climbing. Another floor, they heard swearing and screaming.

Ron reached the landing first. Two workers stood there, one with a cigarette, the other doubled over, vomiting behind a stack of plywood.

The body was in front of them. Caucasian male, maybe mid-thirties, jeans and a plain T-shirt, sprawled on his back with a knife jutting from his chest. Next to him, a long case.

Ron pulled out his phone. "We've got a body. Male, unknown. Requesting CSU and ME."

Ana stepped up. "Did either of you touch anything?"

"Are you kidding? No!"

While Ana questioned them, Ron snapped on gloves and crouched beside the body. No ID. No wallet. But the man wore gloves, thin, tactical. And the case…

He flipped it open. Inside, a custom sniper rifle. Scoped. Precision-grade.

"Could be our shooter."

Ana returned. "They said they were on break. One guy hit the bathroom. The other stepped out for a smoke. Heard a noise, but figured it was just construction."

Ron stood. "So far, it fits. Gloves, long-range rifle. No ID. No one saw him enter."

"But who stabbed him?"

"That's the part I'm wondering about."

She crouched by the spent casing again. "You know, I swear Wagner was hit in the shoulder first. Then he dropped like a rock with that head shot."

"Same impression here. But if this guy was a pro, he

wouldn't have aimed for the shoulder first. He'd have gone straight for a double tap to center mass or head for a clean kill. We need to watch the video again, slow it down frame by frame. If Wagner was hit twice, that means two shooters."

She hopped to her feet. "One's on the floor here. But what if he's not the one who took the kill shot?"

"Then the one who did is still out there."

They stood over the body in silence.

Ana crossed her arms. "Lots of good questions."

Blood gleamed, pooling beneath the body.

"Now we just need answers." He looked toward the stairwell. "Let's start by finding out who this guy is."

"And while we're at it"—Ana slid her arms free—"maybe it's time we dug deeper into Hans Wagner's life."

OLIVIA/PHOENIX

Sirens echoed in the distance as Olivia stood beyond the crime-scene tape, the stench of gunpowder still clinging to the air. Her pulse was steady now, battle rhythm restored, but her thoughts moved fast.

She didn't like loose ends. And Hans Wagner was supposed to be their linchpin.

Then came the voice in her earpiece, smooth and wry. "Phoenix, I found the other sniper's nest."

Her eyes narrowed. "Get out of there. Agents are heading over."

"I know."

There was a grunt, faint scuffling, a breath caught through gritted teeth.

Then: "Coming through."

Her brow furrowed. "Who are you talking to?"

"Why does the elevator have to stop working now?"

She blinked, then understood. He was in disguise. Moving right under their noses.

"Okay, I found his nest," he said. "While I wasn't paying attention, he got the drop on me. There was a minor fight. I used his knife on him. You'll hear about it."

Her chest tightened. "Are you okay?"

"Good enough. A few bruises and cuts. Thankfully, the overalls hide them."

She exhaled, tension bleeding off her shoulders. "Jay isn't gonna be happy."

The Company "didn't" operate stateside. Shadow Shot existed in the shadows—off the books, off the radar. If his identity was ever exposed, no agency would claim him. Jay and his high-level friends would bury the story so deep it'd never resurface.

"He'll get over it."

"You take care now. Thanks again."

"One more thing. If he's who I think, he is, or was, a freelance contractor. Worked for the highest bidder. But he did a few jobs for the BND."

The name hit hard. Bundesnachrichtendienst. Germany's version of the CIA. More ghosts.

"Seriously?"

"Simply passing on some info. Shadow Shot out."

The line went quiet.

Olivia remained crouched, replaying his words. A dead freelancer. German connections. Possibly Chinese blackmail. And now a secondary shooter, also dead.

This wasn't just a rogue operation.

She jogged back toward the elevator shaft where Simon stood scanning the garage as if half-expecting Hans to rise from the ground.

"What do we do now?" he asked. "He was our only lead."

She didn't answer, just motioned for him to follow.

They had to move before local law enforcement tried to drag them into official reports.

She knelt by Wagner's body, snapped on a fresh pair of gloves, and retrieved his phone. The screen was cracked, splattered in blood, but still pulsing.

"Deanna might be able to pull something out." If there was anything left to find. She slipped the phone into her coat.

Simon nodded, but his focus was on Wagner. "This just got bigger, didn't it?"

Olivia didn't respond.

She didn't need to.

CHAPTER 68

TASK FORCE OFFICE, FLORIDA, USA

KYLE

Hans Wagner was dead? Kyle's stomach dropped.

Their only solid lead to Lily gone in a flash?

He sat frozen in the task force's operations room before forcing himself to move. If they couldn't follow the man, they'd follow the money.

And hope it led somewhere fast.

Deanna had Wagner's phone. If she could get anything from it, coordinates, messages, cached maps, it might be the break they needed.

In the meantime, Kyle focused on what he could control and dug through Rifkin's financials with Tommy.

"I haven't seen anything yet." Tommy scrolled through data on one of the laptops Kyle had set up for him.

"Me neither." Kyle's eyes stung from staring at screens, but he wasn't quitting.

"Kyle, did you see this?" Tommy pointed at an old federal tax return on the screen.

"Rifkin's?"

"Yeah. Take a look at the Schedule C, business income."

"I didn't even realize he had a business." Kyle leaned in. "I skimmed the form but didn't really know what half of it meant."

Tommy clicked through to another document. "It's a one-person LLC. According to this, the IRS treats it as a pass-through entity."

"Sorry." Kyle raised a hand. "You lost me at 'pass-through.' Bottom line, please."

Tommy smirked. "He inherited a property from his mother. Then sold it to his shell company, Round Tree LLC. That's why it didn't show up under his name in property records."

Kyle straightened. "Wait. Round Tree? That's it."

He pulled up the property database and began scrolling. "Here it is. Good work. You're not a CPA for nothing."

"Glad to be useful. Let me take a peek at Pearson's taxes."

Kyle let him work. Minutes ticked by.

"He has two properties," Tommy said.

"I didn't see that in the database."

"Yeah. He pays taxes on one listed under his own name. The other's listed under someone named Debbie Wilcox."

Kyle's eyes narrowed. "Who's she?"

"No idea. That's your lane. But here's the address."

Kyle searched the property records using the address. He ran a reverse lookup on the name and cross-referenced it with Pearson's wife.

"She's his mother-in-law. Her name changed when she remarried. Wilcox is her new husband's name."

Tommy raised an eyebrow. "So why is he paying *her* property taxes?"

Kyle clicked through several linked records. "Because she's dead. Cancer. Died two years ago."

"If his wife inherited it, the deduction makes sense. But the title should've transferred to her or both of them."

"My guess? He didn't want anyone to know they still had

that property. That's good work. You ever get tired of being Dylan's sidekick, I bet the Bureau would love to have you."

Tommy laughed. "Thanks, but no thanks. I don't get paid for being Dylan's sidekick. I get paid for doing my job. Besides, I doubt the Bureau can beat what they pay me."

"You got me there."

Time to tell Dad what they'd found.

OLIVIA/PHOENIX

The elevator doors opened, and Olivia stepped into the task force office, Ron and Ana just behind her. The fluorescent lights felt harsh after the chaos of the garage. Shadow Shot's bullet had been clean. Precise. But that second shot, the one no one planned, derailed everything.

Ron already grilled her about the sniper fire. She kept her answers clipped and factual. What else could she say? She couldn't tell him about Shadow Shot.

Her phone vibrated in her pocket. A secure line.

She turned away from the others, stepping into one of the glass-walled offices. Door closed. Head down. Earpiece in. After she went through the authentication process, the click to connect came. "Finally."

She'd been trying to reach Jay since Wagner hit the ground.

"Why do you always make me clean up your mess?" came the dry response.

"I didn't make the mess. Did Shadow Shot check in?"

"Yes. Now I have to go play politician again. Something I loathe."

"Did he tell you who he thought the guy was?"

"Not by name, but yes. Curious."

She about-faced to the window, scanning the bullpen. "What are you thinking?"

"If I were you, I'd investigate your target's history. If, and it's a big if, he was hired by the BND, I can only think of one reason."

It took her a beat to register what he was saying. "A spy? Seriously? Wagner was wanted by just about everybody. Why would they use him?"

Jay's voice didn't flinch. "What if, and again, big if, he'd done wet work for the BND? You think they'd want *us* to know about it? Especially if it involved Americans?"

She paced, the pieces shifting in her head. "How would they know about the exchange?"

"Maybe they were already suspicious. Had eyes on him. Either way, I need to go smooth some feathers."

"Ciao." She ended the call and walked back out to the squad room.

"Update." Ron tapped a button on the wall monitor. "We went frame by frame. Wagner was shot in the shoulder first. Then a second bullet, clean through the forehead."

"Two shooters," Ana confirmed, checking her phone. "The one we found—ID just came in. His prints match a Logan Sullivan. Multiple aliases."

"The question is who killed him. We got there minutes after the hit. No one saw anything. The construction crew didn't spot anyone leaving. My guess? Our other shooter—the one who wounded Wagner—may have killed him. Deanna should be able to confirm if Sullivan fired the kill shot."

Simon spoke up. "So let me get this straight, two shooters. One intended to wound—the other killed Wagner. One is dead— the other's gone."

"Correct. From what I saw, the rifle beside Sullivan likely fired the kill shot. My working theory? He killed Wagner. And someone else killed him."

"Why shoot to wound?"

Ron glanced at Olivia. "I suppose the goal would've been to capture."

She didn't blink. Years of tradecraft had taught her to wear her face like armor. Jay was already dealing with the fallout. No way she was blowing Shadow Shot's cover now.

Ana cut through the tension. "Why don't we move on? Time's a-wasting."

Ron's phone rang as Kyle rushed in, breathless, tablet in hand.

"What do you have?" Ana asked.

"Tommy found it." Kyle tapped and sent files to the wall monitor. "Property 1: Rifkin's shell company. It's in Tosohatchee and matches the last-known cell signal. Property 2: owned by Pearson's deceased mother-in-law. Still in the vicinity. For some reason, he's paying the taxes on that place."

"We need to question Pearson again," Ana said.

Ron ended his call. "I heard. He's holding back. Hernandez, bring him in again. Kyle, you and Hernandez question him when he's here. And give me that address."

Kyle clicked, and the address popped up on the screen adjacent to the pin.

"That tracks." Ron pocketed his phone. "I just got a call from the hospital. Paramedics dropped off a GSW victim earlier. Someone pinned a note to his jacket. Took the ER staff a while to alert us."

"Who is it?" Ana asked.

"No ID at first, but here's the note." He pulled up a photo on his phone and zoomed in. "It says, 'Call FBI Task Force Agent Ron Peters. Find Dylan Roche. Check here.' Includes a crude map."

Kyle stepped forward. "That location is right near one of the properties we flagged."

Olivia's pulse jumped. It was happening. Something was cracking open.

Beside her, Simon's posture shifted. The quiet heaviness in his eyes—gone. There was hope again.

"Let's go," he said.

The office phone rang. Ana picked it up.

"Let's put the map up and do a satellite recon," Ron said.

Ana covered the receiver. "Ron—it's FDLE. SSA Cole."

Ron frowned and took the call. The rest of them studied the map while Ana highlighted possible access roads.

When Ron hung up, he didn't waste words. "The GSW victim is FDLE Special Agent Dante Ortiz. He was undercover, working a case tied to Rifkin. He tried to rescue Dylan and Lily."

"Who shot him?" Olivia asked.

"He's in and out of consciousness, but Cole got the basics. Ortiz got them out, but Wagner caught up. Ortiz was shot and told them to run."

"Has the area been raided?"

"Not yet. But according to Ortiz, Dylan's grandmother may have sent people. They didn't say who they worked for, just asked about Dylan."

Simon was already dialing.

Olivia turned to Ron. "I thought she was out of the game."

"She is. Technically, she was never *in* the game. She knows things because of her husband. And some old loyalties run deep."

Simon came back a few minutes later. "I spoke to Max and Ms. Carol. Neither gave orders, but both admit they asked around. Loyal contacts found Ortiz and another guy in a cabin. Dylan and Lily weren't there."

"Who was the other guy?" Ron asked.

"They don't know, but said he was drugged and now in police custody. But whoever these people are, they saved the agent's life."

The room's energy shifted. Focus. Motion. Purpose.

They gathered around the screen again. Olivia leaned in, highlighting Rifkin's and Pearson's properties. Not far apart. If Carol's people had already cleared the cabin, then Wagner might have moved the hostages.

Deanna burst in. "Ron, I've got Wagner's call history."

"Put it up."

Numbers populated the screen. "The highlighted ones are Pearson's," she said.

Ana squinted. "These area codes. They aren't domestic."

Olivia stepped closer. "Hong Kong and Shenzhen. Mainland China, just north of Hong Kong. And a few scrambled numbers… likely routed through VPNs."

"It still could be the Chinese," Ron said. "Maybe Pearson didn't lie about everything."

Or maybe he lied about the wrong things.

But now wasn't the time to unpack it.

"It doesn't matter. They already searched Rifkin's property and came up empty. Let's hit Pearson's place next."

"Makes sense," Ron agreed. "Let's move."

CHAPTER 69

ON THE ROAD, FLORIDA, USA

RAY HO

"In thirty minutes, we'll have the drive," Ray Ho said in accented Mandarin, his voice calm and deliberate. "Our associates will secure the package soon after. You have everything ready? I want you to put the girl in the elite group. Keep the boy for me. I have another purpose for him."

Across from him in the back of the luxury town car, Zhou Yang's head bobbed, his legs twitching with nervous energy. His gaze kept flicking to the tinted window as if expecting police or worse.

The traffic around them moved smoothly, none of the chaos of Central Hong Kong. Wide lanes. Predictable patterns. The silence left too much space for fear.

Ray sipped from a porcelain cup resting in the armrest console, unbothered.

"Relax." He put the cup back down.

"If the Ministry finds out..." Zhou began.

"Then don't let them find out." Ray faced him. "You've been transferring our cargo for months. You're not new to this."

He let the silence stretch before continuing. "And if you were *that* concerned, perhaps you should've considered the consequences before you took the money. But you did. And now… you belong to me."

Zhou swallowed. "The Americans—"

"Have you forgotten your diplomatic immunity? Or shall I remind you again? You have cover. You just lack nerve."

"But if the Ministry finds out, that means—"

Ho's patience snapped. He jerked the door handle hard. "Enough whining. Do you have everything ready? I won't ask again."

Zhou stiffened. "Yes."

"Good. My courier will deliver the package to your hotel. You'll handle the girl, secure her transport with the elite shipment. There will be people waiting to receive her. As for the boy, leave him. He's mine. Simple."

"Yes."

The town car stopped. Outside, a hotel valet stood waiting. One of the chain's finer locations, neutral territory under heavy surveillance, but only where Ray wanted it to be.

He nodded toward the door. "Go."

Zhou slipped out without another word. The door shut, and the car pulled away again.

Ray sat back while the manicured skyline blurred past. His expression didn't change.

To some, he was a businessman. To others, a kingpin. A criminal in a tailored suit. He preferred the first label. It gave him flexibility. Respectability. A way to play in the open.

His permanent residence remained in Hong Kong, but for this—this inheritance—he'd made the trip himself. His usual entourage remained light, just a trusted driver, a loyal underling, and a bodyguard who didn't speak unless ordered.

"Has Larry checked in yet?" Ray glanced toward the man riding up front.

"No, boss."

Typical.

The hotel manager had long outlived his usefulness. That rat couldn't even keep a girl in place long enough for the auction to be arranged. Now, Ray had been forced to deploy professionals, *his* people, to clean up the mess.

Word had moved fast once the Ghost had been arrested.

The yakuza were circling, hoping to reclaim their Tokyo turf. And Ho, he felt the same urge. Hong Kong. Macau. Shenzhen. The whole of southern China. These belonged to him. For too long, he'd tolerated the Ghost claiming his society as her own.

That era was over.

She had been clever, yes. Ruthless. Well-connected. But her power had never come from strength. It came from secrets. And soon, he would hold those secrets. The girl. The drive. The leverage.

By tomorrow, the underworld would know there was a new Ghost.

And he didn't care about her legacy. Her alliances. Her warnings.

The girl? Just currency. Once the drive was decrypted, her only remaining value would be what she could fetch in a quiet bidding war.

And the boy?

He was blood.

Which meant leverage.

The throne was almost his. All that remained was one final exchange and the destruction of the Ghost's last piece of unfinished business.

CHAPTER 70

TASK FORCE OFFICE, FLORIDA, USA

OLIVIA/PHOENIX

Olivia double-checked the mags in her vest, snapped the last strap into place, and shut the trunk. The gear felt familiar. Heavy. Grounding. That was a good thing.

They had a plan. The team was set, the cavalry waiting.

Kyle had wanted to join them, but he had a job to do. Pearson would be in custody soon, and Kyle and Hernandez must get him to talk.

Simon, on the other hand, had insisted on going. She'd tried, twice, to talk him out of it, but he just looked her dead in the eye. "Don't ask me to sit this one out."

Now he stood behind her in the lot, hands in his jacket pockets, eyes scanning the team as they moved toward the vehicles.

Ron's phone rang. "It's Tanner." He answered. "Go."

A pause. His face tensed, then relaxed.

"Okay, listen, gear up. I'll text you the location. Meet us there."

He ended the call. "They're wrapping up. I told them to meet us at the site."

Simon followed the group out, but he was clearly chewing on something.

Olivia touched his arm. "Ride with me."

They got in her car. She started the engine. Simon stared out the windshield. The others deployed in separate vehicles.

"What's going on in that head of yours?"

He shifted, brows tight, lips drawn downward. "I'm thinking that I really don't like politics."

She snorted, despite herself. "You're a politician."

"Maybe I don't want to be one anymore." He let that hang. "Wagner was a wanted man. Globally. Intelligence agencies from three continents had open warrants. If Sullivan killed him, it's just as likely he was working for someone else. Anyone could've hired him."

"Then we'll chase that lead later. Right now, the mission is Lily. Focus."

They hit the highway. Lights flashing. Sirens muted. It was less than an hour out, but time thudded in her chest like a warning.

She didn't speak. She needed her concentration. Her instincts sharp.

But beside her, Simon clenched and unclenched his fist against his knee. "When that guy pulled his gun, I thought that was it. That I was done. And the only thing I could think about was you. And Lily. I almost never got the chance to meet my daughter. To… make up for everything. For all the time we lost."

Olivia gripped the wheel tighter.

For years, decades, she'd questioned everything. Giving up her baby. Living under aliases. Sacrificing her real name for shadows. She'd convinced herself it was necessary. But hearing him say that, so plain, so unguarded, it cracked something she didn't know was still fragile.

"Simon, I never would've let anything happen to you. You were never in danger. I had your back."

He tilted his head. Studied her. "Is there something you're not telling me?"

"There are a lot of things I *can't* tell you. Different clearance levels. You know that."

He raised a hand. "I'm not talking about classified ops. I'm talking about *you*. Did you arrange for that second shooter?"

She didn't answer. Didn't have to.

"You did." It was a statement. Not a question. "What did they train you to be? An assassin?"

She chuckled. "You watch too many spy movies."

"Then what?"

"They trained me to observe. To extract information. To disappear. I was deep cover for so long I forgot what it was like to speak plainly. It took years to earn Jay and Patty's trust. Then they did whatever they did to send me to the Farm."

"They had to fast-track your US citizenship before you could work for the Agency."

"Ask them how they made it happen. I followed the process. Just… at light speed."

She tapped the screen on the dash. The map blinked. "We're close."

Closer than she liked.

She reached for her comms unit. The team was already checking in. Weapons hot. Eyes open.

She gripped the steering wheel harder as the next turn came up fast. Simon hadn't said another word.

She just hoped—*prayed*—they weren't too late.

CHAPTER 71

UNIDENTIFIED HOUSE, FLORIDA, USA

LILY

The hinge wobbled. Almost there.

Lily pressed her palms flat against the cool stone wall, holding her breath as Dylan loosened the last screw. Dust swirled near the floor, and something metal pinged as it hit the cellar ground.

Please don't squeak. Please don't echo.

The old door inched open, just enough to let in a sliver of stale air. Dylan turned his head, eyes locking with hers. A single finger rose to his lips. Quiet.

Her heart thumped so hard he must hear it.

She hovered just behind him, tension coiled in her shoulders. They had no idea who or what might be waiting upstairs. But that didn't matter now. The stillness pressing down on her said it all. Either they moved now, or they stayed prisoners.

He threw the pin out the door. When no shot or people came, he eased the door aside and gestured for her to move. "It's clear."

They emerged from the cellar. She squinted upward, adjusting to the filtered light.

Not a cabin.

This was a house. A real one. Spacious. Upscale. Foreign.

And somehow more unsettling because of it.

As they crept into the open kitchen, she kept close to the wall. Polished appliances gleamed beneath a thin layer of dust. To her left, a low-lit living room with a massive television and deep-set brown couch. To the right, glass doors led out to a sunlit patio.

Her skin itched. Not from dirt or heat, but from uncertainty. From having no memory of how long they'd been underground. No sense of where they were. Hans had blindfolded them. Even without that, she wouldn't have recognized anything. Not this country. Not yet.

They searched. Dylan opened a door. "Garage. Three bays. No cars."

Lily peeked inside. Empty. Just oil stains on concrete.

"I don't see a phone," she said.

"Not surprised. Most people ditched landlines."

She started to reply, but froze. A sound.

Tires crunching. Then voices.

She pointed toward the driveway. Dylan nodded. A car.

They didn't wait. He tried the garage door again. It led outside. He cracked it open, scanned, then motioned.

They slipped into sunlight.

Hot. Blinding. The kind of sun that sucked the breath out of you.

She pulled her shirt from her skin. It clung, damp with sweat. Her lungs burned. Her legs trembled, but they ran anyway.

The sun stabbed at her eyes as she sprinted through gravel and overgrown weeds. A haze shimmered off the pavement ahead. No cover. No trees. Just wide-open American countryside and a single house in the distance.

Why did this place feel so empty? In Hong Kong, land like

this would be packed with towers. Homes stacked on homes. Here, it was like no one else existed.

"Head for the house?" she asked, chest heaving.

Dylan didn't stop moving. Just nodded.

She wiped sweat from her forehead and pushed herself harder. Her body wanted to crumple. But the voices behind them were getting louder, Cantonese shouts, harsh and fast, punctuated with rage.

They were being hunted.

"We need them to call the cops." She panted. "Let's be loud. Be annoying."

Dylan didn't answer. He was watching the space between them and the house.

They might not make it.

The footsteps pounded sharper behind them.

Too close.

A blur of motion—Dylan shouted as one man tackled him to the ground.

Lily skidded to a stop. Her breath caught. Something shifted behind her.

Hands. Around her.

Instinct took over. She threw her head back, felt the crack of skull against jaw, and dropped her weight.

The arms loosened. She reached between her legs, gripped his calf, and yanked with everything she had. The man went down with a grunt.

She dropped into a horse stance.

Focus. Just like in class. Center weight. Eyes forward. Don't blink.

He got to his feet, slower this time. Blood ran from his mouth, but he smirked.

Then he tossed his knife aside and raised his fists, bow-and-arrow stance.

Recognition flickered through her.

Kung fu.

He knew what he was doing.

So did she.

They clashed. Strike. Parry. Block. He was fast, faster than her muscle memory could keep up with, but not invincible. Her body remembered what her mind hadn't thought about in years. Her breathing found rhythm. Her legs held strong.

She was back in the studio. No audience, just instinct.

From somewhere behind her, Dylan groaned. More scuffling.

She couldn't look.

A faint opening.

She pivoted and drove a roundhouse kick into the man's side. He staggered, and in that heartbeat of hesitation, Dylan surged forward and slammed a pistol across the man's temple.

He dropped, unconscious.

Lily whirled. The other man was already down, face bloodied, unmoving.

She gasped. "What happened?"

"He hit a rock when he fell." Dylan bent down, checked his pulse. "Still breathing." He yanked the knife and gun from both men and shoved them into her bag. "Come on. We need to move before someone else shows up."

They ran again, this time stumbling more than sprinting. The house grew closer. It was nice, white siding, manicured bushes.

"Think anyone's home?" she asked.

"I hope not. Or I hope they have security and call for backup."

He pointed at the window. "Monitored system. Yup. That's something."

They reached the steps. Two bright-red banners flanked the front door. Gold calligraphy shimmered in the light.

Spring Festival couplets. Left up all year—some Chinese families believed they protected the home.

Dylan jerked his thumb toward one. "That Chinese?"

"Yes. We might get lucky."

She pressed the doorbell. Waited. Knocked. Pressed it again.

Her pulse thudded in her throat.

The door swung open.

A poised Chinese woman, maybe in her fifties, stared at them. An elegant blouse accentuated her straight posture. Something about her reminded Lily of actresses from old TVB dramas, controlled, graceful, but with steel under the surface.

"Ma'am, we need help. May we use your phone?" Lily repeated the request in Cantonese.

The woman hesitated, then opened the door wider. "Yes, of course."

Lily exhaled.

"Come in." The woman stepped aside. Locked the door behind them.

"We're sorry to barge in. Your phone, please?"

"One moment. Have a seat." She gestured toward the piano room and disappeared down the hall.

Lily stayed on her feet, breathing in the faint scent of incense and tea. A dark-wood upright piano stood in one corner. A calligraphy scroll hung on the wall above it. On the foyer's opposite side, the formal dining room gleamed with untouched glassware.

"You were a total badass back there," Dylan whispered.

She frowned. "I was a what?"

He smiled. "A ninja. You, those moves, wow."

She rolled a shrug. "I studied kung fu when I was younger. You weren't bad either."

"Agent Peters showed me a few things. Lucky they stuck."

Voices floated in from the hallway, soft, deliberate Mandarin.

"Shush!" She crept toward the sound, careful not to be seen, and stopped just before the corner.

"She is dirty," the woman said in Mandarin.

"Clean her up," replied a man's voice.

"What about the guy?"

"I'll take him."

"Pickup is tonight."

Lily's blood turned cold.

She stepped back, fast but silent.

"They're talking about us," she whispered to Dylan.

He paled. "We should go."

They moved quickly, snatching her bag, stepping toward the door.

Lily's hand grazed the doorknob when her whole body seized.

Electricity shot through her limbs. Every muscle contracted. Her knees buckled.

The last thing she saw was Dylan's face, twisting into a scream that never reached her ears.

Then—

Nothing.

CHAPTER 72

HOTEL, FLORIDA, USA

RAY HO

Ray Ho was annoyed.

Hans still hadn't checked in and, worse, hadn't responded to the text he'd sent over thirty minutes ago. A simple confirmation was all he needed. Just one word, *done*.

Instead? Silence.

He lay face down on the massage table in the Albrecht penthouse, a towel barely covering his lower back, while the masseuse tried her best to unknot his shoulders. Normally, this would've calmed him.

Today, it did nothing.

"Boss." His second-in-command entered the suite with the remote in hand. "You might want to see this."

"I told you, unless it's Hans—"

The television clicked on anyway.

The anchor offered a grim smile. "Good afternoon. We're following breaking news out of the downtown area where a man has been found shot inside a parking garage. The FBI is now on the scene and leading the investigation. We go live to reporter Shannon Lee."

A woman on location took over. "Yes, Steve, I'm standing outside the garage where the shooting occurred roughly twenty minutes ago. The entire structure has been cleared and taped off. Authorities confirm one adult male is dead. His identity has not yet been released."

Steve's voice overplayed her image. "Do we know why the FBI is involved?"

"Well, Steve." She raised her microphone. "They're not commenting yet. But sources tell us this is part of a larger, ongoing investigation. A construction worker we spoke with says he saw two people wearing tactical gear rush up the stairs of the building across from the garage shortly after the incident."

The screen cut to a prerecorded clip of the worker, face blurred. "I didn't hear anything, no gunshots or anything like that. But two agents ran up the back stairwell of that building there"—he gestured to his left—"like they were chasing someone or securing something."

Shannon's serious image returned. "There's also an uncon-firmed report of a second body found inside the neighboring building. Again, authorities are not commenting on that just yet—"

"Turn it off!" Ray Ho sat up fast. The towel fell. He didn't care.

He stood, grabbed his pants, and pointed at the masseuse. "Out."

She bowed once, snatched her oils, and hurried from the room.

"We need to go," he ordered.

His men scattered, wiping down surfaces, clearing prints, and packing fast. The suite would be sterile in minutes.

Ray called Zhou. "Report."

Zhou's voice came back steady. "We have them."

Ray exhaled. Not a total failure.

"Put the girl in the elite group. She'll fetch a high price, clean her up."

"I already told Mama-San. She said the girl was dirty. I said to fix it."

"And the boy?"

"We're bringing him to the jet."

"Good. We leave as soon as we get clearance."

He hung up and glanced once more at the now-dark TV screen.

Hans was probably dead.

But Ray still had the merchandise.

And the game wasn't over yet.

CHAPTER 73

PEARSON'S PROPERTY, FLORIDA, USA

OLIVIA/PHOENIX

Olivia crouched low behind the hedges, her gaze sweeping the sleek angles of the house ahead. Too quiet. Too clean. Like a display model in a real estate brochure. But she could feel it. Something was off.

She tapped her comm. "No movement on the south side."

Ron's voice came through the earpiece. "Copy. Teams, fan out. Approach with caution."

She circled wide, eyes tracking every corner, every window. As she reached the house, something caught her attention. One of the garage doors. Slightly open.

She stilled. Heart steady. Pulse low. Her hand slipped to her holster.

Ugh, how she hated those things. But right now, she was grateful for the weapon in her hand.

She eased forward, weapon drawn, and pressed her back to the wall. A deep breath. Then a peek inside.

Empty.

"Clear," she called.

Another agent echoed, "Clear!"

Ron's voice followed. "It's empty."

Olivia stepped inside. The dust pattern told her the door hadn't been open long. A footprint smudged near the threshold.

"The cellar door is busted." Ana's voice crackled in her ear.

Olivia hurried over. She descended, the stairs creaking under her boots. Cool air kissed her face, tinged with mildew and something metallic.

Then she saw him.

"Body!" Ana hollered.

Olivia toed a sliced-through zip tie. "This is where they held them."

Then she headed back up, glad she'd told Simon to stay in the SUV. He didn't need to see this. No one did.

Back in the kitchen, she went to Ron with Ana on her heels. "Lily and Dylan must've broken out on their own. Someone came for them. They bolted through the garage. That side door was left ajar."

Ron raised his phone. "Calling it in."

She didn't wait for a response. "I'm going after them." She headed back out through the garage, boots hitting pavement, Ana right behind her.

The neighborhood ended in a cul-de-sac. Olivia paused.

"They could've gone either way," Ana said.

"They'd go straight. Out the door, forward instinct. Not a lot of time to weigh options."

"I'll take the other path. Just in case."

Olivia jogged down the drive, eyes sharp for movement, tracks, anything disturbed. The afternoon light stretched long across the pavement. Then, there. Grass pressed flat. Red-brown specks along the dirt.

She knelt, fingers hovering just above the stain.

Blood.

Nearby, a rock. Jagged. Tainted.

She snapped photos and texted them to Ron. Then a second message to Ana.

> Blood trail. Heading to house.

As she approached the neighboring property, Ana jogged up beside her. Ron's SUV rolled up to join them.

The house was quiet. Picturesque. But neither the trim nor the garden attracted her attention.

The red banners flanking the door did.

"That Chinese?" Ana asked.

Olivia inclined her head.

"Maybe Lily came here."

"Maybe." Olivia touched one banner. "But if they did, why not call for help?"

"I can check if a call was made from this address." Ana tapped on her phone.

Ron joined them. He waved to the nearby camera. "I'm sending agents to sweep the first house and the spot with the blood trail. This place has a door cam."

"I'll ask." Olivia pressed the doorbell.

Nothing.

Ron stepped up and banged on the door with the flat of his hand. "FBI!"

After a beat, a Chinese woman answered. "No speak English."

Olivia switched languages. "How are you?" she asked in Cantonese, then repeated it in Mandarin.

The woman responded in crisp Mandarin. "I'm well, thank you."

Olivia held up her phone, Lily's image glowing on the screen. "We'd like to ask a few questions. Have you seen this woman?"

The woman shook her head too fast. "No, sorry. I just got back from the salon."

"We noticed your door cam. Would you mind if we reviewed the footage?"

The woman stiffened. "I don't know anything about that. My husband handles it. You'll have to ask him."

"When will he be back?"

"He's out of town. Come back next week." She began closing the door.

Olivia stepped back, staying just outside the camera's lens. "She's lying," she whispered. "Something's off."

Ron nodded. His phone buzzed. "Pearson's not supposed to leave town.… Ping his phone. And while you're at it, check any traffic cam coverage near our location over the last few hours." He hung up. "Pearson's in the wind."

"Nothing smells guilty like running," Ana said.

Olivia turned back toward the other house. "That property had a security system. We'll get the footage."

"On it," came Tanner's voice. She hadn't even noticed him approach.

Ron's phone rang again. His brow furrowed. "Peters… Yes, that's helpful. Thanks."

"What is it?" Olivia asked.

"That was Max. Dylan recently got a new smartwatch. Max said he just got it synced a few days ago, right after he went back to the estate. He thought I should know, in case we had a way to track it."

"We do. I'll call Deanna." Ana held her phone to her ear.

Olivia scratched her palms, her fingers twitchy to hack into the server herself. She'd be faster. But chain of command and jurisdiction were annoying like that.

Twenty minutes later, they followed the signal Deanna picked up from Dylan's watch. The ping was active. The device was on the move.

Ron's SUV was in the lead. Olivia's behind him. She insisted Tanner stay back with another agent to keep eyes on the suspicious house.

Ana's voice came over the comms. "We just got a call from Hernandez. Pearson's at the Sanford private terminal. And Dylan's watch is heading that direction too."

Ron swore.

"What's happening?" Olivia asked.

"The vehicle we're following has diplomatic plates."

Her heart sank. Ron would go by the book. What to do? Then it came to her. She accelerated and overtook Ron's vehicle, cutting in just behind the target car.

Simon grabbed the overhead bar. "What are you doing?"

She didn't answer. Just tapped the lead car's bumper.

Both vehicles jerked to a stop.

"Stay down. Out of sight. Let me handle this."

A Chinese man stepped out of the driver's seat, all smiles.

"Sorry, sorry." She put on a thick accent. "I just got my license." She scanned the back seat. Empty.

Trunk.

"Chinese?" the man asked in Mandarin.

She nodded. "Yes."

"No problem. It's minor. Don't worry about it."

"But I must pay!" She bent to inspect the bumper and reached for the trunk latch.

The man waved her off. "No, no—" Then he noticed Ron's car. He'd know something was up.

The car shuddered.

The trunk vibrated. A panel on the taillight popped loose.

A pair of bound feet stuck out.

Ron was out with his gun. "Sorry, sir. Hands where I can see them."

Ana flanked him, gun drawn.

"No one's hurt, right?" she asked Olivia, keeping her voice level.

"I hope not." Olivia opened the trunk. Dylan was folded inside like luggage, bound and gagged. She ripped the duct tape from his mouth.

"Ouch." He twisted up his lips.

"Sorry. Where's Lily?"

"Back at the house. We need to get back."

"Why did they separate you? Where was he taking you?"

"I don't know. I was out cold. Came to when I heard shouting. Thank God I've been working out. It wasn't easy kicking out that taillight."

She squeezed his shoulder. "You did good."

The man was now shouting something about ambassadors and immunity as Ron cuffed him. "You'll hear from our embassy! Diplomatic plate!"

"Diplomatic plates don't cover kidnapping." Ron remained grim. "You have the right to remain silent…"

Ana flagged down a local cruiser. Ron shoved the man into the back seat.

An ambulance arrived. Paramedics hopped out to tend to Dylan, who insisted he was fine.

"Let them check your vitals. We'll get her back."

He relented and sat on the back of the ambulance. While the paramedics worked on him, Olivia asked, "Do you know where she is in the house?"

"No, they tased us. She has to be back in the house still. There was a woman… and the man. Talking in Mandarin. According to Lily, they were saying something about her being 'dirty.' About cleaning her up. And a pickup tonight."

Olivia's jaw tightened. That sounded like trafficking protocol. *Oh, Lord, please save my baby.*

"Oh, and two goons were coming after us. We took them

down. They were unconscious, but I don't know where they are now."

"One of you bashed one guy with a rock?"

"Technically, he fell and hit his head. Self-defense."

"You're not in trouble. We found the spot. They're gone now."

"Olivia, let's go!" Simon must have heard the conversation. He hauled her back to the car.

"Go! We're right behind you." Ana waved them off.

CHAPTER 74

PRIVATE AIRFIELD, FLORIDA, USA

RAY HO

The hum of the engines did nothing to settle his nerves.

"How much longer?" Ray snapped.

"We're ready, sir," the pilot replied. "As soon as we have clearance, we can take off."

Ray checked his watch again. Zhou should've been here twenty minutes ago. Three missed calls. No answer. No message. The silence scratched at his patience like a dull blade. Second time this week someone had gone dark.

Unacceptable.

A high-pitched wail cut through the ambient whir of the runway. His gaze jerked to the narrow window. Red and blue strobes bounced across the tarmac as a convoy of police cruisers surged past the hangars, tires screeching.

He stood. "Get us out of here. Now."

The pilot didn't argue. The plane began taxiing toward the runway. Ray's pulse thumped against his collar. He gripped the leather headrest in front of him. Zhou. That idiot must've been caught. If he talked—

A thud followed as Ray's fist crashed into the seat back.

No intel. No Dylan. No leverage.

But he still had Lily. That girl's face—innocent, delicate, perfectly packaged for the collectors who paid well—would drive the auction numbers up. He'd log in once they hit cruising altitude. Might as well salvage something from this train wreck of a trip.

The jet eased to a stop.

Ray didn't wait for permission. He yanked off the shoulder strap, stormed toward the cockpit, and jabbed the intercom. "Why are we stopping?"

"Tower said to hold."

He twisted toward the window. The police cruisers veered, not toward his plane, but another jet farther down the strip. They zipped past without as much as a glance.

Not him. Not yet.

He exhaled, forcing his hand off the bulkhead. He couldn't afford to look shaken in front of his crew.

"Boss, take a look at this."

His second-in-command handed over his phone. A breaking headline blinked across the screen:

FBI Arrests Chinese Diplomat for Alleged Kidnapping in Orlando.

Ray's jaw clenched, and he let out a string of curses.

He pounded the bulkhead, hard this time. How? Zhou was supposed to be careful. Diplomatic plates. Clean handoff. Now the whole damn op was compromised.

And the Ghost? That woman ran circles around the FBI for years. Never caught. Never even touched. What did she have that he didn't?

Connections. Immunity. Leverage.

Maybe it was time he stopped playing clean.

"Zhou needs to go," he ordered. "Now. Before he gets comfortable in some American holding cell."

"We're short-staffed here."

"Then outsource. Use a trusted contact. Someone who doesn't ask questions."

"Yes, boss." His man began texting.

Ray didn't sit. He stayed standing, gaze locked on the police vehicles disappearing into the distance.

Zhou had made a mistake.

Ray wouldn't.

CHAPTER 75

UNIDENTIFIED HOUSE, FLORIDA, USA

LILY

The air smelled of bleach and damp stone.

Lily blinked awake, skin pressed against a scratchy mattress. Cold concrete bit through the thin bedding. She was underground, again.

Once again, Dylan wasn't with her.

Her pulse surged. She pushed up on shaky elbows, gaze darting across the dim basement.

Two girls sat at the foot of the bed. Still. Dressed like beauty queens. Sparkly gowns. Painted faces. Not a hair out of place. But their eyes, red, hollow, betrayed the truth.

She sat up straighter. "Hi."

Neither blinked.

She tried again. "Do you know where we are?"

One girl barely shook her head and pressed a finger to the air above her painted lips. The other just stared, eyes wide, lips trembling. Neither wore restraints. Neither tried to run.

That unsettled her more than if they'd been shackled.

Before she could ask again, the door creaked open.

The woman from before entered, same sleek hair, same clinical detachment, but this time, her English was crisp and cold. "You need to learn your manners. Don't talk unless you're talked to. We'll get you cleaned up soon."

Lily shot to her feet. "Where's Dylan? What do you want?"

The woman's gaze was all contempt. "I don't want anything from you. I'm doing my job. You need to be presentable for the auction."

A chill swept through Lily. "What auction?"

But she already knew. The dresses. The makeup. The dead stares.

"Enough talking." The woman clapped her hands together. "You'd better behave before he comes in to teach you a lesson."

"Who?" Lily's voice cracked. "What are you talking about?"

"Mama-San, we have company!" a man shouted from upstairs.

Both girls flinched. The woman froze, then strode out, slamming the door behind her. A metallic click followed.

Locked.

Lily backed away. Her palms had gone clammy.

The quieter girl edged closer, whispering, "Don't make the guy angry. He'll… he'll do things to you."

Lily opened her mouth.

But the girl had already slunk back to the bed, curling into herself, her expression carved from fear.

Then voices. Footsteps. A crash. More shouting.

"Lily! Lily!"

She darted to the door. Tried the handle. Locked. She pounded. "I'm here! I'm here!"

"She's down there!"

Kyle's voice. Clear. Desperate. Alive.

"Lily, stand back!"

She did, heart hammering as the frame cracked under impact. A second kick blew the door open, and a rush of bodies spilled into the room. A tall guy in tactical gear appeared, then Kyle. She ran straight to him.

"You have to find Dylan!" she cried. "He's not here. I don't know where they took him!"

"Olivia and my dad got him. He's safe. He told Olivia where to find you. He'll be here soon."

Relief crashed into her. She wobbled, breath catching. Dylan was safe. He'd come because of her text. She hadn't gotten him killed.

"Are you hurt?" Kyle gripped her shoulders.

"No." She ran a finger along some dried blood on her shirt. "The cuts and bruises are from before."

Across the room, the tall man knelt in front of the girls. "You're safe now," he said. "I'm FBI Special Agent Tanner. We're here to help."

The girls stared at him like he was speaking another language.

Then—*her.*

A Chinese woman stepped into view. Familiar yet older. The resemblance was sharp, undeniable.

Her mother.

Olivia. And her father was right behind her.

She knelt by the girls, calm and soft-spoken. "You're safe now. I'm Olivia. What are your names?"

"Tosha," one whispered.

"Kim." The other's voice followed, barely audible.

"Okay, Tosha, Kim. Will you follow Agent Tanner upstairs? He'll make sure you're taken care of."

They rose slowly, limbs stiff, like they expected to be struck for moving. Agent Tanner led them up the stairs. Kyle started to follow.

"How's your leg?" Lily eyed the limp.

"It's fine." He patted his thigh a few inches above the

bandage. "I wasn't supposed to be here, but… Pearson—never mind. We'll talk later."

Then he was gone.

Leaving her alone.

With them.

Her parents.

She'd imagined this moment a hundred ways since leaving Hong Kong. In dreams, in silence, in spirals of doubt. But now that it was here, she had no idea what to say.

Her mother's eyes brimmed with tears.

Her father looked like he was holding his breath.

So much unsaid, crowding the room like ghosts.

Then all three spoke at once.

"Lily—"

"Hello."

"Hi."

They stopped. Laughed.

Her mother smiled first. "Okay, I'll go first. Hi, Lily. I'm sure you know I'm still alive by now. I'm sorry for keeping this a secret all these years."

Lily held her gaze, trying to reconcile memory with reality. This was real. A few strands of gray shimmered in her hair. Layers of warmth melded to her voice.

Without thinking, Lily closed the distance and hugged her. "You're real. Dylan told me about you, but I didn't want to get my hopes up. Auntie told me a lot about you."

Olivia clutched her back. "We have a lot to catch up on," she said through tears. "But first, allow me to introduce you to your—"

"Ahem…"

SIMON

Simon didn't want the moment to end, Lily, Olivia at her side, both safe and real.

"Ahem… sorry to interrupt your family reunion," Ron said from the stairs.

Simon turned, heart still pounding. Ron's face was tight. He wasn't the kind to interrupt without reason.

"Check your phone. It's not good."

Simon unlocked it to a breaking headline.

Update: Mysterious Illness

Sadly, the two patients we reported earlier are now in critical condition, oozing pus and experiencing severe pain.

Prayers for them and their families.

Medical teams are working tirelessly to find answers.
Stay tuned. #MysteriousIllness #CriticalCondition

Simon's stomach twisted.

"If they don't receive the antidote in the next few hours, they won't make it," Olivia said behind him. "Even if they survive, there might be permanent damage."

Ron raised a hand. "We need to move."

Simon's gaze slid to Olivia, then to Lily. He wanted nothing more than to pull them both into his arms, hold them, tell them they were safe now. Reclaim a few of those lost years, if only for a moment.

But the moment had passed. Duty pressed in.

"Yes, we do." He faced Lily. "Do you have the intel?"

She hesitated. "I think so."

Olivia sidled up to her. "I'll help you get it off. Did you bring the lotion like I told you?"

"Yes. It's in my purse." Lily glanced around, brow furrowed. "Where are they? I had a purse backpack… and a duffel bag. I think the bag's gone."

Ron radioed upstairs. "Check the trash. Look for a purse and a bag."

Moments later, Ana jogged down the steps with a black purse slung over her shoulder. "This was in the kitchen trash can."

Quick introductions followed. Olivia pulled the lotion out, nodded, and guided Lily toward the upstairs bathroom. "We'll be back!"

Ron watched them go, then crossed his arms. "I thought it was a flash drive or maybe a chip."

Simon shrugged. "You know as much as I do. Report said she'd secured the intel. That Lily would deliver it. Nothing more."

"We got it!" Olivia called from upstairs. "Why don't you all come up?"

On the main floor, paramedics were already tending to Lily. She protested that she was fine. Dylan told her to suck it up, that he had to let them patch him up earlier. Kyle hovered nearby, circling like a worried hawk, asking if she needed water, food, a blanket, anything.

Simon hung back, watching the scene.

His daughter. Alive. Safe. Still strong, still stubborn.

He didn't speak. He didn't move toward her.

Not yet.

Olivia stepped beside him. "We need to head back to the office," she murmured. "The file's encrypted. Once I crack it, the CDC team can begin analysis."

Simon gave a single, solemn nod. "Let's go."

CHAPTER 76

TASK FORCE OFFICE, FLORIDA, USA

RON

Ron entered the squad room but didn't make it two paces before Hernandez intercepted him.

"Boss, Congressman Pearson's in holding. Waiting on his attorney. He was heading to Germany, according to the flight plan."

Germany?

Ron's brows knit. He hadn't pegged Germany as part of this mess.

He grunted in acknowledgment and surveyed the bullpen. The hum of agents, analysts, and caffeine buzzers filled the room again.

Earlier, once the paramedics cleared Lily, Simon and Olivia agreed the girl needed rest. Ron had assigned an agent to drive her to Simon's place. She'd asked if Dylan and Kyle could tag along, understandable she didn't want to be alone. Tommy, of course, had inserted himself without needing an invitation.

She'd lost her duffel too.

"Kyle." Ron pulled him aside before they left. "Call Eva.

Have Lily make a list of what she needs. Introduce them so Eva knows her size. Tell her to get clothes. Toiletries. Whatever she's missing."

"Will do."

Once they returned to the office, Olivia wasted no time decrypting the microchip. Now, strings of equations, notes, and chemical diagrams filled the monitors. Ron glanced at one screen and gave up. Better to leave it to the people who knew what it meant.

When Olivia finished, she uploaded the data to the CDC scientists waiting on standby. They pored over the formulas and charts, praising the intel like it was the Rosetta Stone.

Ron stood back and let them work. The medical part was out of his lane, and with the antidote on its way to production, his job on that front was done.

But more than formulas were on the chip.

Olivia flagged other documents and forwarded them to Simon. Probably intelligence-grade stuff. That suited Ron fine. Once, he would've wanted full visibility. Now? The less he knew, the better he slept.

When the frenzy quieted, he gathered his team for a briefing.

He faced Hernandez. "Germany?"

"According to the flight plan, yes."

Ron rose from his desk and joined them near the monitor wall. "Give me Wagner."

Tanner took over. "Hans Wagner. Born in Davenport, Iowa. Graduated high school in '98. Joined the army right after. Dishonorably discharged in '04, conduct unbecoming of an officer." Images of Wagner cycled on-screen. Military portraits, surveillance shots, blurry passport scans.

Hernandez picked up. "Nothing for years after that. Five years ago, he turned up in multiple murder-for-hire investigations. Now wanted in the US, UK, France, Italy… and a few others."

"Not Germany?" Ron braced back against a desktop.

Tanner hesitated. "No, boss. But…"

Ana stepped in. "We think he worked for Germany. Off the books. I called a contact at NSA. He and Olivia believe Wagner did wet work for the BND."

Ron folded that into the mental pile forming in his head. "Logan Sullivan. Go."

Tanner tapped the screen. A new face replaced Wagner, mid-thirties, clean-cut, dead eyes.

"Normal background. Applied to the FBI. Washed out, failed the psych eval."

"No social media," Hernandez added. "No memberships. No digital footprint."

"But we found a collection of forged passports in his apartment," Ana said. "Deanna cross-referenced the travel data with unsolved high-profile homicides. Every trip matched with a hit."

"A contract killer," Ron muttered. "Who hired him this time?"

Another slide. A bank statement. Hernandez pointed. "He got a wire transfer two days before he was killed. Fifty thousand. Either the down payment or the final installment. The funds came from a Swiss account."

"Deanna's pulling his digital records now, calls, texts, email," Ana added. "We'll know more soon."

The pieces didn't fit. Not yet. Ron's hands lowered to grip the table's edge at his sides.

He cleared his throat, but couldn't clear those pieces from his head. "Pearson made it seem like the Chinese were behind the abduction, but he was flying to Germany. Wagner might have done wet work for the BND. Sullivan was a hired gun. They must be connected, but how? We're missing something."

Ana folded her arms. "Let's say the BND outsourced the hit to Sullivan. How does it connect to the kidnapping?"

"And how do the Chinese fit in?" Ron asked.

Tanner was pumping a stress ball. "Boss, maybe the killing of Wagner was unrelated to the kidnapping?"

"How so? What are you thinking?"

"Let's assume Wagner did work for the BND. We tried to keep the kidnapping quiet, but it probably leaked. Let's say they were monitoring Wagner. If they somehow suspected his arrest and were worried about him talking, especially about his role in killing Americans, it's not too far-fetched to think they would take him out."

Ana nodded. "And use a false flag. Blame it on the Chinese."

Ron held quiet, mentally replaying their theories and everything they knew. "He worked for Pearson. No leak required. Pearson already knew about the kidnapping and the intel. He told us Wagner was supposed to find Lily, not take her. Maybe that's the truth. And Wagner went rogue."

"And Pearson?" Ana asked. "He claimed the Chinese triads were blackmailing him. So why go to Germany?"

Ron exhaled through his nose. "We've got more questions than answers. Get to work. I want connections and evidence."

A chorus of "yeah, boss" rippled back.

He tapped Ana. "Maybe you should stick around. We could use the help."

She arched a brow. "Transfer again?"

"Your call. They can make you liaison. Or whatever title they dream up. It's a task force. You could keep your DIA creds."

"I'll think about it."

CHAPTER 77

THE ROTH RESIDENCE, FLORIDA, USA

LILY

The moment she stepped inside, Lily stopped in her tracks.

"Wow," she whispered. The air smelled of citrus and wood polish. Sunlight spilled across the hardwood floors, making the space feel even bigger. "This house is massive."

The open kitchen stretched to one side, gleaming with stainless steel and marble counters. It could've been right out of a magazine. In Hong Kong, even the nicest flats had walled-off kitchens.

"My entire flat could fit inside this room and the kitchen. And it's considered luxurious back home."

Kyle shrugged as he closed the door behind her. "America has land. You can't compare it to Hong Kong. Everything's big here."

She dropped her backpack and collapsed onto the plush light-gray velvet sectional. "This is comfy. I might not get up."

Kyle gestured down the hall. "According to the senator, you should make yourself at home. Bathroom's that way. There are a couple others with showers, I think. Haven't checked out the rest of the place."

In the background, Dylan and Tommy's conversation shifted from teasing to a full-on argument.

"You need to call your grandmother!" Tommy shouted.

"I will. But you tell her what you said about that agent," Dylan shot back.

"Wait, Agent Ortiz? Did someone find him? He's okay?" Lily snapped her head to Kyle. "And will you sit down? My neck hurts looking up at you all."

Kyle and Dylan plopped down on either side of her.

"Yes, ma'am." Tommy perched on the love seat. "He's in the hospital. Ask Kyle. He'll have the latest."

Kyle gave a nod. "What he said. Last I heard, Ortiz was upgraded to stable. Ms. Marino's fans went out hunting for you and Dylan… and found him instead."

She patted Dylan's arm. "You weren't kidding. Your family really *is* connected."

The doorbell's chime jolted her upright. Dylan and Tommy sat up. Kyle moved without hurry, checked the peephole, and opened the door.

A young woman about their age with mixed features like herself stepped inside and went straight into his arms.

Lily frowned. *Girlfriend?*

Kyle guided her into the living room. "Everyone, this is Eva Higgins."

Dylan squinted. "Aren't you going to be my grandmother's new assistant?"

Eva beamed. "Yes. You must be Dylan." She waved. "And you must be Tommy."

Tommy shook her hand. "You spying on us already?"

She laughed. "Let's just say I've done my homework. If I'm going to work for Ms. Carol, I should know who her family is."

"I'm Lily." Lily stood and offered her hand.

Eva stared for a beat longer. "Sorry, I… You look familiar."

"I doubt it. I only arrived two days ago. But if you've stayed at Hong Kong's Marino Hotel recently, you might've seen me."

"Nah." Eva released Lily's hand. "Must be a coincidence. Anyway, I heard you need clothes. Did you make a list? And your size?"

Lily chuckled. "Kyle made you my personal shopper?"

"Not me. Dad's idea." Kyle held up his hands.

"Don't worry," Dylan added. "We're not going anywhere. You two can figure it all out."

"Okay." Lily smiled, starting to feel normal again.

But across the room, Eva was still watching her.

CHAPTER 78

TASK FORCE OFFICE, FLORIDA, USA

RON

Ron didn't want to face Pearson until he had more than suspicions. He needed leverage.

The ME's autopsies turned up nothing helpful. Sullivan had been killed with his own knife. No prints. No skin cells. Whoever did it wore gloves. Professional.

Ballistics matched the bullet in Wagner's body to the rifle left at the scene. Sullivan's prints were on the weapon, which gave them a clean close to that case. But the shot to Wagner's shoulder was meant to wound, not fill. Olivia must be connected somehow, but again, Ron had no proof. Just instinct. Which also said Sullivan's murder would vanish, buried by someone upstairs.

Deanna burst into the squad room. "Boss, I've got something."

"You could've called."

"Yeah, well, those CDC scientists are still camped out here. Thought they were heading back to their fancy lab."

"I'm sure they will. What've you got?"

She tapped her tablet and sent an image to the main screen. "Congressman Pearson's photo archive. Pulled from his phone."

Family pictures. Birthdays, vacations, barbecues.

"So?" Hernandez asked. "I've got family photos on mine too."

"Right, but Pearson sends photos, different ones, to the *same* email address on a regular basis. No variety in the messages either. Always: 'How are you? We're doing fine. Attached are some photos.' Over and over. Who does that?"

She advanced the screen. Zoomed in. Circled sections of the images.

"There are microdots embedded in the photos. I checked several. All are about something called Project Sandman."

Ron stiffened.

He'd heard the name. Black file. Way above his clearance level. Simon might know more, but he was busy briefing the president and other top brass.

Ana fiddled with the remote. "So he's been feeding classified material to the Germans? I thought he was working for the Ghost."

"He is," Ron said. "We don't know if he's spying for them or selling the information. What about his finances?"

Tanner chimed in. "He's laundering money through offshore accounts. Today, a million landed and bounced. Hernandez is tracking it."

"Cayman Islands," Hernandez confirmed.

"Trace the origin?"

"Bank in Zurich. But we don't have the account-holder info. Maybe Olivia—"

"No," Ron cut in. "She doesn't have jurisdiction here."

Ana stepped in. "Zurich's overseas, Ron. Her contacts can dig faster than we can."

Not a fan of relying on the CIA, he took a deep, calming breath. Ana had a point. "Fine. See if she can help."

Olivia came through faster than he liked to think about. Ron didn't ask how. Didn't want to know. The team still filed an official request, and Simon tapped a few of his old State Department contacts to grease the wheels.

The account belonged to a Wolfgang Beck. An information broker, known for buying classified data and selling it to anyone with the cash.

Now they just had to prove Pearson sent him intel. Ron tried a bluff to see if the congressman would crack.

He did.

"That was easy. Didn't think he'd cave so fast." Ana almost stomped as they left the interrogation room.

"He knew he was finished the moment we caught him at the airport. The rest is up to the US Attorney."

"And Beck?"

"Interpol or Europol's problem now."

Both of their phones buzzed. The same time. The same text.

Ron swore.

Ana's eyes narrowed. "Boy, that was fast. How'd they get to him so quick?"

Zhou was dead. Found hanging in his holding cell.

"Says he killed himself."

Ana snorted. "Yeah, and I'm the tooth fairy."

Ron didn't reply. Either the triads or the Chinese government got to him. If it was the triads, he could dig. If it was the government, he'd let that one lie.

Back in the squad room, he gathered the team.

"Let's recap the cases, then go home. Start with the woman."

Tanner stepped forward. "Mama-San is Rose Chang. Her record's old, mostly solicitation charges. Been clean for the past fifteen years. Lawyered up the second Zhou's death hit the news."

The screen shifted to two mugshots.

"Tyson Gray and David Schultz," Hernandez said. "Multiple

priors, aggravated assault, robbery. Tyson has a couple of sexual assault charges. They both ID'd Zhou as the man in charge. They didn't even hesitate."

Ron nodded. "Zhou's phone?"

"Burner. One call. Disconnected. That's it," Hernandez replied.

Ana moved to the wall screen, already tapping against the digital surface. "Okay, timeline." She began writing using a stylus, the text appearing in neat blocks as she spoke. "Lily arrives. Fake agents try to grab her. She and Kyle run. Dylan joins. Then the car crash. Ortiz and, uh, Randall Hall abduct her, take her to Rifkin's place. She tries to escape. Calls Dylan. They're both captured."

Ron raised a hand. "Let's pause. Rifkin's motive was money, right?"

"Yes," Hernandez confirmed. "Harrison was blackmailing him. We've got messages backing that up. Harrison had found out about Rifkin's involvement with the Ghost."

Ron sighed. "Okay. Go on."

Tanner took over. "Wagner is sent to find Lily and the drive. Kills Harrison and Rifkin in the process. He believed the drive existed, probably after the intel."

"What about those phone numbers?" Ron asked. "We allege Wagner wanted the intel for the Chinese. Question is whether it was the Chinese government or the triads?"

Silence.

Ana offered, "Maybe Olivia can ID the phone numbers. Tell us whether it's gang or government."

"Next."

"Wagner is killed by Logan Sullivan," Tanner continued. "We've confirmed it. Sullivan was a contract killer. He was, in turn, killed by an unknown shooter who also wounded Wagner. Same rifle."

Ana muttered, "I'd like to shake that guy's hand."

Ron shook his head. "Not our call. We'll work it, but my bet? I'll soon get word to hand it over to DOD or Justice. And they'll deep-six it."

"While that's happening," Hernandez picked up the thread, "Lily and Dylan escape. They fight off Gray and Schultz, then get tased by Zhou. He was transporting Dylan to a private jet when we intercepted them."

Ron made a timeout sign. "Did Zhou have a link to Pearson?"

"Not that we can find," Tanner said.

"Pearson was already taxiing when we got there," Hernandez added. "Didn't look like he was waiting for anyone."

"I'm on it." Ana pulled out her phone. Moments later, she looked up. "Another jet was scheduled to leave five minutes after Pearson's. Headed to Hong Kong. Manifest lists 'Johnny Chan,' 'Jackie Chan,' and 'Bruce Lee.'"

"Seriously?" Tanner scoffed. "They're not even trying."

They laughed, but Ron stayed focused. "Are we checking video footage?"

"Running facial rec now." Ana typed.

Tanner continued. "Lily was left with Rose Chang. Based on what she said, they planned to auction her online, along with the two teens we found."

"When?"

"No clue," Hernandez said. "The two thugs didn't know either. Just followed orders."

Ana lowered her phone. "We looped in the FBI's human trafficking team. They've already interviewed the girls. They'll speak with Lily soon."

Ron nodded. "Good. Let's finish this tomorrow. Go home. Rest."

Just as people started to stand, the computer dinged.

On-screen: Hong Kong ID card—Ray Ho.

Photo. Stats. Known associate of the Ghost.

CHAPTER 79

MIRROR ESTATE, FLORIDA, USA

LILY

For the first time since she arrived in America, the pieces of Lily's life were falling into place.

"Once you decide what to do with your flat, you let me know, okay?" Auntie's voice crackled through the screen.

"I will." Lily leaned closer to the laptop on the polished coffee table between her and her mom. They were perched side by side on the parlor's floral-upholstered loveseat, its carved wooden arms cool against her skin. Seeing Auntie's face always grounded her.

"Looks like you're having fun over there."

"It's Thanksgiving here," her mom chimed in. "We're at a friend's house to celebrate. Speaking of, we should head over."

"I won't keep you, then."

They waved goodbye, signed off, and joined the rest of the crowd.

Dylan hadn't exaggerated. Mirror Estate was breathtaking. When Lily first saw it, she had been stunned into silence. In Hong Kong, she'd only seen homes like this on TV. She'd been staying at her father's house for the past few months, adjusting to her new life. Agents had come and gone, asking questions. She'd gone shopping with her mother. She and Auntie video chatted often. And her dad… He wanted to know everything.

The CDC had worked fast after receiving the antidote formula from the recovered intel. But it hadn't been quick enough to save the initial two victims. However, most of the later cases responded well. A crisis had been averted.

She and Dylan had visited Agent Ortiz before the hospital discharged him. He still had a long road ahead, but he smiled when he saw them. Said he was glad they were okay. They promised to keep in touch.

Her parents worried about the trauma she'd endured. Her father suggested counseling. She'd resisted until Dylan told her about Fr. Phil. Talking to him had helped Dylan after his brush with death. Encouraged by her godmother, too, she'd agreed. It was early yet, but the fear of being alone had loosened its grip.

She'd tackled something practical, too, getting a driver's license. It had turned into a whole process involving a social security card, drug and alcohol course, all before even sitting behind the wheel. Simon—*Dad*—had taken her driving before deciding it was safer to hire a professional instructor.

Agents Peters and Ruiz had stopped by several times. They never told her everything, but she'd overheard, er, eavesdropped, enough. Hans had once worked for something called the BND. He'd planned to sell intel to a Chinese triad leader named Ray Ho. The working theory? The Germans had ordered Hans killed and let the Chinese take the blame.

The FBI's human trafficking unit was still digging. They'd already spoken to the other girls. Her turn would come.

"Hey, it's your dad!" Dylan's voice snapped her out of her thoughts.

It was her first Thanksgiving. She'd never understood the hype, but now, she got it. Ms. Marino had invited her whole family, plus Fr. Phil, Agents Peters and Kyle, and Tommy, who'd flown back from visiting his family in Washington State.

The feast was held at Lorraine's Kitchen, which was closed for the holiday. She was used to Chinese banquets with endless courses. This wasn't so different, except the main event was turkey, surrounded by mountains of side dishes.

Dylan had been right. Lorraine, Max's daughter, was an amazing cook. She and her mom, Kate, had done everything. Afterward, the younger crowd insisted the cooks rest while the others handled cleanup.

Now, they'd returned to the main house while Max had stayed behind with his family. The adults sat clustered on couches in the great room or chatted around the TV as Dylan turned up the volume.

A newsclip played—her father's press conference.

"I'm here to announce my resignation from the position of US Senator. After much consideration and soul-search-ing, I've decided it's time to step down and devote more time to my loved ones."

The reporter added commentary. "Senator Roth also expressed condolences to the Burke family…"

"What are you gonna do now that you're unemployed, Simon?" Ms. Marino teased.

He reached over and squeezed Mom's hand. "We've been talking through a few ideas."

While the older folks talked, Kyle nudged Lily's shoulder and whispered, "Are they getting married?"

"Did he pop the question?" Dylan asked from the other side.

She shrugged. He hadn't technically proposed yet, but he'd asked her how she felt about taking his name. Without hesitation, she'd said yes. Finally, she wouldn't be the girl with her mother's surname.

Thank you, Lord! A few months ago, she was lamenting being alone with no family. Now, she had both her parents and new friends.

The moment felt too perfect to spoil.

And then it happened.

Her father stood, dropped to one knee, and pulled a small box from his pocket. Conversations fell silent.

Lily's hand flew to her phone, already recording. Dylan had his out too.

With his gaze locked on Mom, Dad said, "Olivia, I bought this ring twenty-three years ago. I've been waiting all this time to ask, will you marry me?"

Tears shimmered in Mom's eyes. "Yes."

Lily's vision blurred. She blinked fast, smiling through tears.

Cheers erupted. Applause. Laughter. A moment she'd remember for the rest of her life.

Then a ringtone shattered the peace.

Dylan checked his phone. "Nobody panic. An assistant US Attorney just arrived at the gate. She showed ID. I let her in."

Her father and Agent Peters exchanged glances. Everyone moved toward the entry.

Lily followed, her chest aflutter.

A woman and a man approached the open door. The woman, dressed casually, carried an envelope. The man looked like security.

Her gaze scanned the room and landed on Olivia.

"Ms. Tso, I'm Assistant US Attorney Leslie Phillips." Her left hand held an ID card. "I'm sorry to barge in on your holiday celebration. Could we, uh, speak privately?"

Agent Peters held his credentials up. "Special Agent Ron Peters. What's this about?"

"Ah, yes, SSA Ron Peters, head of Task Force 629. Okay, Marge Beaumont is in the process of negotiating a deal—"

"You can't be serious." Dylan stepped forward. "She's my evil aunt. No way you guys are letting her walk."

"You must be Dylan Roche. I'm sorry, and I understand. Unfortunately, I can't discuss it with you." She turned back to Olivia. "Ms. Tso?"

Dylan kept shaking his head and muttering curses under his breath.

Dad sidestepped Dylan. "Olivia is my fiancée. If the Ghost is cutting a deal, what's that got to do with her?"

"Congratulations, Senator." Ms. Phillips presented the envelope. "Ms. Tso, this may explain things." And then she pivoted to Dad and Agent Peters. "Here's the thing. There's no deal yet. We don't know what she wants, if anything. She will only talk to Ms. Tso."

Forgotten Secret, the next gripping installment in the Mirror Estate series, is available on Amazon and Kindle Unlimited. Grab it now!

In case you miss it, here's where you can download book 1, *Buried Secrets - Where It All Begins*, or any previous books you've missed.

THANK YOU!

Thank you for diving into *Living Secrets*! Writing this story has been such a wild ride and knowing that you've spent time with the cast means the world to me.

I hope you loved reading it as much as I loved writing it. If you'd be so kind as to leave a review on Amazon and/or Goodreads to share your impressions with others, I would greatly appreciate it. Your insights will help other readers find the book.

BONUS SCENES

BONUS SCENE 1

HONG KONG

OLIVIA

Olivia adjusted the lanyard around her neck, the badge clipped to it reading "Jade Lam."

Her new skin. Her new life. Her new lie.

She'd worn many faces over the last years, literally. Every time Jay and Patty handed her a new identity, it came with a fresh mask, each more lifelike than the last. The latest was seamless, molding to her like a second skin. No more stiff latex or awkward edges. This one blinked when she blinked, moved when she smiled. A masterpiece of illusion.

Now she worked at Data Solutions, tucked into the hum of the IT security department. Her cover: cybersecurity specialist. Her mission: blend in, excel, and get noticed.

That part hadn't taken long.

When she intercepted a pair of hacking attempts, word spread fast. Jay and Patty likely had something to do with the attempts. But soon after that, Marge Beaumont made her acquaintance at a company event.

Then the real operation began.

A memory flared, sharp, uninvited...

"You can't back out now! It's too late," Jay snapped.

They were in his and Patty's apartment, posing as a married couple again. A cozy flat with minimalist furniture, framed art, and secrets stuffed between the couch cushions.

Patty stood by the kitchen counter, arms folded. "Olivia, you made contact with Beaumont. And she seemed to like you. That's our in."

Olivia planted her feet, arms crossed. "We don't even know if she's the Ghost."

Jay exhaled through his nose like a steam valve. "She's on our short list. If she's not the Ghost, she knows who is. Your job is to earn her trust and dig."

"She's too smart to expose herself," Olivia said. "If she's the Ghost, she's not going to blurt out a kill order over coffee."

Patty nodded. "Of course not. But the Ghost doesn't act directly. Watch closely. You'll feel it, how people orbit her, how decisions ripple outward from her."

Olivia said nothing. But she was listening.

Jay's tone shifted, cool, measured. "You remember the deal, don't you?"

Her stomach knotted. "That was four years ago. Haven't I done enough?"

"Let's count. We fast-tracked your immigration. Got your daughter citizenship. You didn't want to list her father on the birth certificate. Do you know what kind of hassle that is?"

"You told me he'd be in danger," Olivia shot back.

"I don't believe we said he could be in danger," Jay countered. "What we said, and it's still true today, was that if word got out he had a daughter, they wouldn't hesitate to use her as leverage to make him do what they want. Do you want to put your daughter in that situation? Can you risk it?"

Before she could respond, he held up a hand. "Remember the Ghost's people, via Rifkin, tried to kill you? They thought that by eliminating you, they could get him to comply. Well, it seems your man has a spine. He doesn't cave easily. As of now, we don't have any indication he is compromised. But that could change if they knew he had a daughter and she was in danger. Don't you agree?"

"Olivia, they have plans for Simon," Patty chimed in. "We believe they'll pave the way for him in the political arena. What do you think a scandal such as this would do to his political future? A love child with a Chinese spy? That would be their narrative. Never mind you're from Hong Kong and you're working for us. And when it ruins his political future, do you think they'd hesitate to get rid of him and cultivate another candidate?"

"So, to protect your child and your man, we keep it a secret," Jay said.

"Until when?" Olivia asked.

"I'm sure the day will come when she'll learn the truth," Patty answered.

BONUS SCENE 2
Florida, USA

EVA

E va had learned to trust her gut, and right now, it wouldn't shut up.

The moment she saw Lily, something twisted in her chest. A flicker of recognition. A memory buried just beneath the surface, refusing to rise. She'd racked her brain for days, tracing every face, every distant family gathering, every newsclip she'd ever studied. Nothing. Just that gnawing sense that she'd seen her before.

Now Lily was a regular at Mirror Estate. So were Dylan and Tommy. Word was Lily would be working at M&M Enterprises soon.

Eva hadn't ended up at the Marino estate by accident. Agent Peters had made sure of that. Officially, she was Ms. Carol's personal assistant. Unofficially? She was here as a conduit between Agent Peters and certain people in the estate.

Kyle had been right. She'd joined the Bureau for one reason: To find out what happened to her aunt.

The police never believed Clara had been abducted. They'd written it off as another runaway. But Eva *knew*. She remembered the calls that stopped coming. The laughter that vanished from family holidays. The silence that settled like ash.

The door creaked. Eva looked up.

"Earth to Eva!" Lily waved in front of Eva's face.

Eva blinked. "Sorry, zoned out. Does Ms. Carol need something?"

She sat behind the desk in her small but private office. One of the perks of working at Mirror Estate. Quiet, tucked away, and yet close enough to the action.

"Nope. We're planning a trip to Harry Potter World. You in?"

"When?"

Lily shrugged. "Still checking calendars. I'm the only one—wait, hold up." She pointed to the framed photo on Eva's bookshelf. "Why do you have this picture?"

Eva followed her gaze to the photo next to a paperweight and a ceramic mug. Three teenage girls, arms slung around each other. It was the only image she had of Clara. She kept it as a promise: Never stop looking.

"That's my aunt, Clara Wu. She's the one in the middle."

Lily's eyes shot to hers. Then back to the photo. "No. *Way.* Are you serious?"

Now, Eva frowned at her. "Of course. Why?"

"That's your aunt?" Lily nearly bounced in place. "I've seen this photo before. The girl on the left, that's my mom, Olivia. And the one on the right? That's my godmother. You've heard me call her Auntie, but she's Sr. Marie to everyone else. They were best friends when they were kids."

Eva sat frozen. Her pulse thundered in her ears.

"They lost touch after your aunt's family moved," Lily continued. "Auntie told me about it once. Said it was her biggest regret, not staying in touch."

"I'm afraid…" Eva swallowed hard. "I don't think your mom or godmother will be able to reconnect with her."

Lily's face fell. "Why not?"

"She's been missing for years."

FORGOTTEN SECRET

A Psychological Suspense Thriller

BOOK 3
SNEAK PEEK

PROLOGUE

A relentless throb pounded in the hollow of her skull, a rhythmic drumbeat that drew her from the comfort of unconsciousness. She forced her eyes open, wincing against the antiseptic brightness. Stark-white walls towered around her, impersonal and cold, the ceiling sprinkled with tiny fluorescent lights that flickered like distant stars. She was lying on a bed, machines nearby, a thin hospital sheet barely covering her. How'd she end up here? Her breathing quickened, and her heartbeat picked up speed. Her clammy skin threatened to soak the sheet. She couldn't remember.

She blinked two figures into focus—men dressed in white coats.

"Welcome back to the land of the living." The younger, Middle Eastern-looking one leaned closer, thrusting his angular cheekbones and well-defined jaw into view and exuding a sense of strength.

Her brows furrowed. Did she die?

"You're awake." The older white man perused the hospital chart. "You've been in a coma. Because of the angle, the caliber, and perhaps distance, the bullet didn't cause any major damage.

But your brain still needed time to heal. I'm Dr. Lester Cook. This is Dr. Michael Khoury." He gestured toward the young man. "Your vitals look good. Let me have a peek. The police haven't been able to identify you. What's your name?"

Her lips moved, but no sound came out. Did he say bullet? And what was her name?

Dr. Cook did a check on her head, the bandages wrapping it making her feel like she was wearing a turban. He then asked her who the president was, what year it was, how many fingers she saw, and similar questions. She had no trouble answering them. "Now, how are you feeling?"

She tried to reply, but her throat was parched, her voice a mere croak. Dr. Khoury fetched a glass of water from the bedside table, held it to her lips, and helped her to take slow sips.

"I–I don't remember anything," she admitted, her voice barely above a whisper. Why was she struggling to say a simple sentence?

The two doctors exchanged glances. Then Dr. Cook scanned the medical chart, his brows furrowed. "You've been through a traumatic ordeal. You don't remember being shot?"

The words hit her like a gut punch, her heart pounding a frenzied tattoo against her rib cage. "Shot?" she echoed, a trembling taking over her body. "But... why can't I remember anything?"

Neither answered right away. Then Dr. Cook touched her hand. "The human brain is a fascinatingly complex organ. When it undergoes severe trauma, such as a gunshot wound, it sometimes shields itself by temporarily blocking out memories. You're fortunate to be alive."

I'm not feeling lucky! "Will I... get my memories back?"

He gave her hand a comforting squeeze. "In most cases, yes. Memory loss after head trauma is usually temporary. Your brain needs time to heal, and as it does, your memories should begin to return."

"But… who am I?"

When Dr. Cook turned to his young colleague, Dr. Khoury cleared his throat. "We haven't been able to identify you yet. You had no identification when I found you. But don't worry. We're here to help you."

He found her? Her eyes welled up. She clutched the bedsheets, searching for answers that seemed to slip through her grasp.

"Where… did you… find me?"

Dr. Khoury hesitated. "My brother and I and some friends were out on a boat on the Intracoastal Waterway. When our friends dropped us off at the dock, we found you nearby."

Had she been on the Intracoastal Waterway? The blankness in her mind failed her. "Are we… in the Outer Banks?"

"No, we're in Durham. We had to airlift you here because of the seriousness of your injuries."

"How long… have I been out?"

"Ten days."

Ten days!

The room's door swung open, breaking the heavy silence that settled upon them. Her heart quickened. Could this bring a breakthrough or a glimpse into her unknown history?

No. Just a nurse carrying a tray of medications. He exchanged a glance with the doctors, perhaps apologizing for interrupting.

Her chest tightened, but her recovery couldn't be rushed. She took a deep breath and then pushed out words with the air. "Thank you, doctors, for everything you're doing to help me."

"Don't mention it." Dr. Cook wrote some notes on the chart. "That's our job. Remember, healing takes time, and in due course, we hope to piece together the puzzle of your identity. When you feel better, we'll have, uh, a specialist to come and talk to you."

She nodded. What kind of specialist would she need to see?

Surely, a difficult journey lay ahead, but she *would* reclaim her past, no matter how arduous the path might be.

As the nurse finished his task and left, her gaze lingered on the closed door. The weight of her forgotten memories pressed upon her, urging her to seek answers beyond her hospital room.

Dr. Cook said, "Do you have any other questions?"

So many! Starting with her name, but it wasn't the doctors' fault. Her focus was on the sterile white ceiling when she heard:

Clara, Clara!

Was that—? She thought she'd seen her grandfather, but that couldn't be. He died years ago. The hazy figure was retreating, and she tried to stop him. *Come back. Don't go!*

Clara, you need to stay there. It's not your time yet.

Concerned voices murmured around her. She opened her eyes—she hadn't realized she'd closed them. Doctors and nurses now surrounded her. "What happened?" she asked.

"You gave us a scare," Dr. Cook said.

"I thought you'd drifted off to sleep until the alarm started to go off," Dr. Khoury added.

"Clara," she repeated, turning to look at the doctors. "I think… I think that's my name."

A spark lit Dr. Khoury's dark eyes. "That's a start, Clara." The encouragement in his gentle voice warmed her. "Every journey begins with a single step. This is yours. Rest now."

Dr. Cook smiled. "Your memory should start to come back."

As the doctors left, Clara stared at the ceiling, her mind a whirlwind that refused to calm. But amidst the storm, a single thought stood out. She had a name. Clara. And with that name came a glimmer of hope, a tiny flame in the all-encompassing darkness. She wasn't just a gunshot victim or an amnesiac. She was Clara. And she was alive. That had to count for something.

Exhaustion tugged at her consciousness, pulling her toward sleep's comforting embrace. But before she succumbed, she sighed. Dr. Khoury had found her and likely saved her life.

Dr. Michael Khoury, formerly known as Amir, stepped into the doctor's lounge, away from the bustling hospital corridor. He fumbled with his phone, needing to update his brother on the condition of the girl they rescued.

That fateful weekend replayed like a vivid filmstrip. His brother had given his statements to the local police while Michael had been preoccupied with saving the girl's life. After she'd been airlifted to University Hospital in Durham, Michael had gotten the chance to provide his account to the authorities.

Now, in the relative calmness of the hospital corridor, he dialed his brother's number.

When the call connected, Majid's voice broke through the static. "Amir, how's the girl doing?"

Michael had given up trying to make his family call him by his Christian name. He leaned against the wall, finding solace in his brother's presence, even if only over the phone. "She woke up. Still here at the hospital."

"Oh, good. Allah is looking out for her. Come on, what are the odds a neurosurgical fellow just happens to find her?"

"I was there at the right time. But yes, I do feel God's hand in this."

"It's been a few weeks now. Found her parents yet?"

"Nah. I'm more concerned about the cops. They got her fingerprints, but they didn't find anything."

Unspoken worries and shared understanding filled the pause before Majid spoke. "I saw a news report. The coast guard busted a boat full of illegal immigrants from Asia close to where we found her. Do you think she's one of them?"

Michael's brows furrowed as he recalled the news images—the desperation and hope on the faces of those who had risked everything for a chance at a better life. He exhaled, but he couldn't lift the weight from his chest. "I don't know. She's

Asian, but she speaks English quite well, with the slightest accent. British, I think."

"Well, we speak English quite well too. And we weren't born here."

"Point taken. So, maybe she is educated, but… I don't know. Anyway, people don't embark on such dangerous journeys unless they're fleeing something unbearable, whether it's war or political oppression. Maybe that's what she was doing." He rubbed the tightness between his brows. "By the way, her name is Clara, and she doesn't remember anything. So, I can't ask her. The cops think it's a robbery gone wrong."

"Really?"

"What I heard."

"Maybe they won't look too closely, then. And you said she didn't remember anything?"

"Yup."

"Oh, wow. Imagine that. To end up here, injured and with no memory of who she is or where she came from."

Michael nodded, though Majid couldn't see him. "You and I understand what it's like to seek a better life, to escape the horrors of war. While these immigrants may not have come from a war zone, their journey is born out of desperation and longing for a chance at a brighter future."

CHAPTER 1

CLARA

The Florida sun was a mellow presence in the sky, its rays a gentle warmth against Clara Khoury's skin. A soft breeze wafted through the minivan's open windows as she navigated the familiar Orlando streets. She glanced at the passenger seat. "I'm sure you'll make at least JV, if not varsity."

Another grunt from Jason, her freshman son. Sometimes, she wondered if Michael needed to check Jason's vocal cords.

"Dad or I will pick you up."

"Okay."

Boys! At least he said one word.

She pulled into Orlando Christian Academy's parking lot and stopped by the gym entrance. "Good luck."

Jason hopped out.

The school team had a no-cut policy, so it was only a matter of which team—varsity or JV. If nothing went wrong, Jason would make varsity. He'd been playing on elite basketball teams for years.

Her next stop was the store. She strolled through the aisles, her daughter the predominant force in her thoughts. The move had come at a challenging time for Faith in her high school senior year. They'd thought about waiting till after the new year. But the hospital wanted Michael here pronto, and they'd secured spots for their children in an elite academy.

Despite the typical teenage angst and resistance, Faith's recent breakup with her boyfriend eased the transition. The young man had, according to her dramatic narratives, made her life "miserable." The breakup had lessened her initial resistance to the move.

Now settled in Florida, she was adjusting well. She'd even made a friend, Josie. However, Josie appeared to be a trouble magnet, a wild streak visible in her languid swagger and defiant attitude.

At least amidst the upheaval, Faith maintained her grades. But navigating this crucial year of high school, the friendships she forged and the life decisions she made would need their constant vigilance and guidance.

"Ma'am, will that be cash or card?"

"Oh, I'm sorry." Clara slid out her wallet, checked out, and texted Michael for an update. As expected, he had a late meeting. So she'd go back to get Jason.

With twenty minutes to kill, she wasn't going to sit in the car. So, she went inside and joined the other parents on the bleachers, veterans whose older children had already gone through this ritual. They nodded to her, and she joined in polite conversations.

"Where are you from, if I may ask?" Sue Richards asked.

"Hong Kong, originally." Only a handful of people knew about her memory loss, and Clara kept it that way by telling people she was from Hong Kong—it sounded right. It might even be true. "But I've been in America for decades. Looks like your son is going to make a great center this year." And so she steered the conversation elsewhere.

While Jason high-fived his fellow students, Clara texted Faith, checking on her essay's progress in an attempt to maintain balance between Faith's college applications, Jason's basketball dreams, and Michael's demanding job. After waking up in a hospital with no memory, Clara began her journey to where she stood now—a writer for an online Christian magazine, the mother of two wonderful teenagers, and the wife of a successful neurosurgeon. With her therapist's help, she'd accepted that she might never recover her memories.

But sometimes, questions lingered. As the priest once counseled her, she reminded herself daily to surrender to the Lord. *Have faith!*

The cool air of Orlando Hospital greeted Michael Khoury as he stepped through the sliding glass doors. With each step, his dress shoes clicked an echo down the hospital's sterile corridors. When he started not even a month ago, a flurry of activity, sights, smells, and sounds undeniably characteristic of a busy hospital welcomed him.

Today was no different. Nurses hurried by, their shoes squeaking against the linoleum, while doctors huddled together, discussing cases in hushed tones. The antiseptic smell tainted the air, mingling with the undercurrent of coffee from a nearby vending machine.

"Dr. Khoury." Dr. Jenkins, the hospital's robust administrator, approached with an outstretched hand.

Michael returned the man's handshake, his smile easy and welcoming. "Good morning."

"Michael, these are our neurosurgery fellows." Dr. Jenkins led him toward a young man and a woman who looked eager, perhaps too eager.

"Dr. Khoury, it's an honor to meet you." A quiver slipped into Dr. Hill's voice, perhaps from nerves.

Beside her, Dr. Kim, another fellow with an equally anxious expression, nodded his agreement.

Michael extended his hand, shaking theirs in turn. "It's good to meet you both. I hope we'll have a chance to work together closely."

Michael recognized that hope in their eyes, remembered it. He'd stood there once, eager for guidance and approval. He'd offer the mentorship he yearned for during his early years.

Born as Amir in a small Palestinian village, he'd taken on his Christian name during college. Others accepted him more readily with a Christian name, a sad but enlightening reality. But it was as Michael that he had saved Clara's life, built a family, and found a home in America.

However, the path to pursuing a relationship with Clara hadn't been easy. He still remembered his conversation with Dr. Cook so many years ago. He'd been straightforward and requested to be removed from her care team in the event he might want to pursue a relationship, something he couldn't ethically do as her doctor. Dr. Cook had commended him for taking the ethical route and approved the change while warning him to proceed cautiously.

Refocusing,

Michael excused himself with a promise to catch up with the fellows soon. On his way to his office, his chest swelled. The road here hadn't been easy, but he was here now.

Hours later, he slumped into his plush chair, his palms flattening on the polished mahogany desk, such a stark contrast to the crisp white walls. He pivoted his seat toward the tall window offering a panoramic view of Orlando's skyline, the fading sunlight casting an ethereal glow over the city. Yes, this was where he was meant to be.

His cell phone buzzed with a text from Clara. She'd attached a picture of a beaming Jason in his new basketball uniform.

Michael then opened the draft email from Faith, her college essay attached. As he read her words, he let out a low whistle. What a girl! Her writing was poised and articulate. She was so much like her mother.

Dear Clara. He ran a hand over his face. He should have done something long ago. As a physician, he healed patients. But for so long, he'd been so helpless when it came to helping his wife recover her lost memories or her past. Then their move back south had unsettled her more than he'd expected, pushing him to do something he should've been brave enough to do long ago. Why did part of him still fear he might lose her if she found herself?

He typed his feedback, ensuring his constructive words remained encouraging. He was still at it when a knock interrupted him.

"Dr. Khoury, it's time for your last meeting for the day," his assistant announced.

As he closed his office door, he wondered when the PI would report back.

ABOUT THE AUTHOR

S.F. Baumgartner writes fast-paced Christian suspense thrillers. Book 1 of her Mirror Estate series, Living Secrets, was selected as one of the Top Picks in the thriller category at Killer Nashville, 2024. Her love for writing comes second only to her love of reading.

When she's not busy writing about complex characters, secretive operatives, and relentless agents, she spends her time binge-watching crime TV shows, such as NCIS, or playing with her cats. If you enjoy James Patterson's style—specifically short chapters—you'll love her Mirror Estate series.

To be the first to know about any sales, promotions, and new releases, sign up for our monthly newsletter. By subscribing, you'll stay informed about all the latest happenings and never miss an opportunity to explore this captivating world.

ALSO BY
S.F. BAUMGARTNER

Mirror Estates series

Buried Secrets, book 1

Living Secrets, book 2

Forgotten Secret, book 3

Tangled Secrets, book 4

Hidden Secrets, book 5

Shadowed Secret, book 6

Stolen Secrets, book 7

Box Set (Books 1-4)

KC & Orlando Prime series

Christmas Murders, a prequel

Fatal Invitation, book 1

ACKNOWLEDGMENTS

I'd like to take a moment to thank everyone who contributed to the materialization of this novel, a project close to my heart and a testament to the collaborative spirit of creativity.

First and foremost, my editors & proofreaders: Jennifer Collins, an independent editor who brought a keen eye to my work; Emma Jane of EJL Editing; and Chelsea Lauren of Represent Publishing. Their meticulous efforts in combing through my drafts, refining the prose, and catching all the errors have been instrumental in making this book what it is.

A special acknowledgment must go to the talented designer from 100covers.com, who took my idea and translated it into the beautiful cover that graces this book. Their vision and creativity brought the visual aspect of my story to life.

I'd like to extend my appreciation to friends who helped me polish the blurb, turning it into an enticing invitation to readers. Their input was invaluable in shaping how the book presents itself to the world.

Gratitude is also due to all my ARC readers who provided early feedback and encouragement. Their voices helped guide the final adjustments, and their enthusiasm propelled me forward.

Last but certainly not least, I'd like to thank my family for their unwavering support, understanding, and belief in me throughout this entire process. They have been my rock, providing both a sounding board and a safe harbor as I navigated the complex waters of writing this novel.

To all of you, thank you from the bottom of my heart. Your contributions, large and small, have made this book possible, and I'm forever grateful for your faith in me and this project.